PURPOSE OF EVASION

A SAMI LAKHANI THRILLER

J. A. WALSH

MILFORD HOUSE

Milford House Press

Mechanicsburg, Pennsylvania

MILFORD HOUSE

an imprint of Sunbury Press, Inc.
Mechanicsburg, PA USA

For information about special discounts for bulk purchases, please contact Sunbury Press Orders Dept. at (855) 338-8359 or orders@sunburypress.com.

To request one of our authors for speaking engagements or book signings, please contact Sunbury Press Publicity Dept. at publicity@sunburypress.com.

ISBN: 978-1-62006-123-7 (Trade paperback)

Library of Congress Control Number:

FIRST MILFORD HOUSE PRESS EDITION: May 2019

Product of the United States of America
0 1 1 2 3 5 8 13 21 34 55

Set in Bookman Old Style
Designed by Chris Fenwick
Cover by Chris Fenwick
Edited by Chris Fenwick

Continue the Enlightenment!

To victims of hatred, everywhere

To the defenders of freedom, for everyone

"There are indeed gloomy and hypochondriac minds, inhabitants of diseased bodies, disgusted with the present, and despairing of the future; always counting that the worst will happen because it may happen. To these I say: How much pain have cost us the evils which have never happened?"

–Thomas Jefferson

CIA OATH

"I, Sami Lakhani, do solemnly swear (or affirm) that I will support and defend the Constitution of the United States against all enemies, foreign and domestic; that I will bear true faith and allegiance to the same; that I take this obligation freely, without any mental reservation or <u>purpose of evasion</u>; and that I will well and faithfully discharge the duties of the office on which I am about to enter. So help me God."

EISENHOWER EXECUTIVE OFFICE BUILDING
WASHINGTON D.C.

July

Gerald Seymour uncorked a bottle of 21-year old Elijah Craig Single Barrel Kentucky Straight Bourbon Whiskey. He poured two fat fingers on top of the few drops remaining in the cut crystal tumbler. It was a two-whiskey day.

The first whiskey was a longstanding habit. As summer peaked in the brief and quotation-mark-free period that a new White House experienced between the "First 100 Days" and "Midterms," Gerald Seymour accepted that all days in this office were two-whiskey days. The only mystery when he woke each morning was whether the second drink would be in celebration or lament.

He walked across the spacious office, dark but for the glow from a laptop and the flickering of a candle. The candle smelled of Prince Albert's Cherry Vanilla. He quit smoking a pipe eight years ago after mouth cancer fired a shot across his bow, but he could not work at night without the scent on the air. The blue-white glow from the laptop was not so easy to explain, and he passed by his desk to the window.

It was a corner office. The finest in D.C., in his opinion. From one window he looked out over the Ellipse to the National Mall and the Washington Monument. A few steps to the left and he was looking at the West Wing. For years, administration after administration, the Senior White House Advisor kept an office in the West Wing.

Republican or Democrat, proximity to the President was a prize that crossed party lines. It was conventional Washington wisdom. He hated conventional Washington wisdom. He hated everything about Washington. They had come to change it, he and the man he was responsible for putting in the Oval Office.

The window also afforded a view past the southern jutting Oval Office to the colonnade that connected the West Wing with the South Portico, the President's back door. When the leader of the free world started his walk to the office, Gerald could start his. Or not. Sometimes he didn't make an appearance in the White House for a few days, preferring to maintain the mystery and reinforce the notion he was somewhere behind the President pulling strings. Svengali. Rasputin.

During the transition, one of the old Republican hands they hired was shocked to hear where Gerald planned to office. "You have to be near him!"

"I wasn't near him on the campaign," Gerald responded without hesitation. "Never rode on that plane once. And yet everything flowed through me. I was his first call when he woke up, his last before he went to sleep. It's not about proximity, it's about control."

Gerald did not conclude by adding that "The President won't wipe his ass without asking me whether to sit or stand." But that didn't stop the quote from becoming conventional Washington wisdom.

This White House, and everyone associated with it, did things their own way. The mandate of their election required they did, Gerald Seymour demanded they did, and everything continued to flow through him. That was the reason for tonight's second whiskey.

He swallowed something between a sip and a gulp and returned to the laptop. He scanned the document displayed there one more time. It was the final time. As in, final for everyone. He would never see it again and neither would his man at the FBI, who wrote it. No one else at the FBI would ever lay eyes on it.

Seymour didn't ask any questions about the sourcing, though it seemed solid. If the allegations in the document were true, the media would relish spreading the news. If the story ever came to light, he was ruined. So was the President.

After 9/11, it became conventional Washington wisdom that the people who hated America would no longer express their feelings just by blowing up our embassies in the Middle East and Africa, and that the FBI needed to take on more counterterrorism and intelligence responsibilities. The problem with the FBI was they wanted to do things covert agencies had long done but with a bias toward prosecution. The Hoover Building was full of people who liked to arrest and indict and convict.

Langley was different. The CIA traded in information. When they found no willing customer for their reporting, they sometimes conducted misadventures of their own. But their trade was secrets, not justice. They used secrets to compromise agents who were – by definition – liars, and who – in turn – provided more secrets. If the CIA discovered that Mr. Bad Guy would like to harm America, they collected information about Mr. Bad Guy. Information, not evidence. If Mr. Bad Guy developed capabilities to harm America, they degraded those capabilities. If Mr. Bad Guy had actionable plans to harm America, they disrupted those plans. They might even kill Mr. Bad Guy. But they would not arrest him. Information was power, even if they never used it.

Langley's approach suited Gerald much more than the FBI's. The J. Edgar Hoover Building was an insult to its namesake, one of America's foremost secrets-and-lies blackmailers. If the CIA had the same information included in the FBI memo Gerald was reading, the CIA would not have told the White House. Gerald would have found out because he had a guy at Langley too. But if he let this go on any longer, the FBI would be handing this memo around Washington like homeless newspapers at a Metro station.

Soon the dipshit Director would know and while he served at the pleasure of the President, he was not someone that the President appointed. If the Director knew so would the Attorney General. The President did appoint him, but he was a cocksucker who worried Gerald. It could not get that far. He would tell his guy to make sure the FBI backed off.

Still, someone needed to determine if what was in that memo was true. If it was, then it needed to be stopped. If it couldn't be stopped then it needed to be managed. Gerald's problem was that the CIA had limitations. Like the Harlem Globetrotters, they did not play home games. The United States was the FBI's jurisdiction. But the Bureau didn't stop things from happening, they responded to them when they did. Since 9/11, a debate had raged about whether there was a third way that was within the Constitution.

The Constitution went out the window when we let people who hate this country live in it, Seymour thought, as he turned away from the window.

Fortunately for Gerald Seymour, he was not the first person who dealt with a dilemma like this. He might shun conventional Washington wisdom, but some good work had been done over the years. There was a third way. There were people to call who were not concerned with chains of command or jurisdiction. They didn't participate in Washington's wars for bureaucratic turf. Gerald Seymour drained the last of the bourbon and picked up the phone. It was not a call he could have made from the West Wing.

ONE

BATTLEFIELD

Samir Lakhani zipped the weapon into his backpack, hoisted it onto his shoulder, and walked out of the internet café into the heat of a crowded street. He headed east.

A group of young women passed, and he disguised a scanning look over his shoulder as a lecherous glance. Instead of their asses, he focused on the clothing and faces behind him. He would check again in two minutes to be sure no one was following. He kicked his walk up to a brisk pace. Foot traffic was heavy as he weaved in and out of oncoming shoppers on the sidewalk. Next to him, a small lane was filled with bicycle rickshaws. Traffic was snarled on the main road.

Of Pakistani Muhajir origin, Samir's skin was a caramel color and when he grew a beard it was wiry and black. A mustache could age him into his mid-forties. Clean shaven, he could pass for twenty-five. He was tall and thin, and he dressed fashionably but not fastidiously. Nothing too noticeable. He could be a computer programmer or your Uber driver.

Or a Soldier? Freedom fighter? Spy? Terrorist? He wasn't certain where he fit on that spectrum anymore. Whatever he was, he still needed tradecraft. If anyone was following, the Spy would smoke them out with a good surveillance detection route.

His SDR left the busy commercial street for a deserted residential block where no one could hide from his scrutiny. Two blocks from the café, he turned left up a side street that climbed a steep hill. The foot traffic thinned, and the incline would challenge any pursuer to appear casual. There were no vehicles moving.

Stop for a smoke. Now was the time. He had crested the hill and turned left again, onto a street parallel to the main road. He was above and behind the café now.

Stand in a doorway...take out a cigarette...struggle for the lighter...have a little trouble sparking the flame.

All the while he looked through hooded lids to see if anyone was watching from a parked car, or if some amateur would steam around the corner trying to make up ground while line of sight was broken. The cigarette was cover but the smoke in his lungs was not unwelcome.

The world did not know yet, but from the café, with nothing more than an internet connection, he played his role in an attack that killed at least a dozen. Maybe more. He didn't know for sure, Freedom Fighting was an inexact science, but he watched the explosion from 7,000 miles away. It was eerie. Silent. The dust settled without any of it catching in his own throat like it would have in the beginning of the war when he was face-to-face with the enemy and he saw the bodies.

Back then, he went village to village with other soldiers, corn-fed infantry jarheads who looked nothing like him. He entered the homes of Afghani and Waziri families who could have passed for his cousins, and yet no matter how many times the scent of their homes singed his nose, the same re-alization always surprised him. They were strange to him. He had more in common with these boys from Alabama and Mas-sachusetts than he did with his grandparents, who were born in one of these villages.

Clearing homes meant knocking on the doors, if no one an-swered, then they kicked in the door. If there was any resistance inside, they erred on the side of caution and that meant three bullets center mass to any "military-aged male" who stepped up. But how could they not step up? Their wives, mothers, and children were in the house.

As he cleared small home after small home, he watched these men's defiant eyes fill with doubt and then drain to des-pair. The soldiers went room to room in a tight, tactical group. By the time they left, the same eyes bulged like a fish, flayed on bleached white fiberglass.

The women and children were corralled outside. More than once Samir saw that the defiance had not died with the father but was staring back at him from the eyes of the youth, who were scared and innocent just moments ago.

Smoking was part of the routine. The Soldier needed it to decompress, and all the pictures of blackened lungs in the world could not change that. He passed above the café and continued to the next corner, turning left down the hill, back toward the main road. Smoking passed for high risk these days. Now that he was not face-to-face with the enemy. Not on his own ground. No more house-to-house. No more detentions. No more interrogations. The rules had all changed and that changed the war, and the soldiers, and spies, and freedom fighters.

Was that when they changed him into The Terrorist? Bombing from 7,000 miles away?

There had been something courageous about the earlier days of the war, when both sides risked their own. Now his victims never saw him coming. No convoy rolled across the border. No thunder of Humvees passed by. No boots on the ground. Just a glint of light reflected 20,000 feet up in the sky. And then nothing. They had been laughing, or smoking, or doing one of the other innocuous and stupid things that people were doing when he blew them up.

Each generation developed its own rules, based on its own changing values, based on the facts of its own wars. This generation's values seemed especially temporal. They killed in the open now. His side and the enemy's. They carried their weapons in backpacks. No matter which of them struck a blow, there was a press release in the can, and they ran to the computer before the smoke cleared to disseminate the news.

He stubbed out the cigarette. He was glad he quit. Too risky.

He turned back onto the crowded main street and walked east, approaching the internet café again. Full circle. He barely felt the weight of his bag, but his weapon was not some shitty homemade bomb like the enemy might use in a market in the Middle East, but the means to target a Metal Augmented Charge. It was officially a Hellfire missile, but they called it *MAC Daddy* and it was the laser-guided air-to-surface missile that he had helped the drone team to target from his computer.

There were precautions necessary when killing from this far away. As he approached the coffee shop again, he tossed the burner phone on which he received the mission code into a trash can. He had destroyed the SIM card with a multi-tool before he walked out. His black box, an internet device that housed a warren of VPN encrypted proxies to mask his online trail, was stowed in the backpack with his computer. For next time. That was the thing, no matter how many times Sami helped kill the top guy, there was always another mission.

About 20 feet before the café door, he cut left down a small alley. If anyone was on him, he couldn't miss them. He climbed the stairs and tried the door. Unlocked. The way he left it. The world's best spies were taught to be exacting, never to leave a trace. They would never do something stupid like forget to relock the door after an infil. It was muscle memory. *Double check, did we relock the door?*

If they were good, they might remember to leave Sami's door unlocked. If they weren't so good, he might catch them out. Either way, no lock would stop the kind of person who would hunt him, so leaving the apartment unlocked was Sami's safest choice. Just another of the paradoxes that defined his life.

He flipped on TV news and saw that the press release was already being repeated.

"A Predator drone dropped a precision-guided 18-pound bomb..."

Close enough. It wasn't a Predator. And operators like Sami did not call them drones. They were Unmanned Aerial Vehicles. The Americans had not yet gone public with the latest UAV design, its name or payload.

Sami looked out the front window, over the crowd of tourists and college kids on M Street's sidewalks. The rickshaws toting tourists in town for 4th of July were still filling the gutters. Ubers were everywhere. It was summer, a hot weekend night, and it was busy.

This apartment in Georgetown was small, but he loved it. It sure beat the FOBs in Iraq or Afghanistan. He had seen both sides of the war. Wherever he fought from, he was valuable to the U.S. intelligence community because he knew the rhythms and tones of the enemy. He might feel more like the American boys he deployed with, but he was not sure they felt the same about him. He spoke the language of the enemy and worshipped their God. He fought with those boys on far-flung battlefields, but he fought another war too, inside. 7,000 miles from the desert, he still fought on both fronts.

In Yemen, a group of men and boys had been taking a day off from their training for some falconry. They wanted to kill Americans. Their mistake was that some Americans discovered their plan and since the Americans could no longer grab them and hold them forever in a cage on a hot stinking island, the Americans killed them first.

The missile was fired from the sky above them but carried by an unmanned aerial vehicle that was controlled by a twenty-two-year-old kid working a joystick in New Mexico. The targeting was Sami's job. Now that it was done, he was thinking about ordering takeout.

This was unlike any war in history.

Sami loved his country and he did his job. This operation killed fifteen of the enemy, including one of the top targets in all foreign jihadism. It was the sixth such notch in Sami's belt. He followed the rules as they stood each day. He followed orders.

In the lead up to a big mission, there was anxiety, but now he was calm. He killed strangers for a living, but he endured the nature of his work because those strangers had done – or planned to do - bad things to Americans.

His conscience was clear. But maybe it shouldn't be.

TWO

ANNAPOLIS, MARYLAND

Parking in Annapolis was always a pain. Especially in a pickup truck. Although why he was driving a pickup truck, Karim was unsure. Hasan said the Learning Center could use one, but he didn't want to drive it, and he didn't want it to just sit without being driven, so Karim should get one and the Learning Center would pay for it. Karim was still paying off his student loans from George Washington, so the deal was an easy sell for him. Besides, Hasan had grown the Learning Center so successfully that the members rarely asked questions.

Karim never asked any questions, even when he noticed a few other guys pulling up in pickup trucks in the weeks after he got his own. But then they stopped meeting at the Learning Center, where there was a parking lot. Worship still happened at the mosque, which Hasan insisted they always call the "Learning Center," but the meetings of this smaller group, which Hasan called the "Council of Muhammad," were now in downtown Annapolis where parking was always a pain. Karim would be late. He finally found a parking spot for the truck and jogged three blocks. It was only when he pulled open the restaurant door that Karim realized the keys were still in his tightly-curled fist. He didn't like to be late for Hasan.

The hostess showed him to the private room reserved for their meeting, where they could speak freely. Hasan was there with only two others. Karim was late, but not last. He relaxed.

"As-salamu alaykum." Hasan greeted him with a warm handshake. Karim's remaining anxiety melted away. Hasan was an amazing person.

"Wa'alaykumu as-salam." After the Arabic greeting, Karim continued in Urdu. "I'm sorry, brother. Parking!"

"Ah! I understand it's difficult." Hasan's Urdu was clean if a bit clumsy. And then, changing to English, in which their fluency made both much more comfortable, "Now that you mention it, I should make that part of the agenda tonight. We'll find somewhere with easier parking for future meetings."

With that, it was resolved. Hasan *really* was an amazing person.

The restaurant was the recently-opened satellite of a well-established Lebanese chain in Washington. Its presence in Annapolis attested both to the city's status as a college town with global tastes and to the continued sprawl of Metro Washington across Northern Virginia and Maryland. Since the crack-marred 1980s, the U.S. capital had changed into a global and gentrified city. The Northern Virginia county where Karim grew up had a Muslim-American concentration among the highest in the U.S. Annapolis was sandwiched between two counties - Montgomery County, bordering Washington, and Baltimore County, bordering Baltimore - that had Muslim populations approaching 5%.

Every member of the Council of Muhammad was American born. Other than those early greetings, they spoke in English throughout the night. The meal was informal and enjoyable. They discussed everything from politics to the Redskins. Hasan liked it that way. He encouraged them to talk, to enjoy the fellowship of their brothers, and – for a little while - only their brothers.

There was nothing nefarious about that. Nothing like the undertone that captivated the country during the last cycle of national elections and seemed to be taking hold around the world. The tone of us-versus-them nativism that sought to take white, Western countries back and make them great again. No, this was little more than guys' night, as American as apple pie and as universal as a languid chat in the afternoon cool of an Islamic tea house.

"Brothers, thank you." The meal concluding, Hasan spoke in his loud, clear, formal imam's voice for the first time. "Thank you for coming to another meeting. This group is taking off. It is becoming everything I hoped it might be. I understand that several of you had a difficult time parking tonight." No remonstration, just an acknowledgment. "I will keep that in mind for future meetings and choose a venue that offers us parking on-site."

None of the brothers recognized this as the most significant of Hasan's statements that night. They could not have. It was so mundane.

"We meet tonight under the specter of an ongoing war against Islam. A war in which none of us wish to be soldiers, but to which we must never let ourselves become mere observers. Or worse, innocent victims. Just as our meeting began, news broke of another attack on the Ummah. A drone flying over sovereign airspace struck with guided munitions. At least," Hasan consulted his phone, "at *least* twenty were killed. The world will be led to believe that each was a terrorist, rather than a victim. That the strike was not on a settlement, but on a training camp. Many Americans will believe that. Of course, a press release was already written. America no longer wishes its dirty secrets - its dirty war - to be revealed by news agencies, years after the deeds are done."

Hasan positioned himself near the door, so he was speaking back into the room, his voice directed away from the diners outside of their private room.

"No, today, the government positions the narrative of these attacks. It sets the tone. It spoon-feeds the media the only thing that the media wants. A story. But we know that this is not a story. Instead, it is part of a plot. An arc of history. It is an arc that bends toward the injustice of Western imperialism. An arc that has its origins as far back as the Crusades." Hasan often borrowed oratory from Martin Luther King, Jr., in this case turning King's famous "arc of history" quote on its ear. His great gift in criticizing the West was that he was a child of the West. He understood it, as did his flock. There is no more effective criticism than that which is directed inward, emanating from one's own tribe.

"The indiscriminate slaughter of the Ummah was once carried out under the sword, and it continues to be violent. Witness today's slaughter of women and children. But it has become more insidious. The West corrupts governments. It gives money and weapons. America stations her crusaders among the Sha'b. Among our people. On our blessed soil. The world today is no longer the peaceful and beautiful place the Prophet tells of. An oppressive strain, a stain of hegemony, has created violence, poverty, famine, and disease."

"The disease kills slowly. Materialism." Hasan raised his index finger. "The quest to acquire makes its most important acquisition of the soul, bringing spiritual death decades before the wastrel finally shakes off mortal life. Immorality." A second finger ticked up. "A flash of skin, on fleeting view, consummates the betrayal of the flesh. And then it must be had, again and again."

His audience was rapt. Hasan was more acerbic than usual, but still controlled.

"It is no wonder then that the American soul is corrupted. No wonder that the arc of history bends toward injustice even here in the American homeland. For the legacy of American imperialism abroad is American racism at home. Witness our fellowship here tonight, in a private room, for fear that if we were seen congregating – a half dozen young, *military-aged*, males with dark skin - it would arouse fear and suspicion. It may even arouse action. Surveillance. America today listens to every phone call. Reads each email. The FBI visited our own house of worship. Our brothers recruited as informants."

Hasan's eyes flickered around the room. He was looking for something, a subtle hint, any gesture of acknowledgment. A look that said: *Yes, me too, I was recruited.* Or worse, eyes that asked: *How does he know?* He was trying to smoke out an informant.

But he saw nothing. He had not expected to. He selected these men very carefully. They were all Americans, all from families that raised them in the suburbs and sent them to college. They were career men who owned homes and participated in community activities outside The Learning Center. They were no one's radicals.

And if they had been selected with great care, they were being groomed with even greater caution. For if Hasan's plan was to work, he could arouse no suspicions. Not friends or neighbors. Not the FBI's. There could be no interviews after the fact, where one of these men's neighbors reported that they had always wondered. There could be no revelation in the newspapers that these men were suspected by law enforcement, and interviewed by law enforcement, and even surveilled by law enforcement; but, were never arrested because the American system did not permit arrests for things that people might do, no matter how suspiciously those people behaved. If Hasan used men who could fit that narrative, then that narrative – the same old story of homegrown Muslim terror – was what the media would key on. That was not his plan.

When Hasan told those enabling this plan that he would do something never done before, there were smirks. He was telling hard men, men who had seen it all. There was nothing new under the sun. But then he detailed the plan and watched their eyes widen. His sales pitch had wooed the partners he needed. Men of action, mysterious and dangerous. Men of authority, whose influence could shape opinion. He was right, it had never been done. It had never been attempted. But if it worked?

"Brothers, we not only see this hypocrisy, we not only understand it, but we live amidst it. We are soldiers in this war, as much as any of the brothers killed in one of the strikes that are sanitized and justified for TV. We are on the front line." If the plan had not been so novel, now is when Hasan would have called these men to action. But, he did not. He needed their good names, not their good deeds.

"That is why we must build the bridge. We must create the way forward to a new reality that smashes convention. A reality which succeeds in bending the arc. Bending back toward the peace and the justice that the Prophet speaks of. We must embrace our neighbors as our own. They must be as our brothers. The American. The Christian. Yes, brothers, the Jew. When they meet you, they must disbelieve the stories they are told. When they hear that America has killed more radicals, they must distrust it. They must learn that there is no distinction between those brothers killed today, under sovereign skies, and their own neighbor. They must know that the Ummah is one. Then they will know the truth."

And then, Hasan thought, *they must fear us all.*

THREE

NATIONAL HARBOR, OXON HILL, MARYLAND

National Harbor's crowd was at the summer convention season peak. Once a plantation, the land where National Harbor rose was meant to become the end of the Potomac Trail, complete with historical displays and wide bike lanes. Instead, over a period that straddled the financial crisis, a mixed-use development took shape. There was a grand resort hotel, an outdoor shopping mall, high-rise apartments, and the 180-foot Capital Wheel. As Sami walked onto the pier from the grid of streets where the shops were, he scanned the crowd. Near the end of the pier, a long line of families were queued to ride the enormous Ferris Wheel that loomed over the Potomac and boasted views of the National Mall from its apex.

"Over here!" Andy Rizzo's accent cut through the summer air like the scent of the stockyards through a South Side Chicago breeze a hundred years ago. Sami could have heard him a mile away, but he still had trouble picking him out of the crowd. Finally, Sami spotted Andy waving from an iron bench where he had spread his sandwich and chips over greasy wax paper.

Rising halfway, Andy popped a chip into his mouth before offering Sami a fist bump. It was his habit to adopt the latest fads. A straight, white, Catholic man working in government, Andy was forever making concessions to progress.

Andy gestured first to his sandwich. "Italian beef!" And then to the bag that Sami was holding. "What'd ya get?"

The instructions were specific: park in front of CVS, no matter how many times you had to go around the block to get an open spot; do a lap of the shops for SDR; buy a sandwich from Potbelly's; meet me on the pier.

"Hummus and roasted red peppers."

Sami sat and spread his sandwich on his own lap. Andy did not stand on ceremony. Another chip struggled to find a free tooth amidst a mouthful of juicy beef. Sami watched with something like disgust. Andy was short and squat with pasty skin. His hair was so dark that if it were not for the light grey at the temples, Sami would have been convinced it was *Just for Men* bottle black. His eyes were deep set, and even as his jaw worked to chew, the squareness was evident. He resembled no one so much as Fred Flintstone.

And from the accent to the Italian beef, he was pure Chicago. Raised in a South Side home that was half-Irish, half-Italian and all-Catholic, he joked that the most difficult decision in his life had been whether to attend DePaul or Loyola. The life decisions that remained after the Agency got him were easier. He made his name in Lebanon in the 1980s, burnished his reputation in Iraq in the 1990s, and earned his way off the books when the government's black budgets skyrocketed after 9/11. Since then, Andy had been running a small and disconnected team of black assets, beholden to no specific agency or chain of command, but at the beck and call of bureaucrats in need. Freelancers.

Call Andy's number, outline the objective, and a few days later he presented a mission outline and budget. They were expensive and they were selective. "Fuck or walk?" Part of Andy's team since his Army discharge came through after the third rotation of Operation Iraqi Freedom, Sami heard Andy deliver that deal-closing line often. Most of the time whoever was on the receiving end didn't walk.

Andy kept Sami busy. There were highs and lows, busy times and lulls, moments where the political moment darkened the relative opaqueness of their authorization for action; but Sami could not complain about working for Andy.

Not without a little difficulty, the slab of half-masticated beef made its way through Andy's esophagus, and he reacted to Sami's order.

"Hummus, huh?" And then, skeptically, "Well, dig in, Dost."

Dost. Sindhi, for "friend." It was always that way in public. When they were sure they were not being recorded and Andy said Sami's name, he pronounced it as the American "Sammy," with considerable Chicago-inflected shortening of the first vowel. Sami found either form condescending, even though he knew it was not meant that way. Andy wasn't like the soldiers Sami served with in Iraq. They were mostly country boys and they called every Iraqi a "Hajji," unless he was a big-time Iraqi, then he was "Ali Baba."

Andy surrounded himself with people like Sami and he not only saw them as integral to the mission, but he saw them as people. That Andy's use of dialectic nicknames was also integral to his career ambitions made the whole thing a little less comfortable. That Andy Rizzo was Straight, White and Catholic did not make him any less smart. Sami knew that. But it had made his career that much easier all along the way. Sami was not at all sure that Andy knew that. Andy had spoken freely in the past about "hitching his star" to young, first-generation immigrants with the language skills and cultural context he didn't have, but which he marshaled like a quartermaster.

"You watch the game?" Andy exhaled the words before another voracious bite.

"You know I did. I'm sure you checked the tickets."

The webcast of the UAV strike was accessible only under specific circumstances. Sami connected a small black box to his computer's USB port. Once connected to the internet, the box routed him through a web of VPN-encrypted proxies to a verification screen. A day before, he received a burner phone, and the access code was sent by SMS. The black box was reusable. The phone's SIM was destroyed, thrown in the trash can outside the coffee shop on M Street Northwest and buried under thirty feet of trash in a Virginia landfill by now. The point was, Andy knew who had watched.

"Another good win. Built a lot of credibility with the new DNI."

The Director of National Intelligence was a Cabinet position created in the fallout of 9/11. Because the DNI's office had sole oversight of sensitive operations like those run by Andy's team, he was an important constituency.

"This administration has more of an appetite for collateral damage than the last guys. If we can just demonstrate that our targeting intel is correct, they don't care as much about the blowback."

Sami swallowed his first bite. "Just keep finding bold faces then?"

"Not you."

"Why's that?"

"We have a new contract." Andy conceded to the beef and cheese by raising a napkin to his chin before continuing. It was time to talk business. "Something special that is going to tie you down a while."

"From who?"

"Whom. 'From whom,' Dost. I know that you know that. I must have corrected you on that a dozen times."

"You have. And every time it hasn't worked to distract me from the fact that you didn't answer the question."

"I never do."

"Same again, I suppose?"

"You suppose correctly."

"Worth trying."

In the years that Sami had been under Andy's chain of command, the nature of his work had become more opaque. There were operations like the UAV strike where the whole team was involved, and everyone was read in. But there were other operations where Sami would only complete his small task. Like part of an assembly line, his job was to make sure that, as the widget passed by his station, it got what it needed before the next stop on the line. There were operations where his task was completed in a black box. He could not see the widget he was working on, and his own work was walled off from anyone else, even those read in. Operational Security.

OPSEC was not unfamiliar territory. Sami's career started on the military side of intel, and when they were chasing a commander's Priority Intelligence Requirements, the provenance was not always forthcoming. There had been that hairy time, after the *New York Times* revealed several intelligence programs authorized by aggressive post-9/11 interpretations of Title 10 of the United States Code. By then, Sami was on loan to a civilian intelligence agency, and the rules – and his boss – changed each day. The uncertainty was enough for him to take the discharge and join Andy's group. Being off the books had offered its benefits. But Sami was not so sure anymore.

"Anyway, this will keep you tied up a while." Andy continued, "I want you to lead a detachment. Totally compartmented."

"What's the objective?"

"The details are still sketchy, but it looks legit. Domestic attack. Homegrown." Andy responded to Sami's raised eyebrows. "The bad guys, they're enamored of it now. Paris. Brussels. Manchester. The fucking European services cannot get out of their own way."

"Liberal democracies are pesky like that."

Andy ignored the sarcasm. "It's the homegrowns that are tricky. They have unparalleled freedom of movement, cultural awareness, contacts, access to resources. We saw flashes of emphasis on jihadi websites after Boston and San Bernardino, but Paris opened their eyes as much as ours. The comms we have on this, Dost? The U.S. has never seen anything like it before."

"How so?"

"It's not just whack-a-mole with an AR-15. Or some reprobate driving a rent-a-truck into the fuckin' farmers' market. Kill as many as you can before the cops, and glorious martyrdom, arrive. Local law won't be able to stop the bleeding on this one. It's bigger."

"There's a bomb maker?" Terrorists in Nice and Berlin used trucks. Guns in San Bernardino. A large, coordinated attack that didn't involve small arms would use explosives. 9/11 killed the chances of using planes. The scary truth was that pressure cookers, like the Tsarnaevs used at the Boston Marathon, were unstoppable.

As ghastly as those attacks were, they didn't really scare counterterrorism people. Even if there were mass casualties, those kinds of attacks didn't demonstrate any deep embed of trained and bad-intentioned actors. One or two guys following an online cookbook and using consumer products could stay under the radar. Too diffuse.

Sami knew Andy would not take a job like that. Those attacks were low profile until they happened. They were tough to stop and the narrative that inevitably emerged was: "Why didn't they stop it?" If they were stopped, the narrative was that the putative perpetrators were Keystone Kops. There wasn't a lot of upside for Andy, and there was a lot of risk to his success rate.

"I could put a rookie on a bomb maker. Forget the explosive. Completely. That's not where I need you."

"What? Online directed? If these guys are homegrown, where's the foreign angle?"

"That's what's fucking with everyone's head, Dost. The full-time Spooks can't find any connection to al-Qaeda, ISIS, Shebab, nothing. No SIGINT to indicate connections. No travel into a known terror group's area of operations."

These were the common traits emerging from increasing radical attacks on cities in Europe: the attackers were radicalized in isolated, local communities and had identifiable connections to well-known groups, often through travel to an area of operations.

"None of the signatures," Andy continued. "And the attack looks weird. It doesn't look like maximum destruction, or even standard fear and panic. It's something more," Andy struggled before settling on a word. "More *political.*"

Terrorism was always political. Sami failed to see the distinction based on what he knew. And based on what he knew, there was something else that was coming up short.

"I'm missing the plot somewhere. Why pull me in? I'm a foreign intel officer."

Avoiding the question, Andy continued.

"You are my strongest independent asset. You have proven that you can direct a small team and deliver on the objective.

Apart from that, you have been with me as long as anyone. I need someone who can look at this with fresh eyes. I don't want it approached like a government case officer would. It'll be too easy for whoever runs this team to reach back over to the agencies. You don't have as many hang-ups as our newer guys. Look, Dost, you're as far off the books as I am." This last was as much a statement of his qualifications as it was a reminder to Sami. *I own you. You have nowhere to run.* "We need someone who can run this thing independently. Only a cell like ours can crack a cell like this."

"Foreign, Coach. *Foreign.*" Sami interrupted. "Otherwise find someone else."

"You're the one who cited the problems raised by those pesky democracies. There's a new sheriff in town, Dost. You've been around long enough that you are seeing your second paradigm shift. Hang around long enough and you'll see ten more. Change domestic leadership, add in tactical shifts by the enemy, and the game is changing. Just like after 9/11."

"EO 12333 didn't change, did it? Never mind, don't answer. I'm sure it didn't. I have a Google alert set. Until it does, I don't collect on United States persons. I've seen this movie before, Coach. People lost their careers because some Yale lawyer on White House Counsel's staff thought he was smarter than a fifth grader."

"And you almost went to jail, right Dost?"

"That's right. A bunch of others with me!"

"It's been almost ten years. We don't bag groceries at Safeway, OK? Everyone has a close shave now and then. But it's high time you come down off that cross."

"You're mixing your religious metaphors. My people don't do crosses, remember?"

The anger coming off Sami's last comment was controlled but palpable. Both men took a breath. Their sandwiches sat ignored, relegated to their role as props. This was not their first time rehashing this argument. It was nuanced but significant.

In seeking a scapegoat for the 9/11 attacks, the media had instigated a circular firing squad immense in scale even for

Washington. Every three-letter agency had their knives out for the others. The narrative that emerged was one of bureaucratic stove piping. Information gathered by the CIA or NSA in the course of their international espionage, which would have been integral to stopping domestic attacks by al-Qaeda, was being withheld from the FBI. Crimes on U.S. soil were under the FBI's jurisdiction, but the Bush White House concluded that when the global terror threat came ashore, it meant war. Not crime. And regardless of jurisdictional issues, the chain of command for warfare ended with one man: The Commander in Chief.

The U.S. government might – and, in Iraq, did - find venues where they could wage this war with bombing sorties, infantry battalions, and armor brigades, but that would not be enough. It would be a new kind of war, geared toward a new threat: asymmetric attacks against soft targets on U.S. soil. Although POTUS was commander in chief of a military that had starred on global battlefields during the 20th Century thanks to conventional might as measured in carrier groups and fighter brigades, the terror threat was better answered by the clandestine services than the Pentagon. That meant that intelligence agencies were involved in warfare, and they reported to the President.

Promulgated by President Reagan, Executive Order 12333 was always more well known for prohibiting CIA assassinations, but 12333 also outlined who intelligence agencies could and could not surveil, what information they could and could not collect, and with whom they could share that information.

After 9/11, White House counsel and staff counsel at several agencies seized the moment to offer reinterpretations of 12333. The lawyers argued that many of the rules that governed "spying," including those outlined in EO 12333, were no longer applicable because the activities engaged in by the CIA were not intelligence activities, but military activities.

With a broadened scope, and a public skeptical of those few media voices who wondered what became of civil liberties, the administration grabbed the authority it felt was necessary to keep Americans safe and prosecute the War on Terror.

There was fallout from this decision. Some resulted from overreach at the operational level, based on a command directive to kill bad guys and prevent another attack. No one told the twenty-something reservists guarding prisoners at Abu Ghraib to walk their charges on dog leashes and turn the whole exercise into a photo shoot. That kind of stupid couldn't be taught.

But other activities were doctrinal, briefed and approved by the highest levels of government. Seven years after 9/11, many were well-documented. Water-boarding, Guantanamo Bay, and enhanced interrogation had all became household terms.

The Bush doctrine was hotly-debated in a 2008 presidential campaign where the War on Terror was a central issue. When the bottom fell out of the economy, terrorism took a brief backseat in the American zeitgeist, for the first and only time since 2001. But the financial crisis defined the anti-climactic general election.

A defining issue in the primary season had been the War in Iraq. Senator Hillary Clinton's vote to invade was pivotal, as was discussion about the conduct of the War on Terror more broadly. Senator Barack Obama scored points in painting his opponent as too closely aligned with the outgoing Republican administration's position. He also made promises. Promises that people would be held accountable.

Perhaps people like Sami. He was not an interrogator, but he had translated when enemy combatants were being questioned. Some of these combatants had not come off battlefields, where they were bearing arms against the U.S. Instead, they were rounded up in house-to-house raids based on intel provided by analysts like Sami. Did that make them POWs? Or something else? No one was sure. And if they weren't sure what their status was, they couldn't be sure how they should be handled. Some of these guys even ended up being Americans. If they were picking up American al-Qaeda fighters in Afghanistan, what made that person different from an American al-Qaeda fighter arrested in Minneapolis?

When Sami, and thousands of other low-enlisted and junior ranking civilian intelligence agents were given orders, they followed them. When White House Counsel said it was OK to hold someone indefinitely, they were held. When the same lawyer said it was OK to interrogate them, they were interrogated. And when the same lawyer said that if they wouldn't talk, there were enhanced methods that were lawful because – by God – there was a ticking time bomb somewhere, they were waterboarded. Or shoved in a box. Or kept under hot lights. Or barraged with ear-splitting heavy metal music for days.

An embarrassing series of leaks brought many of these techniques to light in global media. When the UK's Foreign Secretary announced that details of a British investigation into the treatment of a Brit held at Gitmo could not be disclosed, for fear it would threaten the "special relationship," a global feeding frenzy was on.

After Obama's inauguration, one UN high official called for George Bush to be prosecuted as a war criminal with the lapse of his head of state immunity. It was a diplomatic crisis for the U.S. before the new president's lawyers arrived in early 2009 and parted with the interpretations of the Bush lawyers and the doctrine that had resulted. Geopolitics demanded a scapegoat.

Individuals who had been in the interrogation rooms worried they would fit the bill. Some were policymakers, like Jose Rodriguez, a former head of the CIA's Clandestine Service who was investigated and ultimately not charged in the destruction of recordings of interrogations of top-ranking al-Qaeda detainees. Many others were junior enlisted personnel associated with defense intelligence, civilian employees of intelligence agencies, or contractors hired for their language skills. Nobodies. People like Sami. Some were even questioned. And their answers to questions about enhanced interrogation, or the surveillance of Americans, or other matters that became the subjects of investigations, boiled down to this: they were following orders. The Nazi defense. Fairly or unfairly, the comparison was drawn.

In the end, prosecutions were few and far between. Witch hunts were more common. Sami did not know how much of his own escape he could attribute to the saving graces of Andy Rizzo versus the inability of Washington's institutions to see anything through to completion rather than to the denouement of their political usefulness.

It was undeniable that Andy became even more highly-regarded under the Obama administration. It was a time for the record books if you worked off the books. Funny thing about Presidents, on the way to the Oval Office they may decry how their predecessors have wielded presidential power, but once ensconced, they were reluctant to leave any of the clubs in the bag.

It was a testament to Sami and Andy's relationship, and to their shared depth of experience, that all this context passed between them in silence over the course of about ten seconds. Sami counted another ten to calm himself before speaking again.

"What you are describing doesn't sound legal. I understand that we take risks, but I'll decide which risks I tolerate or not. I'm not looking for another evasive answer this time. Who are we working for?"

Andy avoided the question, the previous twenty seconds of conversation, and all the post-9/11 political background. He referred to Sami's jibe about crosses. "I'm glad you raised the subject of the mosque. That's the final – and most important reason – that only you can lead this team."

"They're Muslims," Sami snickered. "I didn't doubt it. My denial on this job is a matter of U.S. law, not sectarian loyalty. I remain, ever, the Muslim-at-your-service."

"Homegrowns are like everything else in politics, Dost. Local. By 'the mosque,' I don't mean Islam. I mean Virginia. Masjid Almaany."

FOUR

GEORGETOWN

It took the better part of two hours for Sami to cover the distance from National Harbor to Georgetown, but his ongoing annoyance at Andy for scheduling meetings in places with poor Metro access never broke through. He was too distracted by the revelation that Andy reserved for the final moment of their discussion. *Masjid Almaany.*

He accepted an assignment he did not want. This one, probably illegal. Not knowing where his orders came from was a huge problem. Who requested what information was something that mattered. His orders might come from a U.S. spy agency, but which one? Andy might have signed on with a non-spy agency or even a specific government official. Unless that official was an NSC member, the operation was illegal. The homeland angle made it unlikely, but the objective might have come from a U.S. ally. It was possible it all emanated from Andy himself. If that were the case, there was almost no circumstance in which Sami's actions could be justified under law.

But even the gravity of those concerns was subjugated to the thoughts that had been roiling since Andy mentioned Masjid Almaany. Prosperity Mosque. Built on a cul de sac in Loudon County, Virginia that was intended for a subdivision, the mosque bought the land at a fire sale when the developer needed cash to defend himself against securities fraud during the junk bond years.

Since its construction in 1984, a community of prosperity, worthy of the name, had risen in Loudon and Fairfax counties. And there had been precious little controversy. Almaany was a mainstream mosque for D.C. types. The congregation boasted a fair number of members from the foreign embassies, heads of NGOs, and of late, a few high government officials. It had been under the direction of the same imam since the cornerstone was laid. Abu Muhammad. Legal name, Tahir Lakhani. Sami's grandfather.

But Andy didn't mention Abu Muhammad. The rest of the conversation on the bench at National Harbor centered on another connection to Sami. Karim Sulemani was a childhood friend and college roommate. Sami's work made it difficult to keep close ties to anyone. But it was the complications of Sami's relationship with his grandfather, and his grandfather's mosque, that had riven Sami and Karim's relationship. Still, they met for dinner or drinks at least once a year. Sami knew Karim's wife and children. Karim was not a terrorist. Not a radical, at all. He didn't fit any profile.

But Karim was all over the intelligence. There was little SIGINT, collecting that would be Sami's unpleasant – *illegal?* – task. But there were connections all over the metadata. The known bad guys were talking to someone in the U.S., and soon after, that person was talking to Karim. There was no solid financial trail; again, it would be Sami's team who would have to connect the dots, but there were red flags. A large cash transfer went into Karim's account and went out again. He was driving a new truck.

"Why does a guy with over $60,000 in student loans pay cash for an F-150?"

It was Andy's question, and despite Sami's irritation with the source, it was a good one.

"This is a huge break, Dost. You know it is. We don't get this kind of break. Treat the case like you would any other. Put together your team for the supporting pieces but work Karim. He'll trust you."

Sami pushed his confusion over the case aside. It was early and the picture would resolve as more information was gathered. His bias now should be for action. At the small coffee table in front of the TV, he started up his laptop and put out feelers to his preferred experts. Get the band back together. He dashed off his first secure message, hoping that the cyber guy he wanted from New Orleans would be willing and able to sign on. One thing he concluded before he even sent that first message was that his personal relationship with Karim would be close-hold. In fact, he would keep all the intel on Karim to himself until he had more pieces of the puzzle.

Andy's insistent avoidance of mentioning Abu Muhammad still gnawed. Whatever other issues he had with Andy, until now Sami never violated the one maxim that Andy preached when he joined.

"We're going black, Dost. Off the books." It was the recruiting speech of a lifetime, and almost ten years ago now. "There will be no more rules. And no cavalry. If we fuck up, we wear it. We keep the circle tight. We only read in people who need to know, and they only get as much as they need to perform. You have to trust me. More than that, we'll have to trust everyone we work with."

Only now, Andy wanted Sami to walk back into the orbit of the one man they both knew he could not trust: the grandfather who raised him.

FIVE

ANNAPOLIS

Hasan drove home from the Council of Muhammad meeting in a rare state of mellow satisfaction. Born in the U.S. and raised in comfortable suburban circumstances, Hasan Hamad Khalifa was - like all the other men in the cell he was building - a child of America. But he was a zealot for Egypt. His sense of the homeland's history was well-informed, even if the solution he advocated for Egypt's problems had changed little since he became convinced of its righteousness while a student at Columbia. The return of Sunni Islam rule was Egypt's part to play in gaining back the glory lost with the fall of the Ottoman Empire.

During college, he developed an impassioned academic case for the ills that had befallen Egypt since it opened to the West. The privations of the French during the Suez partnership led to British occupation, which inexorably led to the disastrous Six-Day War with the Zionist state and the humiliation of the Camp David Accords. Nasser cozied up to the Soviets. Sadat to the Americans. And all along, Egypt grew poor and – worst of all - secular.

For the self that Hasan willed into being in the Columbia years, this academic case had become a lifelong obsession. Every effort to restore Sunni traditions – the assassination of Sadat, the Luxor attacks, the installation of a Muslim Brotherhood government – was met with global sabotage and internal treachery. No longer would he opine. He acted.

Just how he actualized this self – Hasan the zealot, Hasan the imam, Hasan the jihadi – was a mystery to those who knew him best. His mother and father slipped into the U.S. after the passage of the 1965 Immigration and Nationality Act allowed for the cherry-picking of doctors, scientists, and engineers for special immigration status. The Egyptian beneficiaries of this treatment were mostly Copts fleeing persecution after the Six Day War, but America was glad to take a world-renowned petroleum geologist of any faith.

Given his academic accomplishments, Hasan's father was more noted for the fact that he had only won the Vetlesen Prize (geology's Nobel) and not an actual Nobel Prize. His otherwise sterling academic career was augmented by generous stipends from global oil companies, willing to pay exorbitant fees for their association with a decorated scientist of Middle Eastern extraction.

Hasan attended an elite New England boarding school where he starred at squash while his parents rotated through the series of college towns where his father taught and his mother charmed tennis clubs. Ann Arbor, Berkeley, and Boulder were not places where people thought twice if a local kid came home from college wearing a keffiyeh. Hasan's rising activism was chalked up to youthful exuberance. There had been a knock-down-drag-out fight with his father when he announced that the next step after Columbia would not be graduate studies in the sciences, but in the Qur'an and Islamic law, at Al-Azhar University in Cairo.

Even those disagreements were confined to the usual ebb and flow of parent-child relationships. They were disagreements over the course of Hasan's career, his financial future, and his parents' view that it was a bizarre choice to move back to a country from which they were grateful to have fled. No one thought the path would lead to terrorism. And maybe it would not have. If he had gone to Cairo five years earlier, it was impossible to say whether the path would have led to Annapolis, with Hasan in front of this keyboard, on an Internet Relay Chat with a bomb maker.

But Hasan wasn't there then. He arrived at Al-Azhar in 2010. Rather than assimilating himself among the mystic Sufis at the university, he fell into an activist social circle that included a good many members of the Muslim Brotherhood. As the calendar moved toward December's parliamentary elections, his friends began to disappear. After the elections became an internationally recognized sham, President Hosni

Mubarak's forces ratcheted up their already heavy-handed tactics. A fruit peddler set himself on fire in Ben Arous and for the next month, Tunisia burned. Looking across the Maghreb as President Ben Ali was ousted, Mubarak tightened his grip. He only fanned the flames in his own country.

On January 25, 2011, Hasan joined tens of thousands that descended on Tahrir Square to sue for their freedom. The police came, and he stayed. The plain-clothes baltagiya came, with their truncheons, and he stayed. The government shut down the internet. They opened the prisons. Mubarak went on TV to promise a new government. Hasan stayed.

He was witnessing a dream come to life. It was not until the Army defied orders to engage the protesters with live ammunition that there seemed a glimmer of hope this uprising would end differently than past movements across the Arab world, recorded as mere challenges to the authority of their targeted strongman. On February 10, Mubarak made further concessions but still, he refused to resign. The protesters stayed. On February 11, Mubarak was forced out. Hasan and his brothers won. Or so it seemed.

Hasan did not need to rehash what happened next in the IRC chat, for his counterpart had already established his bona fides where it came to America's history of interventionism. The promise of a Muslim Brotherhood government was betrayed when newly-elected President Muhammad Morsi's coalition partners abandoned him, and the military deposed him. Islam was routed again. And the American Secretary of State described the coup as a "restoration of democracy."

That lament was not one Hasan shared with his correspondent. What they shared was an agreement that America was too involved in Muslim affairs. They agreed that America was once a Christian nation and now it was a *kafir* nation. Secular. The nation had no connection to God, and indeed it denied God's dominion and authority, supplanting it with the worship of secular deities, a culture of celebrity, an obsession with materialism, and overt and immodest sexuality that inevitably transmogrified into homosexuality and transgenderism. They agreed on all those things, and they agreed on one more point. America needed a wake-up call. A violent rending that could not be fitted into the usual narrative.

The computer chirped, shaking Hasan from his Egyptian reverie.

The plan is sound. The final stroke is ingenious.

Hasan had laid out the operation for this stranger. It concerned him to share the details with anyone, let alone with someone he did not know and was assured he would never meet. But it also unburdened him.

Hasan witnessed Tahrir Square. He was on hand for one of the greatest uprisings in modern history. But he was a graduate student, not a soldier. Not a terrorist. His activist ideas had formulated over a long period of intense thought, but he was not operational. He was not even connected to people with the capabilities and knowledge he needed. The attack that he had planned could not be carried out with a rifle or a rice cooker. It was much grander. As grand as anything since 9/11.

That was why he contacted the Sheikh. And the Sheikh sent him to the man he was chatting with now. The plan was satisfactory. What next? It made him feel like an amateur to ask, but this man knew he needed help.

"What next?" Hasan typed and clicked SEND.

The chat window stared back at him, indicating that his correspondent was typing a message. As Hasan waited, he thought about his cell. Men like Karim, who would soon have their faces and life stories flashed across television screens throughout the world. He felt a pang of sorrow. Not for their glorious martyrdom, but because they would have to be deceived. But it was only a glimmer. In Egypt, he saw better men suffer much worse fates. And the stranger was right to tweak the plan. Keep Karim and the others in the dark. The better to carry off the mission, inshallah.

A final IRC message flashed across his screen.

Continue to prepare your team. We will prepare the packages. I will make contact.

SIX

ALEXANDRIA, VIRGINIA

Motorcycle or Mustang? Back tattoo or sleeve? Do I try to marry this girl, or just make this the best night she ever had working at *Rumors*? Whether in Fayetteville's heat, Colorado Springs's snow, or Southwestern Kentucky's hills, outside of the Battalion Gate these were the decisions that awaited the mostly-male teenagers and twenty-somethings returning from Iraq after the first few rotations of Operation Iraqi Freedom.

Some of the Geardos would already have blown their wad in country, buying extra Kevlar, night vision goggles, and Garmins. These were among the most popular items that would become standard issue later in the war, but which Uncle Sam didn't think to provide in the early rotations through Iraq.

With nine to fifteen months of tax-free paychecks sitting in a bank account untouched during deployment, many soldiers came home from the War on Terror with more money than they had ever seen or imagined. The businesses that lined the streets of America's military communities were waiting, as if in formation, to receive the bounty of these returning heroes.

When Sami returned, it was a different decision about a soldier's life in garrison that confronted him. On base or on the economy?

"On the economy" was soldiers' slang for choosing to accept the government's housing allowance to live in private housing, rather than in the unit's barracks. The financial windfall of a few hundred extra dollars a month was strong motivation for many, never mind that they might have to pile into an apartment with half of the platoon. Hey, it beat a dusty tent packed with fifty cots.

After fourteen months living in a Conex with his whole platoon, Sami's decision was easy. A private studio would give him some time alone. And if he didn't come home alone some night, then the private studio would come in even more necessary. If no one asked, he wouldn't tell.

There were no such conundrums now that he worked for Andy. Life was always "on the economy." Sami had no access to government facilities. If he were running an official Op, all secured compartmented information would have been handled in keeping with procedural requirements. Such information would only have been briefed, discussed and stored in a government accredited Sensitive Compartmented Information Facility, or SCIF.

For Operation Home Game, Sami improvised with a key man office near Old Town. Andy's security and communications chiefs met with Sami in the morning, erecting electronic barriers to ensure that the facility was protected from eavesdropping. They also set up elaborate measures for the internet connection and created a storage system.

The Comms Chief was impressed with the view of the Potomac. Riffing on that fact, the team's OPSEC measures called for him to comment on the room's favorable Southern exposure at 11:10 AM. As he finished his work, he noted, "You get great sun in this room in the morning."

Even with his most advanced listening equipment, the Security Chief sitting in his car down on Duke Street could not hear them. At 11:11, he texted the code to indicate that the countermeasures tested operational. The SCIF, as it was, was buttoned-up.

Sami sent out for lunch from Panera and sat alone as the afternoon sun cleared the height of the building and began its journey toward the Blue Ridge. Or was it the Shenandoah? Or the Allegheny? Sami was not expert in what each segment of the Appalachian range was called by its locals. The realization reminded him of what Andy said.

"Homegrowns are like everything else in politics, Dost. Local. Virginia. Masjid Almaany."

A knock on the door revealed that Alexa was the first arrival.

If global politics in recent years taught Sami anything, it was that most people didn't give a second thought to the details that elites and insiders spent most of their time worrying about. That lesson did not stop him from assessing that Alexa's summer suit was Dior, completely New York, and not something that a woman in D.C. would ever wear. No surprise. Everything about Alexa was completely New York. Finding Princeton to be insufficiently feminist, even after her four-year assault on the place's traditions, after graduation she took a job at what she called the "Bear Stearns Boys' Club," and set about attacking Wall Street from the inside.

Over drinks once, Sami saw her smile as he had never seen her smile before. Another member of the team accused her of orchestrating the 2008 financial crisis, which resulted in the ultimate death of her firm.

"I can't claim the credit for that," she said. Taking a small sip from her cucumber gimlet she added, "Not *all* of the credit."

"How's New York?" Sami asked.

"Hoboken actually, I can still see Wall Street, but I like to have the river between me and the Huns, now."

Hoboken. Manhattan. That was another distinction without a difference to most people. She still carried a $10,000 Birken bag, which she placed in a chair by the window before hugging Sami.

Her job was to unravel an adversary's web of financial transactions. Terrorists needed money. It was a fact of life. Without moving money around the world, the only targets accessible to terrorists were the places they lived and the people who lived there with them. Those places and people were still global terrorists' bread and butter, despite all the focus on U.S. and European "homeland" attacks since 2001. But, when they attacked in the West, there were financial signatures. Wires, transfers, Western Union, PayPal: all these modalities left digital fingerprints.

A smart and skilled money man could route funds through enough countries and enough entities to conceal the evidence, but they were no match for a money woman. Alexa would find the trails. No one could do it better. If she discovered the complicity of a multi-national financial institution along the way, all the better. She was spooning salad onto a small plate when the door swung open again, admitting Marc.

"Ich! Is that 'fast casual?' It is, isn't it? Alexa, call me an Uber." It was the first of many jokes Marc would make that day about the commonality between his teammate's name and the ubiquitous Amazon device.

Marc Yoderman was Sami's expert in the cyber domain. Unsurprisingly, given his name and profession, everyone called him "Yoda." He was the only member of the team with an official connection to the U.S. government, by virtue of his ongoing service in the Marine Corps Reserve. It was not an exaggeration when Yoda claimed that he almost single-handedly created MARFORCYBER's offensive capabilities in 2009 and 2010. For that, the Marine Corps was anxious to keep him around, even if it was ludicrous to expect him to remain a junior enlisted Marine.

A gourmand of the highest order, Yoda joked that MARFORCYBER was in New Orleans because the Marine Corps knew he wouldn't visit if he had to eat somewhere else. He lived in a French Quarter walk-up just across the river from the Marine Reserve headquarters SCIF in Algiers, where he came and went with an impulsiveness that rarely corresponded to one weekend a month and two weeks a year. He spent more time than his reserve duty required and offered a hell of a lot more value, and the Marine Corps had shaken off bureaucratic resistance to his comings-and-goings in the interest of the bargain they were getting.

For Yoda's part, he visited the SCIF so often for the same reason that he continued to serve in the Marine Corps at all. "They have the best toys!" With regular access to a near limitless budget for cyber, Yoda brought Sami ancillary benefits beyond his own skills. Yoda was on Silicon Valley's short list when they needed outside perspective on a security challenge and his resume was rounded out by a steady rotation of consulting gigs with tech companies that were household names.

"I know that this town stopped trying after it discovered the steak house, but was this the best we could do?" Alexa could only laugh as Yoda prodded a limp heart of romaine with a fork. Forging a relationship on past operations, somehow their strong personalities clicked, and they enjoyed working together.

Emily was the last member of the core team to arrive. She slipped in almost unnoticed. No hugs or handshakes were offered, and before anyone knew it, she had her computer open and propped on her knees. Small and birdlike, with large glasses in a cat-eye shape out of favor since the 1950s, she was the natural enemy of the Security and Communications types that had "buttoned up" the room earlier in the day.

Trained by the Air Force, and later a quiet but critical contributor to technological advances pioneered by the NSA, Emily was a rare Signals Intelligence talent who was as skilled at collection as she was at analysis. Sami nicknamed her "Section," because she could replace the entire SIGINT section of an intel team. He would have wanted her for any operation, but for Sami, her demeanor was as critical to Home Game as her skill. If he was going to keep his own connection to Karim quiet from the rest of the team, he needed someone as discreet as Emily working on comms.

His team was smart and experienced. Sami was fortunate to get his top choice in each of the key disciplines. As lunch mostly sat on the table, he briefed the intel Andy provided and then laid out their operation.

"You all know how this works. The Incumbent," that was how the unknown client was always referred to, "won't give us much in the way of source intel, so we'll have to reinvent the wheel on some of this. They have provided phone numbers and emails for targeting. We are in early stages on this, but I am confident it will be a brief operation. Someone is being overly-cautious, guys. If you ask me, this looks like amateur hour."

"You said it's not small arms?" Yoda interrupted. "What are you thinking then? Bomb?"

"I think so, yes."

"Then we follow the explosive. That's always the path of least resistance. It has the additional benefit of focusing effort on the weapon. Prevents distraction. That's the best way to prevent an attack from happening."

"I agree, but we have specific direction not to follow that trail." Even Emily looked up at that. "I assume the Incumbent is working the bomb from their side. Our direction is to identify members of the cell, own their comms, track their movements, figure out the flow of money, and identify links to the plot." No one was satisfied with the answer, least of all Sami, so he continued quickly and finally. "We start now."

Sami left his team to their work, with plans to regroup the next day. He had his own work to do on Home Game, which he kept it to himself, except for a brief conversation with Emily on the way out. For a previous operation, she had devised her own mobile phone tracking software that captured voice, images, emails, web activity, keystroke data and other important data from a target's cell phone. There were cheating spouse apps on the app stores, but Emily's software was unlike anything available commercially. To truly own a target's phone, Emily's app made use of a combination of zero-day exploits that intel agencies had been hoarding for years.

What made Emily's solution so elegant was how she designed it to be uploaded to a phone with minimum access and few steps. To make the installation a success, Emily needed to be standing by. Sami reviewed the plan and the timeline with her. Then he left for drinks with a friend.

NORTHWEST WASHINGTON

The invitation came out of nowhere. Karim hadn't heard from Sami in months. Then again, ever since that night in college, "out of nowhere" was Sami's modus operandi. If you had asked Karim to list his friends who were most likely to join the Army after college, Sami would have been dead last. But that's what his friend had done. And then, after months of mysterious obfuscations about his civilian work after he was discharged, Sami told Karim about his "consulting job." Sami wasn't trained in business, economics, or anything else where his skills could help on a consulting gig.

He was an American-born Muslim with the ability to speak several languages and a past in military intelligence. Karim knew what kind of consulting Sami did. It didn't bother Karim. Everyone needed to feed their family. Except Sami didn't have a family.

After that night in college, Karim watched his friend drift away from the life that everyone expected for him. He drifted away from Karim and Masjid Almaany, too. He drifted away from his grandfather.

"What is he supposed to do?" Karim's wife asked him. "Go to one of those brainwashing places where they cure people so that his grandfather will talk to him again?"

"I don't know!"

"Exactly. There is nothing he can do. Besides, people change. You can't hold it against him that he isn't the same guy he was in third grade. Or freshman year. He's your friend." She was right.

Like Sami, Karim was not the same guy he had been in college, or during their shared childhood in the Northern Virginia suburbs. That would become evident as soon as he ordered a club soda with lime at the bar. He wondered what

Sami might say about that and dismissed the thought just as quickly. Sami wouldn't say anything. They were friends.

Sami barely raised an eyebrow, but Karim had no idea how heavily the decision not to order alcohol would weigh on Sami's mind.

The boys were raised within a mile of each other in the same suburb that Masjid Almaany occupied. They met because both families were communicants at the mosque, but their parents shared much more in common than religion. They were all of Pakistani extraction and their stories of childhood in the old country were as familiar as the tales told by Irish immigrants a hundred years before. Sometimes happy but also wistful. Mostly happy that they now lived in the United States.

Both sets of parents were highly educated and had taken jobs in the Washington-based economic development and foreign aid sector. Despite his grandfather's fervency, Sami's parents were casual Muslims. Almost secular. This was something else that they shared with Karim's family.

Both boys were less concerned with Islam, Pakistan or foreign aid than they were with the NBA. Most conversations turned on questions like should Allen Iverson have won the MVP in 2001? Karim didn't think so. Iverson shot too much. Karim was a Jason Kidd fan.

They went to mosque on Friday, just like other kids went to church on Sunday. But that was it. Karim and Sami were normal kids. Just who had changed that paradigm first would be a point of debate between them. One night, Sami had told Karim things that not many high school buddies and college roommates were ready to hear. Sami himself was forever coming to terms with those things, and how those things impacted his life as a Muslim and an American; but he had settled on one thing for certain. It wasn't wrong. It was how he was born.

After the two drifted apart, Sami was surprised when he heard that Karim married a devout Muslim woman in a traditional Nikah. At a past meeting, they discussed the matter, Karim wondering aloud whether Sami had expected him to marry a Presbyterian girl in the National Cathedral. They were

Muslims, and while Karim was forever coming to terms with how his religion affected his life as an American; he had settled on one thing for certain. It wasn't wrong. It was how he was born. And it was how he raised his children.

That was why Sami made so much of Karim's club soda with lime. Intel officers tried to inhabit their subjects. Even with a lifelong friend, behavior could only reveal so much. Sami could not know that Karim's abstention – while in stark contrast to some of their nights in college – was very much in keeping with his life as a thirtysomething husband and father. There was no alcohol at Karim's wedding, and there was none kept in his home. Was that radical?

They met at a busy, upscale place near Metro Center, and rather than sit at the bar they took two seats at a high countertop along the windows. After they ordered, Sami stood and pretended to struggle with removing his keys and phone from his pockets.

"Let me see pictures of the kids, man!" He gestured toward Karim's phone. From his standing vantage point, Sami carefully observed Karim's password as he unlocked the phone. Karim held the screen toward Sami.

"Oh, man! They're so big. How old now?"

"Muhammad is 8 and Mariam is 5."

"Let me see." Sami grabbed the phone and made an exaggerated pop of his eyes. "It sucks getting so old, I can barely see anymore."

Sami noticed his friend flinch almost imperceptibly and he hoped he hadn't overplayed his hand already. Worse, he hoped that what he witnessed was not the panic of an operative in a homegrown cell, alarmed that a former Army intel officer and "consultant" now had hands on his phone. It was neither. Sami's use of the expletive caused Karim's reaction. That seemed a little puritanical, which Sami registered, but he also noticed that Karim didn't seem bothered at all by relinquishing control of the phone.

Sami returned it and retook his seat.

"Well, if you're not going to drink, let's get food, man. I'm not just going to watch you drink a club soda. I'm starving!"

Sami rubbed his hands together over the menu. It was a gesture matched well with his casual enthusiasm. It had been too long since he had a conversation that was not orchestrated. He needed to remedy that, but it would have to wait for after Home Game.

They shared hummus and pita and shared a few laughs over how every restaurant in D.C. tried the Mediterranean chickpea dish now. The conversation was casual. They were once so close that they slid into a rapport more easily than Sami expected or could have hoped.

Sami directed the conversation back to their shared passion for the NBA.

"You won't believe who I met, man!" Sami almost shouted. It was enthusiasm. Excitement. Setting the hook. Karim's eyes lit up.

"Grandmama!" Sami shouted.

"What!" Karim was impressed.

Larry Johnson, AKA "Grandmama," was a 1990s basketball star who won a national championship at the University of Nevada Las Vegas and was drafted 2nd overall by the Charlotte Hornets. He gained wider fame for the Converse shoe commercials where he dressed as an old woman in a long gingham dress. An old woman who could ball.

"We didn't do a selfie— "

"Oh, come on!" Karim interrupted.

"I know. I blew it, but I was trying to play it cool. I got a picture though."

Sami tapped away at his phone, sending an SMS to Karim with a photo of the erstwhile basketball star that he and Emily had downloaded earlier in the day from Google. He put the phone down again. "Check it out!" He indicated that Karim should check his phone.

When Karim received the SMS, Sami encouraged him to click on the photo.

"Zoom in. Check out his right hand." Sami stood, walked behind Karim and looked over his shoulder. To his friend, and to anyone watching, it was a simple gesture of excitement. But Sami did it to make sure that Karim clicked on the photo, which would upload the malicious file. "Boom! Right there. UNLV championship ring. I shook that hand, dude!"

While Karim registered the impressiveness of his friend's feat, Emily's app was uploading.

The tricky part was installation. Any good tracking software used the phone's own systems as its backbone. The interoperability that Global 100 companies programmed into even the most basic phones was an unintended boon to SIGINT collection. But phone programmers required a user to approve every app's access to the phone's hardware and other apps. Anyone downloading and installing an app was familiar with the series of pop-up windows that would have come next.

Can this app access your camera?

Can this app access your contact list?

The elegance in Emily's coding was the combination of zero-day exploits that bypassed this entire process.

Next, apps ask to be configured. This process takes time, creating the slowly-filling progress bar scenario familiar from spy movies. Not with Emily's app. Stage two allowed for remote configuration. The design had the immense benefit of allowing for the detail work to be done remotely. Sami hoped Emily was starting the configuration from Alexandria, without risk, even as Sami retook his seat.

Sami's own phone vibrated with the text he was waiting for.

Can you do the call tomorrow at 1?

It was the confirmation. The seed was planted. Emily was beginning configuration back at the makeshift SCIF. Sami's work was done.

Karim's wasn't. Soon after the plates were cleared, Sami realized that his friend had been screwing up his courage throughout the meal.

"Have you spoken to Abu Muhammad?"

"I haven't even thought of him," Sami lied.

"He's a wise man, Sami. You can't blame him for—" Karim stopped, unsure what to say. A word danced through his mind. It was a word he was never comfortable with and one he had never spoken until that night in college. He had never spoken that word since and he would not say it now. "He is from a different place and time. They had different attitudes. That is not his fault."

"I don't fault him for his place or time. I blame him for his attitudes. It is ironic that I should not fault him for when and where he was born. I only ask not to be judged for *how* I was born."

Even this oblique conversation was too much for Karim's sensibilities and his cheeks flushed. Sami was returned to that night, in their dorm room. He remembered how brilliantly his strategy worked. He knew what he had discovered and how it drove him away from his grandfather. But Karim never found out. No one ever would. Sami's deception was carried off so perfectly that he not only fooled Karim, he fooled himself.

For a few moments that night, the biggest problem in his world was that he was gay. On that excuse could be hung the reason Sami would never see his grandfather again. But sexuality was not what had driven Sami from his grandfather. It was something else. Something Karim never heard because Sami told no one.

His betrayal of Karim's trust today was on par with that night. If Karim was embarrassed now, Sami wondered how the anger would look on his face. Would he turn redder still if he knew what Sami had done by exploiting their friendship? With the spy software uploaded on Karim's phone done, and the topic of his grandfather broached, Sami suddenly wanted their meeting to be over. He decided that he would deploy the same tactic that had worked to such tremendous effect before.

"I'm gay, Karim."

If he could have, Karim would have burst through the plate glass window. The night in college was a vivid memory he did not wish to relive. He asked questions then that he wished he did not know the answers to. Karim rose to his feet, marking his imminent intention to leave.

Even though the misdirection worked as Sami planned, it had infuriated him. A voice rose within, repeating *I am a person. I am your friend. Your friend!*

But then another voice rose. *A friend? A friend? Do you spy on your friends?*

There were parts of himself that Sami did not like. They were not the same parts that Karim and Abu Muhammad had a problem with.

Karim was confused by Sami's sudden distance and he broke the silence. "I know that he would like to see you. That's all. He raised you. He deserves to see you before he dies."

"You don't know what he deserves," Sami deadpanned. He resisted the urge to say more.

And you don't deserve what I am doing to you. Unless Andy's right.

If he was, Sami would know soon enough.

EIGHT

ALEXANDRIA

"We have nothing," Sami said.

"You know I want details, Dost. Let me hear from the team."

"You want the details of nothing?"

A weekend of work complete, the Home Game team were in the temporary office-cum-SCIF and Andy Rizzo was visiting for an update. His mere presence indicated the speed of the operation. Andy thought something was imminent. Which only made Sami more suspicious, because he wasn't lying. They had nothing. He nodded at Alexa to begin.

"The money trail is real, but it's low-tech." She began before Andy interrupted

"No signs of sophistication?"

"I didn't say that. Someone is moving it through several cutouts. There's a combination of fake PayPal accounts, some Western Union cash transfers that are U.S. to U.S. But it doesn't add up. We're missing money. Which leads me to believe that there have been hand to hand deliveries. Or at least cash drops."

"It's homegrown," Andy added.

"We already knew that—" Sami interjected before Andy raised an annoyed hand in his direction.

"The weird thing about the trail," Alexa continued "is that it's there at all."

"How so?"

"If you can do cash drops, why not just keep it up? If you ask me, the online and wire activity is there for a reason."

"Don't keep me in suspense, darling," Andy said, after a brief silence.

Alexa blanched at Andy's term of address. She reminded herself, as she had each day on Wall Street, that Andy's money was still green.

"Either it's a false trail, to make someone not as smart as me, think the money is not coming from someone in the U.S., which it is..."

"Or?"

"Or, the trail is there just so we would find the recipient."

Andy flipped pages of the team's briefing binder before saying, "Hasan Khalifa." It was a charade. The name was front and center in his mind.

Sami picked up the narrative from there.

"The money all goes back to Hasan Hamad Khalifa."

"Who is he?"

"Imam at a new mosque in Annapolis. American. The parents left Egypt in '67. His father was a famous geologist— "

"There are famous geologists?" Andy was feigning perusal of the bio on Hasan.

"He was as famous as they get. Hasan has no notable history. No notable ties. His Arab Studies Masters comes from a school in Cairo. He was there during the Arab Spring, but it was dumb luck. No other foreign travel to indicate international connections."

"Not in person, but there's a virtual world out there. Where has he gone online?"

Sami gestured his approval and Yoda responded.

"Hasan's internet history is similar to the rest of the group. They are clearly part of a group. The internet histories establish a connection. But it seems like a religious studies group. They look at the same passages from the Qur'an on the same day. Nothing that stinks, on any of them. One spends a lot of time on his fantasy baseball team. Another on Redskins blogs. Looks like a couple travel heavily for work. They spend a lot of time cruising hotel websites."

"Nothing that doesn't fit?" Andy asked.

"Hasan has an IRC chat client on the computer. Internet Relay Chat. Everyone knows Signal, because Snowden endorsed it, but it is for mobile devices. This is the laptop version. That's notable I guess."

"Use history?"

"The app erases any exploitable usage data. Even if we were online with him when he was chatting, it's encrypted."

Sami waded back in. He voice was tinged with impatience he didn't have to try hard to feign. But it was feigned. In part to disguise him cutting off the briefing before Emily was put on the spot. He also broke in for the benefit of his team, he wanted them to witness what happened next.

"That's it, Coach. All we have are a whole bunch of U.S. Muslims who have normal jobs and spend a lot of time playing fantasy baseball and trying to figure out which hotels to stay in when they take business trips."

"Who, we can assess, are connected in some sort of group based on their internet activity," Andy added.

"They study the Qur'an together." Sami dismissed. "They all attend the same mosque."

"What about the cash?" Andy countered. "By whatever means, it enters Hasan's accounts and then goes out to buy these guys trucks."

"Agreed. That's the smoking gun right now. But we need more. If you think something is happening, and happening soon, we need the raw intelligence. Or we could watch these guys until there's an attack and get nothing."

"I can't give you any raw intel. Because I don't have it. You know that."

"Then we need the analysis on the explosives, at least."

Andy's expression flashed anger at Sami's breach of the chain of command. Sami might have confronted Andy with the supposition that this was a potential bombing on day one, and the team might all have concluded the same thing, but Andy never confirmed that. He didn't appreciate being dressed down by a subordinate in front of a team of contractors. A deep breath allowed him to compose himself.

"Look," the words came out through a clenched jaw. "We do our job. We do what we can with what we have. Keep watching. If something is happening, you'll catch it."

"And hope it's not too late?" Sami had emboldened Alexa, who was happy to have Sami's back and strike a revenge blow for Andy's earlier condescension.

Andy ignored the comment. "Dig deeper into the data. We're a small team, so prioritize. Who are we watching? Get eyes on, ears on. 24/7. Use the access to the group that we have." Andy stared daggers at Sami, clearly indicating he was disappointed with the lack of development of the Karim connection. He turned back to Alexa before finishing. "And if something is happening, you need to get us there on time."

A look around the room was met with four tight nods. The briefing book could not leave the SCIF, so Andy dropped it on the table and headed to the door.

"Walk me out, Dost."

They rode the elevator down in silence. Outside, a mild breeze off the river reduced the day's heat index to mild. Andy walked about thirty feet away from the door and turned on his heel.

"I appreciate the need for the theatrics. I'm not pissed about that, OK?"

"OK. Good."

"The reason I'm pissed is that you haven't gone after Karim Sulemani."

"I got"—Sami almost slipped up but caught himself before he revealed that he had complete access to Karim's phone. Nothing had come from it yet, but if there was anything, he wanted ownership of the information and the ability to massage the sourcing before he gave it to Andy. "I met him, Coach. We had dinner. There's nothing."

"Work him harder because he's connected to Hasan Khalifa. The truck proves it. And Khalifa is dirty." Andy took a step closer before continuing. "If I didn't make this clear enough at the outset, this is a whole new ballgame, Dost. For all of us, but especially you. You're not bird-dogging PIRs that may lead to a UAV mission, OK. This is a domestic attack. Imminent. People in the U.S. will die."

"Then the FBI— "

"We've had this conversation."

"I understand, but we don't have a domestic intelligence service in this country, OK? We don't do secret police. There's no Lubyanka. I can't grab people off the street. I listen. I watch. I gather evidence. I build a case."

"Then what? You tell us who blew up the buildings after they killed innocent people – and themselves – in an attack? No! That's the fucking FBI's job! Not good enough! We're talking about counterterrorism. With these stakes, there's only one way to do it. Given the players, there's only one person who can do it. You need to step out from behind the keyboard. It's not a shroud that separates you and your job from the spies and theirs. There's nobody waiting for the intel. No one will read a report and decide to launch the drone strike."

Andy gestured with his shoulders and Sami followed him down the sidewalk. "We will not get caught standing around like the Europeans. London. Paris. Berlin. The fucking continent is gone. And we'll never be a police state like Israel, you understand? As long as Congress has their thumbs up their asses, those of us in the field need to chart the middle ground. To protect America *and* American values. We will act before we are attacked. I don't care what the history with Karim Sulemani is, or whatever reason you have for the kid gloves treatment. You can't run an operation with your team in the dark."

"What am I supposed to say? Tell them that one of our targets was my best friend growing up. And my college roommate! I lose credibility. Nobody in their right mind would work with me on the job."

"Throw out the rule book! I know that's not your strength, but— "

"You know that! Then why put me on the job?"

"I told you why!" Rizzo grabbed Sami by the elbow and turned toward him, almost nose to nose as pedestrians passed on Duke Street. "Masjid Almanny!" Andy let the words linger. He was good at what he did. He knew that letting Sami marinate in the name of the mosque would work on Sami's memory. His grandfather built the mosque from the ground up. Abu Muhammad was shorthand for Masjid Almanny. In the U.S., and especially the D.C. area, the mosque and the man were interchangeable.

"It doesn't stop with Sulemani." Rizzo's words hung in the air between them a moment, before a fresh breeze seemed to blow them away. Rizzo's implication crowded the space between them, and they both took a step back.

"What's going on here, Coach? You're talking in riddles. From the beginning, this operation has been a cluster. The whole thing has been closed book. OK, fine, I haven't told the team about my relationship with Karim, but we're in the dark on more than that. It's not OPSEC. You are keeping something. And now," Sami hesitated before continuing, "We've done this a million times, and his name has never come up before."

"It's not normal. I agree. But there is nothing I have that you don't have. The Incumbent is shitting bricks. It's local Muslims and it's not an exercise. They're fucking scared, Dost. You are great at your job. The best I have. But you're not exactly entrenched with local Muslims."

Local Muslims aren't my job! Sami wanted to yell. But he had made his point and Andy didn't slow for a moment.

"Estrangement from your grandfather is estrangement from the whole community. The threat was never here before. Never at home, in D.C., in our own backyard. In *his* community. If Abu Muhammad can help us, then you need to talk to him. Same as Karim."

Long ago, Andy told Sami they had to trust each other because they could not afford to trust anyone else. Long after this operation concluded, Sami would still wonder what Andy Rizzo knew and when he knew it. Why had he told Sami to treat his grandfather the same as Karim? Karim was a suspect.

Years ago, Sami explained his grandfather to Andy. Andy knew Sami's sexuality was not the seed of their estrangement, just the final straw. Once it had broken the camel's back, Sami flogged the beast by joining the U.S. military to fight in the War on Terror.

Iraq. Afghanistan.

It wasn't the whole story, but there was enough red meat there for Sami to satisfy Andy and pass a poly. No one knew the truth.

NINE

KARACHI, PAKISTAN 1941 – 1962
LOUDON COUNTY, VIRGINIA 1962 – 1993

Abu Muhammad was Made in America, an identity adopted by Tahir Lakhani, born in 1941 on the outskirts of Karachi, Pakistan. Then populated by fewer than 500,000, by the time Tahir left for the U.S., his childhood home was at the center of a metropolis that had grown to over 2 million souls. Other cities in Pakistan grew during this period because rural people moved to cities as the country's population exploded. But, more than any other city, Karachi bore the brunt of the religious-political upheaval of India's immediate post-independence period.

With the split of the British Indian Empire into two independent countries that have been enemies ever since, Muslim Muhajirs were driven from secular India. They settled in Karachi by the millions. Muhajirs eventually outnumbered native Sindhis and the city became the center of Pakistani Sufism. A land that was unchanged for millennia, and then experienced the violent influence of the British Raj over the course of 100 years, suddenly experienced kaleidoscopic urbanization, modernization, and globalization in a single generation.

Tahir's family were not spared. His parents were subsistence farmers under the Raj but spent Tahir's childhood working in factories. Neither occupation invested them with much aptitude for educating their son to live in a modern world they barely understood themselves. So, they turned him over to the most well-funded school in their area, a Hanafi madrassa.

By twenty years old, Tahir was a promising scholar of Islam. His marriage to the daughter of the madrassa's founder was a testament to his ascendancy. He studied in Egypt and Saudi Arabia. With his wife and young son Muhammad in tow, his first experience with the U.S. came in the throes of the turbulent 1960s. Studying in a U.S. exchange program near Washington, within six months of arriving in the country he witnessed the assassinations of Martin Luther King, Jr. and Robert Kennedy. Power struggles were being fought in the streets. History was being made by assassin's bullets. The U.S. never seemed more like a Middle Eastern kingdom. But for one difference. Islam.

In the mid-1960s, the religion was known among Americans for the strain proselytized by Malcolm X, who was shot and killed after his own power struggle with Nation of Islam leader Elijah Muhammad. With the passage of the same 1965 immigration act that permitted Hasan Khalifa's parents to enter, immigration from majority Muslim countries grew exponentially. Tahir thought the time was right to build a meaningful home in the U.S. for traditional, Middle Eastern Islam. He raised money from local communicants and contributors around the world, and while the mosque that was completed in the early 1970s would pale by comparison to the Masjid Almaany project completed in the 1980s, it was during this time that Tahir adopted a name worthy of his ambition. Abu Muhammad. Father of Muhammad.

The son, Muhammad Lakhani, grew up at his father's knee. The mosque was central to his life and not just as a place of worship. The construction projects defined his father's life for decades, and young Muhammad traveled with his father to far-flung places in search of support. It was during his early twenties that a former general named Muhammad Zia-ul-Haq rose to power in Pakistan. The rise was contemporaneous with Reagan's in the U.S., and the two governments collaborated with mujahideen to expel the Soviet Union from Afghanistan. Abu Muhammad was uniquely situated to support communication and the strengthening of relations between two nations allied against the Communists, each for their own reasons. He not only raised funds for his mosque, but he raised his profile. And became a political player.

Aided by the CIA and Pakistani ISI, the mujahideen garnered valuable combat materiel during this period and learned the insurgent tactics necessary for a small, disjointed group of tribal forces to defeat a military superpower. Some said the CIA also taught them how to scale production and distribution of heroin. The residue of war with the Soviets also included the displacement of millions, many of whom settled into refugee camps in northwestern Pakistan. Muhammad and his father visited these camps during the mid-1980s.

The father saw more evidence than ever of the need for Zia-ul-Haq's campaign of sharization or Islamization in Pakistan.

The son saw something else. Frequent trips with his father, the construction of the first D.C. mosque in the 1970s, even the ambitious second and grander mosque in the 1980s, could not remit Muhammad of the influences of his American childhood. Seeing the millions starving, sitting at the seat of power as meetings to address the issue were held, Muhammad Lakhani did not think the solution was Islam. It was politics.

Global cooperation was routing the Soviets. The wealth of the West brought to bear not for military conquest but to feed the starving. Foreign Aid. Economic Development. With his father's growing political contacts, it was not difficult to get a foreign aid appointment. Thanks to his own intellect, ambition, and experience, he rose swiftly. Along the way, he met a woman who shared his commitment to the work. In 1982, their son Samir was born.

Abu Muhammad was not considered radical in the mid-1990s, as Sami entered his second decade of life. He was a Muslim, but an Americanized one. He was connected to the Reagan and Bush White Houses. His overt religiosity left him at arms-length from Clinton, but he was still relevant, given his prominence as an interlocutor during the Afghan war against the Soviets. Clinton valued the imam's political ties to both American Muslims and to the region of his birth.

But rapidly, more rapidly than anyone realized, Abu Muhammad and his adherents were finding fault with Muhammad and his benefactors. The simple geopolitics of the Cold War - the enemy of my enemy is my friend – had allied them against the shared threat of Soviet Socialism. But as the last decade of the 20th Century dawned, the mujahideen turned their ire on the formerly allied Americans with quickness and completeness that affirmed they had learned more from the Cold War than how to take down Russian Mils helicopters.

The withdrawal of the Soviets from Afghanistan created space in a failed state. Disgruntled ex-holy warriors radicalized, and radicalized others. The Iraqi invasion of Kuwait and the decision by Arab states to allow America to ride to the rescue, solidifying its role as regional strongman, shocked the consciences and stoked the grievances of militant Islamist groups. A group of innovators saw the potential to scale fragmented, regional operations that they had directed against Soviet Communism into a global war against capitalism, colonialism, and secularism. By the middle of Bill Clinton's first term, Usama bin Laden was a name well known to U.S. intelligence.

The U.S. was living in its post-Cold War fantasy. The lone superpower, it was exalted in the decade between the fall of the Berlin Wall and the fall of the Twin Towers. The nation that had bled the Soviets dry had not yet been bloodied at the nose by fewer than two dozen twentysomethings. The environment in embassies and foreign service posts was incomparable to the security footing of what would become the "post-9/11" world.

Sami was 11. He was at home in Northern Virginia. At his grandfather's home. As Sami reached school age, his parents' steady rotation of foreign postings were anathema to his consistent scholastic and social development. His mother and father were due back by mid-summer, in time to enjoy extra time with him while school was out. Calls were infrequent, but there was a letter or two a week.

He was sitting at the kitchen table of his grandfather's home. Abu Muhammad, the fearless, had brought over a friend's mother to help deliver the news. She was a close friend of his mother's. The virtuous imam left the room, leaving her to the task.

"Sami, there has been a horrible tragedy..."

TEN

ANNAPOLIS

The highlight of Hasan's week was the time he spent with the Islamic Center's burgeoning Youth Council. The Council was composed of boys aged 13 to 18, all of whom reminded him of his own teenage years. Each of them were devout and striving in their faith, but they were distracted. As much as they sought to know the truth, they were tested. They were tempted by sex and the objectification of the female form. Alcohol was ever present in their suburban high schools and they were challenged by a culture that encouraged experimentation. If they pushed the boundaries and succumbed to these temptations as a normal part of life, America had so much more on offer. They were not children of Allah, but children of America, and it had poisoned their minds.

He hoped that someday there would be a girls' council, but it would not do for him to minister to girls. When he started the Center, he dreamed that he would meet the woman who could. Perhaps she would even be his wife. A devout, Muslim woman, committed to Allah and to him, with whom he could build his community. As time went on, the fantasy became harder to maintain. The activities that had become the primary purpose of the Center would not allow him time to create a girls' council. And he would never have a wife. At least, not here.

As Hasan considered this, his phone chirped a unique, new tone. It was an incoming message on Signal, an encrypted messaging app. Without looking, he knew it would be the man who called himself Zechariah. Whatever Hasan had once imagined for the Center, everything was directed to Zechariah's purposes now.

Hasan excused himself from the boys and closed the door to his private office. It took a moment to acquaint himself with the app. It was one he had never used before. When Zechariah communicated, it was always by a new, encrypted channel he used one time only. He was a wise man. And a man who agreed that America was a poisonous place. A place without piety. *Taqwa.*

Without his time in Egypt, Hasan never would have found the purity that cemented his own faith, and which opened the world to him. His purity made him an imam, allowed him the opportunity to lead his own congregation, and recommended him for Zechariah's mission. Hasan would not sit idle in the face of doubts about whether the boys in his Council would ever find a culture of purity in which to develop and practice Islam. Zechariah had given him an opportunity to act. The American culture of sin was the basis of their partnership, in fact.

Where Zechariah's purity was found, Hasan did not know. Sometimes he permitted himself to imagine. His fancy settled on great scenes of the Muslim world. Zechariah in a gleaming thobe, stood on a balcony outside Masjid al-Haram as a throng crowded Mecca and genuflected to the Kaaba in searing heat. Zechariah in the dusty streets outside of Masjid Al-Aqsa, answering the call to prayer in the Holy City's Muslim Quarter, even as Jews and Christians turned their covetous stares toward the four minarets that mark the holiest place in all Abrahamic faith. And because Hasan was born into a time when Muslims worldwide were called to jihad, he had visions of Zechariah the *mujahid.*

In their ignorance, Americans called those who brought holy war jihadis. This was nonsense. A child's word. *Mujahid* were the warriors. Hasan imagined Zechariah shouldering a rocket launcher in Beirut, even as Hasan was only a child. Or Zechariah kneeling in prayer next to Sheikh Usama himself, outside the mouth of a mountain cave in the Spin Ghar. The visions of Zechariah the soldier were the most vivid because this was their shared mission. Or, Zechariah's mission. He was the holy warrior. Hasan was but a weapon.

If Hasan was certain of this, he was also sure that Zechariah had been routed somewhere in the service of Allah and forced to come to America. Zechariah was devout, he was righteous, he was experienced, he was ingenious; but he was also American. Hasan knew this. He had picked up on cues even in their limited communication. At first, this had thrown Hasan. Unnerved him. But their mutual friend had vouched for Zechariah. Hasan had never asked for details. And then the time for asking had passed.

The instructions came. Hasan formed the Council of Muhammad. Hasan handled the money as instructed. He bought the pickups. He provided information on the members of the mosque who now drove the trucks. He bought new phones, he changed sim cards, and he downloaded apps. All as he was told.

And now he looked down at a message he had been awaiting with anticipation. It was the message that signaled a start to Zechariah's plan.

Hasan returned to pray with the boys in the Youth Council, for now, they might be saved.

ALEXANDRIA

If Home Game were on the books, Sami would have had a variety of resources at his disposal. Metadata on the targets' phones would lead to clear connections that could be investigated more closely. Corresponding warrants from the Foreign Intelligence Surveillance Court would have permitted surveillance of the targets' telephonic and electronic communications, and those of their close, frequent or suspicious contacts.

If Sami were on the books, he would surveil Hasan's home and office. They would make surreptitious entry to implant listening devices and cameras. Technical Services ("OTS") could install wireless cameras and microphones in an amazing variety of household objects.

Various and sundry case officers and technical support staff would have rotated through shifts, on fixed and mobile surveillance. The objective would have been to gather intelligence that allowed for disruption of any mission or objective of the cell before an attack. If the time came when Hasan's cell was poised to act, and disruption was inadequate, paramilitary officers from Special Operations Group ("SOG") would be summoned.

Home Game wasn't on the books. There were a number of reasons for that, not least that all the targets of Home Game were so-called "United States Persons," and legally exempt from any action of a U.S. intelligence agency. This fact was still stuck in Sami's craw. But today, immediate practical concerns were edging out the persistent, gnawing worry that had dogged Sami since Andy brought him the mission. There was action from the enemy, and he needed to marshal his meager resources in coverage.

OTS's gadgets and SOG's soldiers were a remnant of life on the light side. Here, in the black, there were limits. In recent days, Alexa had confirmed that the bulk of cash transiting into and out of Hasan's accounts was not being transferred by electronic means. Cash was changing hands directly, but with personnel limited to his small team of collectors and analysts, Sami had no one to surveil Hasan.

Unsure that he wanted to divulge the depth of his relationship with Karim, Sami was cryptic with the team about where the intel had been gathered, but through Emily's access to Karim's phone, they had the emails of each Council of Muhammad member, including Hasan. There was nothing enlightening in the email traffic.

But the team knew where Hasan banked, so Yoda proposed a simple spear phishing gambit. An email purporting to be from his bank would elicit a password from Hasan. If he used the same password for his email, they would breach the inner sanctum. It succeeded, and it gave the team access to Hasan's entire email history. Sami hoped that would put an end to it. Like the amateur he had so far proved himself to be, Hasan might discuss an operation or reveal a contact on his personal email account.

Sami's hard-won experience had proven to him that it was in mundane matters where the cohorts of an operation slipped up. Some things cannot be faked, lied about or covered up. He implored the team not to get discouraged, to keep collecting and analyzing data as planned, and to keep holding twice-daily meetings to discuss any developments. They were in one of those meetings when they got their first break.

"Not much new to report." Yoda was concluding his briefing on Hasan's email communications. "Tonight could be big, but without some technical help, it will be tough to hear much. According to Hasan's latest email, they have a private room reserved in the restaurant for the Council of Muhammad meeting. 7 o'clock. At..." Yoda consulted his computer screen, "a Hilton out on the West side of Annapolis. Going toward Interstate 97."

"They moved it." It was Emily, quiet as ever, but in the face of quizzical glances from the team, she was certain. She looked at Sami, offered an apologetic shrug, and then continued, "I have an SMS from 45 minutes ago to Karim Sulemani. They changed the meeting location to the Marriott on Compromise. Downtown, by the harbor."

Sami frowned, "What is the recency on both data points?"

"Mine is this morning's email from Hasan to the group," Yoda said. "Standard reminder. It was at 0821."

It was five minutes into their 2:30 meeting. 1435.

"And yours is 45 minutes ago, Em?"

"Yeah. That's not all. Hasan asked to meet him ahead of time. He said," Emily quoted from the transcript in front of her. "Need to talk with you before Council meeting. Nothing bad. How about coffee?"

She continued, "Karim accepted and suggested they meet at the Starbucks out by the Islamic Center. He said he could be there by 17:30. Hasan responded, 'That's another thing. We moved the meeting to the Marriott downtown, by the harbor. Long story.' He suggested another coffee shop for the meeting. On the other side of the Naval Academy from the Marriott."

Sami was leaning forward now. "Anything else?"

Emily looked up from the transcript before reporting the next part of the communication. "He told Karim exactly where to park."

***

The energy in the room was palpable. It was the first potential break the team had seen. After ferociously tapping at the keys of his laptop, Yoda was the first to speak.

"There are no emails to the rest of the group, or to any member of the group, after this morning's email."

"No one else was told that the meeting was moved?" Sami's intonation barely registered as a question.

"We don't know that." It was Alexa, as excited as the rest but always glad to designate herself the Devil's Advocate. "He might have texted them all and we don't have their phones like we, apparently, have Karim's."

Alexa's disapproving look went to Emily, who ignored it. Sami noted it though. He needed to come clean but opening the book on his connections to this investigation – all his connections – was still too risky.

Yoda filled the silence. "He has a group email thread, about the meeting, and he sends individual texts instead?" Yoda was incredulous. "Why would he do that?"

"The problem is that we don't know what he would do," Emily added. She, along with Sami, had been struggling the most with the team's limitations and blind spots.

Sami waited another moment, to clear the air in case anyone else had a strong opinion. But he already knew his answer.

"It doesn't matter. We know where Hasan will be before the meeting, wherever it ends up being. He'll be having coffee with Karim. We have to be there, too. If his instructions to Karim indicate deception, we're there."

"We have nothing to lose," Alexa said looking at Yoda. Sami was the boss, but they were all freelancers. Yoda's would be the decisive third vote.

"Be there? Us and what army?" Sami walked to the window as Yoda continued. "Look, I'm not as bothered by the leap of faith. That's what intel operations are, take a data point, tease it out, analyze it; but then we're supposed to brief someone and make a recommendation. Someone with guns. Someone with a mission. There are four of us! To do this right we need static surveillance on-site. That needs to arrive well before Karim and Hasan. For surveillance to get us any sound, we would need at least two or three people on a team. Plus, a counter-surveillance team of two or three, minimum. Then the technical side. Two vehicles, not counting the vehicles that deliver the people in play. One for command. One for collection. That's four drivers. And an extraction plan, staffed by a vehicle with driver and two principals who would be armed."

Sami stared out at Duke Street. "That's not possible."

"Neither is the mission!"

"We have Karim's phone," Emily said, all pretense to the contrary now abandoned. "We can listen without being there. That's our best bet." Her tone suggested a compromise.

"You're both right, but it's not enough." Sami walked back to the table and sat next to Alexa. "This is our first opening. It might only be a sliver of daylight, but we have to take the chance."

"This isn't Berlin 1950, right?" Alexa said. "We should be fine without all the bells and whistles."

"I'm a Marine, Lex. OK?" Yoda was standing. "This isn't about balls. It's about what's practical. We can't pull this off."

"As ever, it comes back to a guy thinking the decision has something to do with his balls."

Sami wasn't sure Alexa was joking, but she relieved some of the tension. Yoda was right, and Sami knew it. But he had not heard anything he had not expected, and he had already weighed the risks.

"We have to pull it off, guys." He told them how.

TWELVE

ANNAPOLIS

Karim found the open parking spot where Hasan described. He was early and with parking so easy, he was relieved to know that he would make the meeting with plenty of time to spare. His relief was such that he never considered why Hasan had been so specific about where he should park. He also never noticed the car that had been trailing him since the interstate and right into the hilltop neighborhood looking down on the Naval Academy campus.

They had Karim's phone and Emily believed that they would hear the conversation without anyone from the team being in the coffee shop. Her personal vehicle was sitting in the hourly lot at BWI and she was in a rental car a block past the coffee shop with no line of sight. It was not ideal. They hoped no one would notice her sitting in the car, and if someone did, they hoped that person would not think twice about a woman sitting in her car with headphones on and a computer on her lap.

Yoda had placed a GPS beacon on Hasan's car over the weekend. They could track him, but without all the additional support that Yoda correctly outlined back in Alexandria, there was nothing they could do if Hasan drove by Emily in her static post. By then, it would be too late. Sami told her to pretend to be working and hope that Hasan would not pass her way when he arrived. The rental car was their only concession to OPSEC and it was a meager one. It was a risk that Sami never would have tolerated if this were a full-blown operation.

Worse, Alexa was in her own personal vehicle. After Sami outlined the mission plan, she had immediately gone to shadow Karim. There was no time for her to swap out her vehicle. She followed him from work, ready to alert the team if he deviated from the plan, they had picked up in the SMS traffic. Karim drove straight to the coffee shop, no surveillance detection en route, nothing to indicate purpose of evasion.

Alexa remained in her position now, a half block away from where Karim parked, with a view of his car. They assumed that Hasan might park here, too. Otherwise, why had he been so specific with Karim? It would be a rookie mistake to have both vehicles in one place, reducing any opposing force's surveillance requirements, but Sami had no sign that Hasan and Karim were professionals.

There was no indication that Karim and Hasan would be covered by a counter-surveillance team of their own, but if they were capable of an armed attack in the U.S., then Sami needed to consider the possibility. Sami should be the spotter because that role held the greatest risk, but he would be exposed and given his relationship with Karim, Sami could not hide in plain sight. The job fell to Yoda.

That left Sami where a team leader belonged, controlling the operation. All communications came through him. He didn't want the team looking at their phones, checking communications traffic. If they had something to report, they passed it through him. If someone on the team needed to know something, he sent the message. After everyone notified him they were in position, there was a tense period of waiting.

The team was using an encrypted chat app for their communication, and the first message came from Emily. When Sami read it, he could not believe the demure tech had written it.

FUUUUUUUCK!!! ANTHONY HERE. CRUZNG ST WHR I PRK. LOOKING FOR SPOT???

Anthony was Hasan's cryptonym. He was looking for a parking spot on a residential street around the corner from the meeting place. As bad luck would have it, the same street where Emily was sitting in their makeshift listening post.

Sami responded. *OK. HANG TIGHT. LET ME KNOW WHEN A ON FOOT.*

***

Hasan found a spot on his second pass around the block, and parallel parked his car. He didn't drive a truck. He had no need for one. In fact, in about four hours, this car would no longer be his. Nothing in the world would be the same as when he awoke that morning. The life he knew would be over. *Inshallah.*

He stepped onto the sidewalk and could not help a nervous glance around. It did not betray a lack of commitment, but a lack of training. As he rounded the corner, he put his phone to his ear, pretending to be on a phone call. For verisimilitude, he decided that he would pretend to be talking to the restaurant where that night's meeting would be held. As he walked to the front of the coffee shop, he muttered: "that's right...the final number will be seven." He looked through the windows, straining to see past his own face reflected in the afternoon sun. He spotted Karim, offered a wave, and gestured to the phone with the universal shrug for *Sorry, I'll be done in a moment.*

Hasan turned away from the window, counted to five, and then took the phone down from his ear, pretending to conclude a call. He opened a chat app and sent the message Zechariah had told him to send. He was told things would happen quickly, but he didn't know how long he needed to keep Karim. He would wait for a message back and then conclude the meeting.

***

Across the street from the coffee shop was a laundromat. In some ways, it was like other laundromats: dryers along the walls and washers standing in the center, a large plate glass front that afforded fishbowl views, and a window sill littered with dozens of copies of a local independent newspaper.

In at least one way, it was remarkable: behind the pages of one of the newspapers, a Marine Corps reservist and freelance spy was working. Yoda's chair afforded a direct but oblique view of the coffee shop. He peeked out and watched Hasan thumb the text. He cursed under his breath because he did not know what the SMS said. It was annoyance at their meager resources but also a commentary on Yoda's worldview: if something went typed, texted or talked, his skills entitled him to access.

Instead, he was limited to dashing off his own text.

ANTHONY IN HOLE

Sami responded to Yoda's message with a note to the whole team.

A IN HOLE. HOLD POS.

Less than a minute after Sami's message came through, Alexa saw a black pickup stop near Karim's truck. It had to have been close, but Alexa did not see where it came from. The driver put the truck in reverse and backed into a position where its bed was adjacent to Karim's, as if to transfer something from one vehicle to the other. The driver of the black truck got out, pushed a button on a key fob and unlocked Karim's truck. He opened both tailgates and climbed up. It all happened so quickly that Alexa barely registered the need to send a message.

SOMEONE HERE!!

Alexa didn't even have a camera. To hold up her cell phone camera would have been out of the question, even if she didn't need to use the phone to message Sami. So she stared. The black truck man was white, between 35 and 45 years old. Despite her panic, it did not fail to occur to Alexa that as ever her adversary was a middle-aged white guy. He reached into his own truck bed and grabbed something. It was heavy. He didn't lift it up. It took considerable effort for him to slide it out of his own truck and across the divide into Karim's. Her phone buzzed.

WHO? And then immediately after, *WHAT'S GOING ON?* It was Sami.

The man struggled for a moment, trying to find a place to get sure footing on one of the two tailgates as he pushed and pulled the heavy object between the vehicles. He straddled the vehicles, a foot on each. That didn't work so he hopped down and pushed from the ground.

WHITE MALE.

Why am I writing this like a bad police drama? She shook her head and continued.

WHITE GUY. NEVER SEEN HIM BEFORE. LOADING SOMETHING INTO

Fuck! What is Karim's cryptonym? Brutus!

INTO BED OF BRUTUS TRUCK.

HOW DID HE GET INTO THE TRUCK? Sami asked.

HAD KEY!

WHAT DID HE LOAD?

IDK. CAN'T SEE. I'LL GET CLOSER.

Sami responded immediately. *NO. DO NOT MOVE. TRY TO GET THE TAGS BUT HOLD POSITION.*

Get the tags! That was something. Alexa looked up. Black Truck Guy had pushed the object as far into the bed of Karim's truck as he could. He slammed his own bed shut and moved to the driver's door. He never saw Alexa watching. He never raised his eyes at all. He pulled his own truck forward a few feet and jumped out again. The few feet of space between his own truck and Karim's was just enough for him to step between the trucks and push the object with leverage enough to load it all the way in Karim's bed.

Alexa had a split-second view and the black truck was gone.

***

Two minutes after Alexa messaged that the guy was gone, Sami got into her passenger seat. She was uncharacteristically ruffled.

"I'm so sorry, Sami."

"For what? No way. You did the best you could." The pep talk was brief. Sami was commanding the operation and two of his team were still engaged. "Did you get the tags?"

With tears in her eyes, Alexa shook her head. Sami reached out and touched her arm.

"It's alright. This was something, Lex. This is the first break we've had. Don't beat yourself up for getting it. Did you see what it was?"

"I saw it, but…" Alexa's essential strength was already building back. She was cycling from disappointed, to frustrated, to pissed. "I don't know what it was. It was black. Big. Like, I don't know, like the size of a trunk."

"A trunk? Like a footlocker?"

"Yeah, right."

"It was a box? Rectangular? With a lid, or…"

"No. It didn't look like it had a lid. It looked like it was wrapped. Maybe wrapped in a tarp. I think I saw bungee cords around a black tarp."

There was one way to find out, but as soon as Sami considered the idea, he dismissed it. It wasn't part of the plan. Sami may not have been a covert action expert, but he knew that there were too many variables outside of their control for him to add complications. Stick to the plan. Adjust the plan based on new facts, but don't wing it. Not in the field. There was too much at risk.

THAT WAS QUICK!

The message came from Yoda, still in the laundromat.

THEY DONE? Sami replied and then thumbed out a message to Emily. He waited before hitting send.

DONE. BOTH ON FOOT. Yoda replied.

Sami sent the message warning Emily that Hassan was coming.

SIT TIGHT.

The rendezvous point was Alexandria. Unless Sami texted the distress code. Then everyone was to make a hasty retreat to their vehicle and meet at a gas station three exits away on I-50. Sami waited. He hoped he would see Emily's message that Hasan was gone before he saw Karim. He didn't. Maybe Hasan was sitting in his car checking his phone. Maybe Karim was just a fast walker. Whatever the case, Sami saw Karim coming and he sent the distress code. He hoped that Emily would be patient, stay in place, and not put herself or the operation at risk. He turned to Alexa.

"We have to follow him, Lex. Just like you did to get here. You did a great job. Remember, we know where he's going so just stay cool. Give him space. We won't lose him."

"What is it Sami? What did they put in the truck?"

"Start driving and I'll check in with Emily and Yoda as soon as we can." He messaged them to check in by phone as soon as it was safe.

"Why is he taking it to the hotel?" Alexa asked.

"He doesn't even know it's there."

"What?" Alexa was incredulous.

"Think about it, you come back to your vehicle after getting coffee. You don't check the trunk. The bed of the truck. You have no reason to." Alexa pulled into traffic behind the pickup. Because regular vehicular traffic couldn't go through the Naval Academy, they would circumnavigate. The route would add a few minutes to a trip that was less than a mile as the crow flies.

"What is happening, Sami? What's he doing?"

Sami's phone buzzed. It was Yoda.

"Where are you?" Sami asked.

"Back in my car, headed to the interstate. What happened?" Yoda asked.

"I'm with Alexa. We're tailing Karim."

"What the fuck, Sami?"

"Someone delivered something during the meeting."

"No, they didn't, I watched it," Yoda replied.

"No. Not to Karim. To the truck. Alexa saw it."

"Delivered what?"

"We don't know. Black. Bigger than a breadbox."

"Fuck! What did Emily get?" Yoda's voice was level but tinged with annoyance. This was going where he predicted it would, and where none of them wanted it to.

"I don't know, I haven't heard from her yet."

Alexa turned onto the traffic circle that wound around the Maryland State House. She was 50 yards behind Karim, and they lost sight of him as the circle turned. Sami covered the phone to speak to Alexa.

"If you lose him, just take the exit toward the church. That'll put you into the Church Circle."

"I remember." In the frenzied pre-mission briefing they reviewed a map. The two circles were the most memorable of

Annapolis' roads and the only roads in this section of down-town that were instantly distinguishable from ground level.

"Good. Get on Duke of Gloucester."

Duke of Gloucester Street paralleled Main Street, the commercial avenue of ice cream parlors and trinket shops that ran down to the harbor. There, another traffic circle offered a split onto Compromise Street and the hotel where they assumed Karim was heading.

Yoda was screaming on the phone. Sami brought it back to his ear. "What?"

"...Call him, Sami! Call Andy. It's a fucking bomb. Get out of there."

"He doesn't even know he has it," Sami said.

"That's bullshit! Or a guess, but- "

"No way. If it is a bomb, he doesn't even know they delivered it. They're using him."

Alexa pointed ahead. Karim's truck was turning left, cutting across Compromise to the hotel entrance. Sami nodded and pointed to indicate that she should follow.

"I can pull him out."

The plan was only emerging in Sami's mind as he spoke and it was half-formed, but he knew Karim. No matter how much their last meeting confirmed their estrangement, his instincts told him that his friend was not a suicide bomber. Yoda was trying to speak over him, but Sami continued.

"I know him, OK? I should have told you guys, and I'm sorry. But I know this isn't what it seems. I'll talk to him and when he sees what they sprung on him, we'll have one guy from the group--"

"Have him? Where? You're not thinking, man." Yoda was pleading. "If you're wrong, which you are, and it is a bomb, you're dead. Even if you're right, we can't hold the guy, Sami. They'll find him and you are going to get us all killed."

"If it's a bomb, we won't have to hold him long. I call Andy and then we have resources."

"Don't be crazy. Get to the rendezvous point, call Andy now. Get the cavalry."

Yoda heard only silence from the other end of the phone. Sami had pulled it away from his ear to look at the screen. Emily was trying to call in.

"Look, man. If he doesn't know, then where is he driving? Why is he going to the hotel?" Yoda paused. Sami could feel his desperation through the phone. "I know you want to help this guy, but you won't talk him out, man. Not with both of you alive."

"Maybe not, but maybe I can get other people out of there," Sami spoke over Yoda's continued protestations. "I gotta go, man. Emily's calling in."

Sami switched calls. "Hey, Em. Hold on." He looked over at Alexa. "Where did he go?"

"He was in front of the hotel on the phone, but he went in."

"Where's the truck?"

"I don't know."

Sami returned to the phone. "Sorry, Emily. What did you get?"

"Nothing much. I think Karim is as confused as we are. It was a useless meeting."

"Did Hasan say anything?"

"They talked about their meeting. Hasan told Karim he wanted him to read a passage from the Qur'an during dinner. Told him to head to the hotel right away and review it for a few minutes. To text him when he looked it over. Where are you?"

Sami ignored the question. "That's it?"

"You saw," Emily said. "They were in and out in less than ten minutes. Hasan was straining to think of things to tell him, and then he couldn't get out of there fast enough."

"You said Karim was confused?"

"Yeah, at the end. You could almost hear it in his voice. Hasan told him about the meeting agenda and then he went on a tangent about the importance of family. He told Karim he should call his wife and kids before dinner. Tell them he loved them— "

"Fuck!"

Emily had never heard Sami curse. "What?"

"Nothing. Go on."

"Sami, when will you be at the rendezvous? What's going on?"

"I can't explain right now. Was that it?"

"No. He told him to use the valet. Made a big deal of it." Sami didn't hear the rest. He had his hand on the door handle before he pressed END.

He turned toward Alexa as he threw open the door. "Go find Hasan!"

Before Alexa could respond, Sami was running across the street toward the hotel.

***

Hasan was a perfectionist, and to him, nothing was as perfect as Islam. That much Karim understood. That was why Hasan asked him to early coffee, so he could be sure that Karim would get to the hotel in plenty of time to read and review for their meeting. And so, he was reading the passage.

The command for Karim to call his wife made less sense. Why he obeyed, that made no sense at all. He just did what Hasan said. Karim trusted him. Hasan had picked the perfect one of the Council for tonight's objective. If Karim had resisted, and it had been necessary, Hasan could have called upon the one who identified Karim in the first place. The Mutual Friend. Karim would obey him.

After reading the passage through two times, Karim glanced at his watch. There was an hour before the rest of the Council would arrive for the meeting. It was a simple passage. Karim was wondering how long to wait before texting Hasan, and how to pass the rest of the time. Then he saw Sami.

"As-salamu alaykum." Sami walked over to hug his childhood friend.

"Waʿalaykumu as-salam" was all Karim could muster, but his expression spoke volumes.

It wasn't just surprise, it was fear. He was not enthusiastic about the auspicious reunion of old friends, the second in the space of a week. *My gay friend, an estranged Muslim, here at my meeting. What if someone sees him? What if Hasan asks about him?* It was only after these thoughts ran through his mind that Karim registered how bizarre it was that Sami used the traditional Muslim greeting.

"What are you doing here, man?" Sami asked.

"Me?" Karim's eyes were darting around behind Sami. He tried to relax, told himself he had an hour before anyone would arrive for the Council meeting. "This is my side of town. What about you?"

"Having dinner with a buddy from the military. He teaches at the Academy." Sami tried again. He wanted to give a clear path to test Karim's evasiveness. It wasn't taken. "You meeting your wife?"

"My wife? No. She's home with the kids. It's a meeting for the mosque."

As Karim spoke, his phone vibrated in his hand. It might be his wife or his children, but Sami guessed Hasan was impatient. It reminded Sami how little time they had. He needed to act. As Karim raised the phone, Sami stopped his hand.

"There's no meeting, Karim."

***

Outside, Black Truck Guy completed a half-mile loop around the hotel. After making his delivery near the coffee shop, he drove the same route that Alexa took minutes later and parked within sight of the hotel. When Karim pulled up, the driver watched him leave the car and complete the phone call to his wife. Only when Karim entered the hotel did Black Truck Guy text the confirmation code to his boss, the man these ragheads knew as Zechariah.

By then, Alexa and Sami had pulled up. No one could blame them for missing the black truck from the coffee shop, the same one that Alexa had seen moments before, parked just three car lengths behind. It was a tense few moments and neither was trained for covert operations or surveillance. Black Truck Guy started his circuit just after Sami ran into the hotel.

He and Sami had been trained by the Army at the same Basic Infantry School. A decade earlier, they had been stationed at FOBs less than twenty miles apart in the Sunni Triangle. They both learned a lot there and both were putting those lessons to use tonight. Neither had the endorsement of the government that trained them, though both were confident they were acting in its interest; perhaps even with its tacit approval.

Black Truck Guy began a second ½-mile circuit. He would circle until his boss told him it was time.

***

Sami grabbed his childhood friend by the elbow and moved him out of the hotel lobby. Down past the elevators and into a plushly-carpeted hallway, he looked for a stairwell. He knew that hotels had stairs near the emergency exit doors. Nearing the end of the hallway, he pushed Karim through a grey steel door.

When the door slammed shut behind them, Karim shook his arm loose.

"What are you doing?" He asked, more confused than annoyed.

"Do you know?"

"I have no idea, Samir--!"

"Do you know what's going on? With Hasan?"

Karim started to respond, then his face registered a surprised recognition. "How do you know Hasan?"

"Answer me."

As if on cue, the phone vibrated again. Both men looked down. Karim was still holding his finger inside the Qur'an to mark the page for his reading.

"That's him. That's Hasan. We know him." Karim stared back blankly. "C'mon, Karim. I'm giving you a chance I shouldn't be. Do you know?"

"I don't know what you're talking about!"

Karim was telling the truth. If it had been someone else, Sami wouldn't have been so sure, but he knew his friend. It was a gut reaction and that was why Andy put him on the operation. Still, it was only a gut reaction. Sami didn't have time to probe any deeper. To leave alive, and stop whatever was planned next, Sami needed to act.

"Give me your phone!" Sami reached as he spoke.

"No!"

Sami didn't think Karim's phone would detonate the bomb. It left too much to risk for Hasan. Somehow, he would need Karim to dial the number of the dummy phone wired into the bomb. What if Karim didn't make the call? What if he got suspicious? No, Hasan's text was for another purpose: to make sure that Karim was in the hotel. Sami felt a prick of understanding.

"OK, but do not text him back!"

"Sami—" Karim protested.

"There's a bomb. Hasan had someone place it in the bed of your truck while you were having coffee. You drove the bomb to this hotel. We have to get out, and we have to get everyone else out before he dials the number of the cell phone detonator wired into that bomb."

It was on the table. Breaking every rule of intelligence and covert operations, Sami just told his target everything, but it wasn't enough. He understood Karim's confused stare. He felt the same way until about two hours ago. Then Black Truck Guy showed up and confirmed Andy Rizzo's worst suppositions about Hasan Khalifa.

Sami knew how Karim felt because he had experienced the feeling once himself. When he discovered his own betrayal. The memory came to Sami as a chill that crept up his spine and made the hairs on the back of his neck stand. He lied to Karim about it once before, to save himself from admitting the truth. Maybe now he could right the wrong he had done to his friend and save them both.

"That night, in college- "

"No, Sami."

Sami had just told Karim that his truck was rigged with explosives and a friend had betrayed him, making him complicit to a terror attack. His reaction was stupor. But, as soon as Sami alluded to the night he came out of the closet, Karim reacted forcefully. It was remarkable how much this said about Islam, and America, and the men of both.

"Do you think I trusted you because I thought you would be accepting? Because you would help me? Or even understand me?"

"Sami— "

"No, listen! I told you I was gay because I knew you would accept that excuse. There was something so menacing, something else eating me up so badly inside that I could not keep it secret. It would have killed me, Karim."

"Ok, but it's not for me or you..." Karim struggled before settling on the explanation he sought. "It is haram."

"Not that! I am gay, but I only told you so I could continue hiding the truth. My grandfather, Karim. Abu Muhammad."

The phone vibrated one more time. Sami was at the end of his rope. He needed to tell Karim what he had hidden for so long. If he didn't do it now, neither of them would make it out alive.

***

Black Truck Guy completed his second circuit of the hotel and still, there was no response from his boss. He pulled to the side of the road before thumbing out his next message. When you are engaged in blowing up a building, you don't want to get pulled over for texting while driving. If Sami and his team were operating with a slim margin for error, the driver's was even narrower. He made his delivery. The package was now in place. He knew what the man who developed this plan would say, but he waited patiently, confident that time was not of the essence.

The text he expected came through.

MAKE ANOTHER LOOP. IF YOU DON'T HEAR BY THEN, PROCEED.

Black Truck Guy shifted into drive and eased back into traffic. Now, or in five minutes, their mission would be complete. They were not starting the war. It had already raged for decades. They were not even the first to bring it to America. They were a long way from the beginning. But he was confident this would be the beginning of the end.

***

Sami grabbed Karim with a pincer grip on the tender tissue just above the elbow and pulled him down the concrete stairs. It was a stairway like those in every hotel in the U.S., unfinished and almost cavernous in its high ceiling and lack of carpet. The faux brass sconces in the guest hallways were replaced by emergency floodlights mounted to battery boxes. The stairs wound up and down in an endless line of tubular steel railing. If Sami was correct, there would be one other common feature.

He scanned the first landing and found nothing. They were halfway to the garage level and Karim was screaming and thrashing to break loose. Approaching the second landing, Sami saw a blue beacon. Below it, behind a clear plastic housing, was an emergency call button. Sami pulled the box free and mashed the button. A wail went up throughout the hotel.

"Are you crazy?" Karim yelled over the shrill echo in the concrete stairway.

"We need everyone to get out of here. Let's go." Sami started down again.

"Where?" Karim asked. And then, with just a second's thought. "No!"

"Come to the truck! I'll show you."

Above them, hotel guests and staff were responding to the alarm, but laconically. Sami and Karim should have been evacuating with everyone else. Sami should have been in the lobby, pushing people out the door and yelling "Bomb!" But he didn't just want to save people, he wanted to stop the bomb.

He still assumed that Karim was innocent, and if that was the case then he would not be the one detonating the bomb. He hoped that when fire trucks and police cars and ambulances arrived in the next few minutes and clogged the driveway and street in front of the hotel, it would be enough to scare off whoever was activating the bomb. It was an assumption that a covert operator never would have made.

Sami wanted to save Karim from more than just the bomb. He wanted to save Karim from whatever he had been dragged into. He also knew that Karim was his best way into Hasan's plot. He wasn't thinking like a covert operator. He was thinking like an intelligence analyst. Someone who wanted to collect data. To crack the case. To do that, he needed his friend to see what was in the truck.

Sami burst through the metal door and into the subterranean parking deck, still and silent except for the hollow echo of the alarm. Karim was still lagging.

"Come on, I don't know how much time we have, but it's not much."

Karim caught up and then they were jogging. Neither of them knew where the valet had parked the truck and Sami was scanning the lot for the truck, or a sign that marked the valet area. He saw the exit ramp ahead and he knew it would be there. On the top level, near the ramp, where the valets could access vehicles quickly. He led Karim in that direction.

Running behind, Karim spoke through ragged breath. "What did you mean? Upstairs? About your grandfather?"

Sami winced. His natural hesitation rose first. It was an instinct he developed after the confrontation with his grandfather, a day he still remembered vividly, down to the smells, the angle of light. The instinct was honed by years lurking in the secrets. He turned his new preference for secrecy into a profession. And no one really knew him again.

Karim knew him. As they scanned the vehicles, looking for the white pickup, Sami decided he had hidden long enough.

"You can't trust him." Sami couldn't see Karim's expression, but he knew what it showed. "He introduced you to Hasan, right?"

"You haven't been to the mosque in years. How do you know Hasan?"

"My grandfather is too lax in his embrace of zealots." Before Sami could go on, they found the truck.

They stopped running, the heavy breathing modulated and the sirens' wail now a far-off cry. Karim wanted Sami to continue. *What about his grandfather? And Hasan?* But Sami wasn't speaking. He looked at Karim with a curious expression.

"The keys. I need the keys."

Both of their hearts sank.

"I'm sorry, Sami," Karim said.

"You don't have them?" It was more of a realization than a question.

"The valet does."

***

Yoda continued texting and calling, but Sami never answered. Yoda met Emily and Alexa at the rendezvous point and they filled each other in on what they knew. Alexa shared Sami's instruction. *Find Hasan.* That should be easy. They knew where the Council of Muhammad meeting was being held, and they all got into Alexa's rental car and headed in that direction.

On the interstate, Emily opened her computer to pull up the GPS beacon on Hasan's car.

"Get off the highway."

"What?" Alexa was driving. She and Yoda both looked back at Emily in confusion.

"He's not at the meeting."

"Where is he?" Yoda asked, regret in his voice. Everything was out of control.

"He's on the move. He's heading west. On the Beltway."

Alexa signaled to reverse direction on the northbound highway. "He's going back to D.C.?"

"Fuck!" Yoda was the first to realize. "He's heading to Dulles."

***

Sami darted away and left Karim by the truck. He returned on the run with the heavy road sign that marked the cross-walk by the elevator. He barely slowed as he approached the truck, flinging the sign's heavy iron base at the rear driver's window creating a spider web of cracks. The truck's alarm bleated an urgency much louder and closer than the hotel si-rens.

Sami tried to remove the base, now wedged into the tem-pered glass. Karim helped and together, using the stand like a battering ram, they struck a blow forceful enough to knock the window out of the frame. Sami reached in and unlocked the door.

They moved to the rear of the truck and Sami opened the tailgate. Sitting in the bed obscured by darkness was a black tarpaulin-wrapped bundle. It was four-sided and looked like a large box or trunk. The tarp was held on with bungee cords, also black.

This was the box Alexa described. Sami looked for any ob-vious sign this was a bomb, but it was too neatly packaged. If there was any conventional explosive inside, something from the plastic explosive family - Semtex or C4 - a bomb this size wouldn't just destroy the parking deck but was a threat to the hotel above and all the emergency personnel outside. Sami needed everyone away. But he also needed Karim to under-stand. He looked at his old friend.

"Hasan? He..." Karim could not formulate the words, but Sami knew what he was thinking.

"We watched him. He lied to you, so they could get this in the truck, and he tricked you into coming here. He's not com-ing, Karim."

"Why? I would...this would kill me."

"It will kill everyone in this hotel." Sami grabbed Karim by the arm again, pulling more gently this time. They ran back to the stairs and started up two at a time. "Someone will detonate the bomb with a remote device, probably activated by a cell phone wired into the explosive. I know that you weren't, Ka-rim, but you need to tell me. Were you going to detonate the bomb?" Sami shouted.

"I didn't even know it was there!" Karim said through ragged breath.

They arrived back at the door to the lobby hallway. Sami reached to pull it open and Karim stopped him.

"Your grandfather? Abu Muhammad, he..." Karim could not form the words.

THIRTEEN

LOUDON COUNTY 1993 | WASHINGTON 2001

"Sami, there has been a horrible tragedy."

Souteli Khala was a pidgin Urdu nickname that Sami developed for the step-aunt who was standing in the bright light of his grandfather's kitchen. She was his friend Karim's mother and a good friend of his own mother.

Dust motes encircled her. They were so numerous and phosphorescent that Sami could not pay attention to what she said. But she spoke of Sami's mother, again and again, starting and restarting the same sentence with tears streaking her walnut-colored cheeks and she couldn't complete the thought.

Sami realized it was something serious. Too serious. He tried to change the subject.

"Is Karim here?" he asked. "I can go play with him." He rose from the chair. The strategy had the added benefit of appearing to be appropriate behavior when a child was confronted by their Auntie crying.

"No, Samir. Karim isn't here." Souteli Khala said. She exhaled violently and pressed the tips of all four fingers hard into the high, round cheek below each eye to staunch the tears. "You need to sit. I'm sorry."

When Sami's grandfather brought him into the kitchen, Souteli Khala was already there. Now Sami's grandfather was gone, and he said nothing before he left. Karim wasn't there. Sami had never been alone with Souteli Khala before and he did not understand why he was now.

"Samir, your mother, and your father...there was a bomb today." Her words caught on a lump in her throat. "The embassy was destroyed. A section of it. Your parents' residence was part of that section. It seems the bomb was close to them.

Maybe even within their apartment, they don't know yet. But, Samir, they are...There is nothing left of either of them."

Sami thought he might ask after Karim again, but Karim wasn't there. He could go find his grandfather and tell him that Souteli Khala was saying awful things. Anything not to think about what she said. Sami knew that Souteli Khala feared his grandfather, but so did he. Just like everyone else. He didn't run to Abu Muhammad. He regretted what he did instead, but he was only a child.

"Maybe they weren't hurt then?" he offered. "If there is nothing left? Maybe they were out?"

"I'm afraid...it is certain." Souteli Khala was not entirely prepared, but she was prepared for this. He was a child. He would see it as a problem, a riddle, and he would fantasize a solution. But it was real. His parents were dead.

***

BAKU, AZERBAIJAN (May 22, 1993) - A massive explosion destroyed several floors in one wing of the U.S. Embassy here this morning, killing at least 7 people, 4 of them Americans, in what officials are calling a terrorist attack. The enormous explosion disrupted the busy downtown shopping district where the U.S. Embassy has been located since the two countries established diplomatic relations in 1992, after the fall of the Soviet Union and Azeri independence.

The bomb exploded as the business day began and as night fell crews from the embassy and from local Azeri emergency services were still sifting through the wreckage attempting to locate bodies. The loss of life is thought to be high because the bomb was somehow placed within the embassy's living quarters. Investigators believe the attack was the work of terrorists but have not released details on how the attackers accessed the residential area of the compound.

While U.S. officials have not commented on claims of responsibility, Azeri officials are directing blame at Sunni terror groups. The country is predominately Muslim, but the majority Shia population is considered to be much less adherent than in neighboring Iran. Experts on the region say an ongoing war with Armenia over the disputed territory of Nagorno-Karabakh, the recent collapse of Soviet rule, and other political disputes have contributed to the creation of an opportunity for Islamist attackers who have recently attacked western Levant countries – such as Lebanon, Israel, and Turkey – to gain access to Azerbaijan.

President Clinton called the attack "a cowardly act of terror," and vowed to bring those responsible to justice "no matter what or how long it takes."

Witnesses said the explosion was concentrated in the residential wing, with a blast radius that traveled up and down within the building rather than outward toward the street. It appeared to emanate from the second floor, where embassy staff apartments are housed. As of this evening, embassy spokespersons could not comment on how an attacker would have gained access to that part of the building, which is tightly secured.

***

It was Friday night at the George Washington University Gelman Library. Again. Friday nights always seemed to find Sami in the same corner carrel on the seventh floor, reading microfilm from newspaper stories recounting the attack that killed his parents.

Though only 20 miles from home in Virginia, during his first two years at George Washington, Sami felt like he was on the other side of the world. He was raised in a secular style. Even with the heavy influence of his grandfather after his parents' death, his upbringing had still been mainstream American. College - with alcohol and drugs, profanity and pornography - felt like another world.

Had he confided his fears to his grandfather, he would have been reminded of Iblis, who – made from fire and permitted to linger among the angels - told Allah, "Because You have sent me astray, surely, I will sit in wait against the human beings on Your straight path. Then I will come to them from before them and behind them, from their right and from their left..."

Sami didn't need reminding. He knew the story well. He preferred the movie trope, well-worn in everything from Westerns to spy movies, where the hero was tempted by illicit enticements which only held his doom. Pussy Galore.

Sami was struggling to acknowledge that he felt no temptation from that enticement. That was another reason to sequester himself in the Gelman; the better to avoid confronting the creeping fact of his own proclivities.

His grandfather would have seen a connection between Sami's preferred metaphor, and his own failing. His sexual deviance was grounded in his secularism. And both were grounded in *American Sin*. The phrase was forever capitalized and italicized in Sami's mind and was – as Sami completed his freshman year - often given the same treatment in the Op-eds of major American newspapers.

American Sin was the title of a successful book that his grandfather published just before Sami arrived at GW. The book was written during the waning days of the Clinton White House, published during the Gore v. Bush campaign, and became a cause celebre among Christian conservative ideologues who saw their own words in its pages but spoken by a conveniently exotic mouthpiece. Here was a way to beat their drum without being accused of blowing their dog whistle. When Bush won, and Beltway insiders attributed the win to a resurgence of religious fundamentalism at the ballot box, Abu Muhammad's book got its fifteen minutes among D.C.'s cognoscenti.

His grandfather. Sami thought about the man more than he cared to admit. The voice was a constant presence in his life, creating an inner dialogue with Sami's own thoughts. It was the cartoon: an angel on one shoulder, a devil on the other. But which was which?

Even as his grandfather's public image grew, the man diminished in Sami's estimation. As his voice gained more adherents, his words rang hollower to his grandson. As Sami wiled away another Friday night at the Gelman, reading stories about his parents' murder, he felt himself drawing closer to something, a new truth. The closer he drew, the more distant he felt his grandfather becoming.

The Gelman was a very good university library. Other than a musty 1970s interior, which Sami found suited to hiding, what recommended it most were the special collections: the Kiev Library of Judaica; the Global Resources Center, a super-sized version the CIA World Factbook; and the National Security Archive.

The National Security Archive was an institution which described itself as "an investigative journalism center, research institute on international affairs, library and archive of declassified U.S. documents, leading non-profit user of the U.S. Freedom of Information Act, public interest law firm defending and expanding public access to government information, global advocate of open government, and indexer and publisher of former secrets."

It was a librarian of the National Security Archive who noticed Sami every Friday, when he borrowed every newspaper and magazine microfilm available on the 1993 embassy attack. Some he had reviewed half a dozen times. Already taking a liking to Sami, when he told her why he read those stories, again and again, she took pity on him.

She suggested that a FOIA request might bear fruit on some information outside the media record. Beyond that, she suggested that Sami – having gained as highly-developed an understanding of the public narrative on the attack as anyone – could use his understanding of the players to cross-reference other available research documents in the library. That librarian gave Sami his first lesson in the craft of open source intelligence collection.

Sami had been kept in the dark about the facts of the attack, his grandfather always receiving the investigators' updates privately, and rarely passing any information along to Sami. He was grateful to have tapped into another trove of documents, matching his own endless appetite for information about the attack that killed his parents. Sami's attitude of simple succor soon evolved. He saw connections in the public record; connections that FOIA requests revealed government investigators had seen too.

Sami had an advantage that the government investigators had not. In his youth, he made trips to Pakistan and to the Holy Land with his grandfather. On these trips, he met people, stayed in their homes, and shared their food. They were his grandfather's hosts. His grandfather's friends. That unique insight allowed him to make connections the government investigators never made. Connections between his own grandfather and people who the investigative documents revealed were suspected of organizing and funding the attack.

From what the documents reported, and what he had seen with his own eyes on trips with his grandfather, Sami developed a theory. It hardened into a belief. And then, into a horror.

FOURTEEN

ANNAPOLIS

Sami hesitated. His stomach flipped. There was no time left. Ten minutes ago, he had opened this can of worms. It was time to tell Karim the truth.

"The bomb that killed my parents. When we were in college, I became interested in the story and I discovered things I never expected. The bomber got into the embassy because he was meeting with my father. My grandfather arranged the meeting. He never confessed that he arranged the meeting to the FBI. Or that the bomber was someone he knew. I confronted him and he admitted it. I didn't want you to know, I wanted no one to know, so I told you the secret that scared me much less. To explain why I wouldn't speak to him anymore. I blamed him for instigating our estrangement because I was gay. Rather than anyone finding out, I exiled him for letting terrorists into his confidences." Sami felt a weight lifted. "I didn't want the same thing to happen to you."

"Sami!" Karim's face was a mask of terror. Despite the last few minutes' frenzy, only now did he look afraid. "Your grandfather! He introduced me to Hasan!"

A black veil fell over Sami's vision. He needed to know more. Was it possible that his grandfather had made the same mistake again? Or worse? Is that what Andy knew? And who else knew?

He had been right to risk coming after Karim. Whatever the personal risks, getting his friend out and interrogating him was imperative. They needed to get out of this hotel. Delirious with a million other questions, Sami recovered quickly.

He threw open the door to a hallway that was the length of a football field. At the end, the lobby was crowded with hotel staff, first responders, and a few guests still milling around.

For the first responders, it was their third or fourth false alarm of the day. Their casual calm was settling over the others.

Until they see two military-aged males of Pakistani extraction, Sami thought, but he reminded himself that only he and Karim knew there was a bomb. The responding authorities thought, at worst, there was a kitchen fire, or someone had a heart attack.

Sami faced an awful choice, but he knew that as bad as he wanted to stop the attack, he could not be the one to tell the police about the bomb. If he did, he and Karim would be arrested and questioned. They were not registered guests, the truck downstairs was smashed and if their story could hold up, it would take too long.

The alternative was to make a scene. Enough of a scene to clear the building. Yell *"BOMB!"* Better yet, run down the hallway and scream *"Allahu Akhbar!"* And be sure they didn't wind up in police custody. Sami needed to catch Hasan and he needed Karim's help. As they approached the lobby, and the time when Sami needed to decide, he turned to Karim. His friend was gone.

A door clicked a few feet behind and Sami turned back. The door was metal with a large stainless-steel handle. It was not a hotel room or a ballroom or a stairwell. There was a large glass window, reinforced by chicken wire. *VALET* was stenciled on the door in frosted white letters. Inside, Karim was scanning a wall-mounted key cabinet. Sami reached for the handle.

"Hey!" A firefighter called to Sami from the lobby. Not aggressive, not accusatory. More annoyed than anything. "Pal, you need to clear out."

Sami threw the door open but stayed in the firefighter's view.

"Karim, it's too late. Let's go!"

"I have to get that truck out of here." Karim was frantic, scanning the keys hanging in the cabinet. They all looked the same.

"Yo! Let's go!" The firefighter started down the hall toward Sami.

PURPOSE OF EVASION · 93

They had to go. All of Yoda's worst fears were coming true.
Sami was not a covert operator, but he knew one thing. *They
could not stay.*

"Karim!" Sami shouted through a clenched jaw.

Karim stopped and for a moment Sami thought he would
come along.

Instead, he turned and said, "When Calamity befalls them,
they say, 'Verily, unto God do we belong and, verily, unto Him
we shall return."

Al-Baqarah. Sami forgot the exact verse. It was something
heard commonly in his childhood. At funerals. At his parents'
own funeral.

The firefighter was only fifty yards away now.

"Here they are." Karim held the truck keys in his hand. "At
least he told me to call my children. Alhamdulillah."

Karim was not leaving without trying to move the truck,
which meant that Karim was never leaving. They had waited
too long. Sami stepped back and closed the door to the Valet.
The firefighter was closing in, but if Sami stepped back now,
the man might not see Karim in the Valet office.

"Sorry. Sorry about that, man." Sami shouted down the
hall.

"We need you out now!" the firefighter said.

Sami feared that one of his team might have called in the
bomb threat, but if the firefighter's demeanor where any indication, they had not.

He held up his hands and responded. "I know. I know."

The exit door at the end of the hallway was only five steps
away. The firefighter made the same mistake that Sami made
with Karim and turned on his heel expecting Sami to follow.
Sami took off in the opposite direction, threw his weight into
the push bar and was outside before he heard the firefighter
shout after him.

Sami sprinted across the parking lot and he kept running.
Only a quarter mile of downtown Annapolis remained before
the Spa Creek Bridge. Like downtown Annapolis, Eastport was
another finger of land that jutted into the Severn River. He
sprinted across the bridge, his breath ragged now. Sami saw

a busy commercial area to the left, down Severn Street. He ran a little further and turned right, onto a well-traveled residential street. He could get lost here.

He was thinking about Karim. If the firefighter chased Sami down the hall, he might have seen Karim in the office. Even if he didn't give chase, someone might have seen Karim when he came out of the office. He would have been caught or at least chased. If Karim was caught, he would tell them about the bomb. He might tell them about Sami.

Sami turned off the main road onto a cul-de-sac. He was a mile away from the hotel and he stopped running. He stopped worrying about Karim. Karim was gone as soon as he closed that Valet door.

Sami was hunched over, hands on his knees to catch his breath when he heard the explosion.

PART 2

FIFTEEN

WASHINGTON D.C.

Gerald Seymour knotted a lush silk tie. It was bespoke. As
was his shirt. Both were made by a haberdasher whose only
shop was in Jackson Hole, Wyoming. Years ago, when the tailor mentioned that he was getting close to retirement,
Seymour ordered 100 of the Supima broadcloth shirts he favored. When the tailor chuckled at the request, Seymour
returned a baleful glare. He wasn't joking.

All the shirts were white. Seymour didn't precisely think
America's problems could be traced to men wearing shirts of
other colors, but he had entertained the idea. He seldom
turned out in a shirt and tie anymore, but when he did, he
preferred to wear each shirt only once. Any more than that
and the collars became grimy.

He was wearing a tie today because his presence in the
West Wing demanded it. Certain things even he conceded to,
and the pageantry of the Oval Office was one. Particularly now
that its occupant was under his sway. The concession was not
to the man, but to the office. To the Constitution and to the
Federalist Papers, and to the ideal of a libertarian, North
American, Christian republic. He had only recently renewed
this concession, after eight years of decrying trespass into this
sacrosanct space by a globalist, socialist, Islamist, un-Ameri-
can interloper.

The conversation this morning would be as brief as possible, and cryptic.

There's a problem. Don't ask me what it is.

Do I have your permission to solve it? Don't ask me how.

*Under no circumstances, Mr. President, consider the possi-
bility that this has anything at all to do with that pesky little
hotel bombing thirty miles up the road.*

It wasn't important for the President to get bogged down in details. The important thing was to stop the next attack, an attack that Seymour knew was imminent. *Actually, that was not the most important thing. Attacks would happen in a free and open society. If it wasn't the Muslims, it would be...someone else.* The most important thing was managing the fallout from the attack. Or attacks.

Days ago, he hoped the threat to him and to this White House might have been managed. Quietly. It had not been. There had to be a formal response. The country had to act. Seymour needed to control that action. He needed to guide it. *Because if things headed in a certain direction, there were consequences he did not wish to consider. They were unthinkable.*

The source of the bomb used in Annapolis could never be revealed. The contents of the FBI file that crossed his desk in early July must never be known. The organizing force behind these attacks against America could never be discovered.

The revelation of any of those facts, or even the future availability of any of the raw intelligence which analysts had used to assess the truth of these matters, would jeopardize this White House.

No. In point of fact - a fact that Seymour was loathe to acknowledge – no matter how integral he was to the campaign, and no matter how much POTUS trusted and relied upon him, the truth would jeopardize Gerald Seymour.

He would be the fall guy. Because that was how the White House worked.

A ready solution awaited. It would leverage a narrative that had been building for years, and which the American people understood instinctively. The great benefit for Gerald Seymour was that this would vitiate the need for any fabrication on his part. Just leave the blanks blank, and the American people would fill them in.

His plan would get an assist from the news networks and the last gasping breaths of the print media, ironic since he painted them as the true adversary during the campaign. The people who had opposed his candidate would now save the presidency.

With the President's endorsement and the media's support, he would tell the American people a story they wanted to hear. The resources he needed to extinguish this threat would have been inaccessible a few months ago but were now at his fingertips. They would be meager really. A discreet and well-trained CIA SOG team, directed against one compound.

The enemy were a dozen men. Men that no one in America would ever hear about. They wouldn't believe it anyway. Americans knew that "others" threatened them. Their jobs. Their safety. Their values. Solving this problem should not come at the cost of shattering that certainty.

The plan was instinctive. Like the campaign. Seymour's instincts had never failed him. Or POTUS. He was so certain of this plan, so confident, that he thanked God for the opportunity now. He remembered a poster on the wall of a company he bought and liquidated in the 1990s, something about how some Asian language used the same symbol for two words. Crisis. Opportunity.

He finally understood the stupid poster. He had to get this right to save himself and save the White House. But he would get it right, and he would show America that the threats he had come to snuff out were real. Crisis. Opportunity.

As the most powerful man in the world entered the Oval Office, Seymour felt a surge of pure joy.

"Good morning, Mr. President."

SIXTEEN

CULPEPER COUNTY, VIRGINIA

Sami woke suddenly, as if from a nightmare. He blinked hard. It was real. He was in the upstairs bedroom of a safe house tucked into a hollow between two hills about 75 miles southwest of Washington. The area had once been horse country but was fast being threatened by the sprawl of Metro Washington.

"Safe" was a relative term for a place off even the non-official grid. Rather than one of the well-protected and well-provisioned houses that the CIA kept outside of D.C., they were in a property that Andy maintained with a slush fund. "House" was hardly more fitting. There were four rooms downstairs and this one bedroom upstairs. Like most everything else about the house, the weathered wood frame was original. The farmhouse's only renovation was concealed below grade, where Hasan Khalifa was imprisoned under control of cuffs and a Propofol and Lorazepam cocktail.

Sami heard the distant white noise of breaking news downstairs: the droning anchor, an occasional reporter on-scene, an expert on the phone. He could picture the images being cycled on the screen, a formula familiar to anyone who lived in post-9/11 America. Police cars arriving. Ambulance lights flashing. Wreckage seen from a helicopter. A trail of smoke diffusing into the sky. More than imagining the video, Sami could visualize it. Because he had been there.

The hotel in Annapolis. Karim's truck. The bomb. It was real. Sami hadn't stopped the bomb. His friend was dead.

As Sami descended the creaking stairs, he saw that the sun had not cleared the hills east of the house. Emily and Alexa were watching the TV. Neither of them had slept much, if at all. The network bug in the corner of the screen read 6:21 AM.

Yoda was in the kitchen, Hasan's laptop open on the table in front of him. Andy was on guard duty, sitting on a kitchen chair by the door that led to the basement. The dungeon. A small monitor sat on a coffee table next to him, broadcasting a fisheye view of the subterranean cinder block room.

"Sleeping?" Sami asked.

"Like a baby, Dost," Andy said. "I relieved Alexa at 0500. Gave him another cocktail just before then. We can get him up soon."

Hasan was lying prone on an Army cot, his hands and feet cuffed to the frame. Another chain extended from a restraint belt to an iron loop installed in the wall. It was meager as secure holding went, but adequate. Why Andy had the foresight to construct it, Sami could only wonder. Who paid for it was another question outside of his understanding.

What he knew was that he and Andy had no basis on which to hold this man. No matter their intentions, the legal status of their actions was not in doubt. Kidnapping. And a dozen other charges.

They arrived at the safe house at 11:30 the night before. They secured Hasan and by the time they debriefed Andy, it was 3 AM.

It was a frantic night, but they grabbed Hasan at Dulles. There were no FBI or TSA agents there to make the arrest. There were not even any black-and-whites from local law enforcement. After all, they had enforced no laws. They had abducted a grown man. That was not a novel feat for the CIA, but there were exigent factors.

The grown man was a U.S. citizen. He was taken in a busy international airport. They were on American soil. And they were not the CIA. They had no resources, no authority, and no legal grounds upon which to claim either.

If that swirl of factors had been last night's dilemma, this morning's was much clearer. They did not stop the first attack. Any chance of preventing another attack seemed to rest entirely in their hands. Or, at least, in their basement.

At 6:30, through the haze of coffee, Sami heard the TV anchor updating the facts for the bottom of the hour. Confirmed

18 dead, 71 injured. So far. The wreckage was still smoking. After running pictures of the scene, the entire night, the network was teasing its morning show coverage, beginning at 7. The pictures would be more compelling when lit by the sun. There was one more item to report.

A FEDERAL GOVERNMENT SOURCE WHO IS REMAINING ANONYMOUS BECAUSE THEY ARE NOT AUTHORIZED TO SPEAK ON THE RECORD, HAS TOLD US THAT THE FBI ARE SEEKING TWO PERSONS OF INTEREST. THEY ARE DESCRIBED AS MILITARY-AGED MALES, MIDDLE EASTERN, WHO WERE SEEN IN THE LOBBY OF THE HOTEL JUST BEFORE THE BOMBING. THERE IS ALSO A REPORT OF AN OLIVE OR BROWN-SKINNED MAN WHO RAN AWAY FROM THE HOTEL JUST BEFORE THE EXPLOSION OCCURRED. AT THIS POINT, AUTHORITIES CANNOT CONFIRM WHETHER THIS WAS A THIRD MAN, OR ONE OF THE TWO PERSONS BEING SOUGHT.

Alexa turned toward Sami and Andy. "Fuck!"

"Just wait until they have pictures," Sami said. Chances were that a surveillance camera somewhere would have recorded him. He turned back to Andy. "Get him up."

"You going to interrogate him?" Andy asked. Sami's clenched teeth said he was. "He'll be useless to you," Andy checked his watch, "for another 60-90 minutes."

"Is that enough time for you to get the cavalry here? A real interrogator?"

"The cavalry ain't coming, Dost."

"Then get him up."

***

The first time Sami tried to talk to Hasan, the only response was some gurgling and a wide-eyed stare. He went back upstairs, had coffee and breakfast, and tried to collect his thoughts and prepare an interrogation plan. Rather than administer a drug that would accelerate Hasan's wake-up, they wanted him to come around naturally so that Sami could maximize the time when he was awake and responsive, but still under the beneficial effects of the drug cocktail. An hour later, Andy reported signs of life on the monitor and Sami went downstairs for the second time.

The only concession to Hasan's comfort was rolled up under Sami's arm. He brought nothing else. Not a cup of water, nor a scrap of food. These would be rewards for cooperation. The air conditioning in the room was at full blast, bringing the temperature down into the high 50s. That was not cold enough to break Hasan, but it was uncomfortable. As the July sun rose, it would be difficult to keep the room cool, even underground, but if Hasan wanted a blanket, it would come at a price.

The conditions were imperfect, but as much as possible they wanted to mimic a real interrogation at a real CIA safe house. One of the most imperfect of their circumstances was that the Sami was not trained as an interrogator. He had seen it done.

In person, in Iraq, where he was part of a small HUMINT team that rode outside the wire on the tail of a mounted patrol. On video, at Langley, where he often referred to taped interrogations as part of the analytical process. But he had never done it himself.

That made all the difference. He had watched Bryce Harper hit dozens of balls into the right-field deck at Nationals Park, but Sami had no hope of stepping up and doing it, too.

He tried to focus on the PIRs. Priority Intelligence Requirements.

Where did the money for the trucks come from?
Who made the bombs?
Who was the delivery man?
What was the next target?

Even those four questions almost overwhelmed Sami's ability to collate them. They were huge questions. Getting answers – even from a cooperative subject, which Sami was not sure he could expect Hasan to be – would be a challenge. If this were a covert Op, CIA would have had dozens, maybe hundreds, working the operation. Off the books, as leader of the Andy Rizzo Five, it was down to Sami. Which led to a different set of questions.

Why had his team been denied the raw intelligence?

Why was Andy pushing back on pursuing the bomb maker?

Why now – even after an attack – was someone in the government not offering Andy everything he needed?

Why wouldn't Langley take it from here?

The second set of questions had to wait. Sami needed to focus.

On the monitor, Hasan still appeared to be restrained, but nothing could be taken for granted. As Sami descended the stairs, he listened for any sudden movement. Having had the worst of last night's ordeal, Hasan looked as haggard as everyone else in the house, but Sami saw that the young imam was more alert than he had been an hour ago. Sami placed the two rolls under his arm onto the plastic chair opposite the cot. Hasan immediately recognized these objects. Sami checked the cuffs and restraint belt. All were still fastened.

"As-salamu alaykum." Sami's greeting was not amicable, but it was polite.

"Wa'alaykumu as-salam" came back from Hasan, in kind.

"If you promise me you will pray in peace, I can have your restraints removed."

"This is more than the concessions given at Guantanamo." Sami expected a sneer but saw a glimmer in the prisoner's eyes. "I am in the States still." The first PIR point on the board went to Hasan.

For a moment, Sami's heart sank. Hasan was clever. Far from cooperative, he would be difficult for an experienced interrogator to crack. Then, spurring himself, Sami bucked up. *The cavalry ain't coming.*

"You'll never know where you are. And neither will your brothers in arms. We can take up that discussion now if you like. Or we can pray."

"Hayya alas salah." Islam's equivalent to *Let us pray*, the Arabic phrase translated literally as *Hasten to prayer*. It had been years since Sami heard it and the inflection and pronunciation were his grandfather's own. A chill ran down his spine as he climbed the stairs to retrieve the keys for the cuffs and restraints.

The keys were kept upstairs as a security measure, in case Sami were overpowered. It also supported the ruse that this was a fully-staffed operation. In a proper safe house, he would have been accompanied back downstairs by beefy guys in balaclavas, but only Andy was waiting at the top of the stairs to hand him the ring, and Sami returned alone.

The restraint belt and cuffs removed, Sami handed one of the prayer rugs to Hasan. They unrolled them, Hasan hesitating just a second for Sami to confirm the orientation of his rug toward the East. There was no hesitation in what happened next, Hasan needing no indication that it was he – the imam – who would recite the Adhan.

"Allahu akbar. Allahu akbar. Allahu akbar. Allahu akbar."

***

When they finished praying, Sami fastened the cuffs again. He placed the restraint back around Hasan's waist to allow the prisoner to sit up on the cot. He returned the keys to Andy at the top of the stairs. He barely settled into the chair before Hasan began.

"You pretend to be a Muslim— "

"No." Sami interrupted. The next sentence came out as if there were periods after each word. "You pretend to be a Muslim."

"I have only stopped pretending to be an American. The rest of the country stopped pretending that one could be a Muslim and an American long ago. I made my choice." Hasan said.

Things were beginning as expected, if not as planned. The team understood that the conversation could get confrontational. It was an interrogation. Sami could let Hasan speechify, but not filibuster.

Don't let him kill time.

Don't let him distract from the priority intelligence.

If he gets too far off track, shepherd him back by revealing what we already know.

Sami ran through these instructions in his head as Hasan continued.

"The American Dream is tragedy clothed in myth. Americans are the only people in the world who don't know it. The stories of American greatness are varied, but many more are the stories of great loss. A father, a brother, a mother, sons, and daughters. They come here, but few of their stories adhere to the global myth. Freedom. Safety. Wealth. I have lived this fantasy. I have traveled the world. And I have studied politics and literature and culture. The whole of the American Dream was a post-World War II amplification of the 19th century's Horatio Alger stories. And now the world is catching up."

"Technological parity is America's enemy. Their longstanding advantage, the investment in resources to deliver propaganda, has been decimated by global connectivity. When people discover these myths of America, when they are presented with alternative facts, they see the truth. There is no opportunity here. 1% of your people hold your wealth. Mexicans are your modern field and house slaves. The blacks, who had the audacity to throw off that yoke, now wallow in prisons or ghettos. Asians, here or in their home countries, are your garment workers. And Muslims," Hasan paused, "we are your whipping boys."

Sami drew a breath to speak, but Hasan had only paused.

"When that myth fades away and America's moral decrepitude is exposed, there is but one American export that remains. Murder. American history is murder. American Indians felt the sword first. In Mexico, they bore the brunt of your muskets. Americans could not resist the urge to divide by North and South and murder each other. A hundred years later, the only country ever to drop a nuclear bomb. The My Lai massacre. Juntas and coups in South America and the Middle East. And now, the forever war. Until Islam is gone."

This time Hasan paused long enough to warrant a response. Interrogation is about control. Asserting it and then leveraging it. Like poker, winning by bluff was more indicative of skill than winning with good cards, for it concealed much. Like a game of chess, the speed to victory matters to virtuosos.

How many moves does it take? How few will it take to win? Sami's team expected that they might get to this point, but they were here already. No interrogation had been necessary. Sami waited, replaying Hasan's words and combing his memory for the right response before he began.

"For his willingness to expose this hypocrisy," Sami said, haltingly at first, "Karim Sulemani takes his rightful place among the *Shahid*. Allah's chosen martyrs." Now he gained speed. "And from Karim's brave act of *shahada,* we must all take a lesson. If a normal American like Karim could strike a blow to explode these myths, then so might any Muslim."

On the cot, Hasan's eyes widened in surprise. Sami stood and walked to the stairs. He didn't look back when he spoke.

"I've heard that speech. I know every word." Sami hoped this would make it obvious to Hasan that they had his computer and were inside of it. When Sami turned back toward Hasan, his expression of deflation confirmed this.

"We have everything. Every word you have written and spoken. Every email sent. You may be an educated man and a smart one. But not in the ways of war. As you have so eloquently indicated, we are rather knowledgeable in those ways. You have won a victory. A painful one for us, yes, but not a decisive one."

"You were prepared to sacrifice others to inflict harm on America. Perhaps we are matched in our cowardice, because we are willing to sacrifice you to protect America. Someone else was willing to sacrifice you as well, Hasan." Sami climbed the steps.

"I'll let you think a while." Just before he closed the door, Sami shouted down "Come up with something new to say. You have been successful. Your attack has changed things. The next time I visit you, something that was written before the attack will not suffice for you to avoid punishment."

***

When compared to humanity, psychology is in its infancy. Psychologists sought to identify sufferers in the 19th Century so they could be quarantined and to analyze everyone in the 20th Century so they might be treated. Still, in the 21st Century, there is much to learn about the pathology of the mind. Unfortunately for Hasan Khalifa, when it comes to the normal and expected behavior of a subject when responding to certain stimuli, American intelligence knew more than he would have wanted.

Interrogators at the Intelligence School in Fort Huachuca, Arizona, or at The Farm near Dam Neck, Virginia learn techniques that will make a subject to talk. The wise old hands at those schools also know how to break the will when someone does not want to talk. These techniques all make use of psychology.

The first lesson? Interrogation mind games were for city detectives and FBI agents in golf shirts. That's how they play the game when the Constitution was in play. In law enforcement, they had to sit there and let some little shit act hard and clam up. All those guys have is their wits. It was chess. Chess isn't war.

When hotels are blowing up, its war.

It is said doctors can develop a God complex. They save a life or bring someone back from the dead and the feeling eclipses pride. It becomes compulsion. But the doctor moves on to the next case. He gets in his Benz and gets stuck in traffic. He goes home and the dog puked on the rug in the front hall. The God complex takes hold only where the pathology is strongest.

Interrogators also develop a variation of the God complex. Despite the horrific - and sometimes apocryphal - stories of torture training academies where sadism is fine-tuned, it does not take much training or creativity to figure out how to fuck someone up bad. Especially not someone who is tied to a cot without food or water for days on end. It doesn't take waterboarding.

Put someone in a cell alone for a few days – no lawyers, no phone calls - and you control their world. Interrogation is about control. Not manipulation. Control. Putting someone on, like a puppet you wear, and pulling the strings they didn't even know were there. Control their thirst and hunger. Decide if they sleep and for how long. Control whether they shiver or sweat.

If you do all of that, and you do it right, you can control the beating of their heart. Food, water, light, dark, pain, comfort. That's not psychology. That's reality. God made real.

Sami was not a professional interrogator, but he understood the biggest misconception about interrogation. People think it is about getting answers. Big answers.

Where did the money for the trucks come from?
Who made the bombs?
Who was the delivery man?
What was the next target?

Sami needed those answers, but he didn't think he would get them. From a true mujahid? No chance. Hasan? Maybe.

Hasan was not likely to give answers to questions like that. No amount of control can compel a person to say something they don't know. Sami's instinct was that Hasan was isolated from the operational side of the plot. What Sami needed were the missing pieces of the puzzle.

If you can starve a guy for days until he's catatonic, then wake him up, force feed him, throw him in an ice bath and ask for one small but critical piece of uncertain data, he will lack the ability to deceive. He doesn't know whether you are asking something he wants to keep secret, or why it might be important. Even the best in the world cannot cloak their deception under those circumstances. That was the game.

Sami did not have days. They knew there were more Council of Muhammad members from Hasan's cell, more guys with trucks. These trucks were bought and given for a reason. There was a plan.

The team met around the dining table, in a small alcove at the back of the kitchen. There were three chairs around the table and a bench seat built into a bay window, affording a view of dense overgrowth behind the house. It was Sami's turn to face the team's questions. Known as a debrief, this was the first chance he had to talk about the events inside the hotel.

"Karim was shocked. He had no idea he was being set up," Sami told them, after recounting the frantic rush to the garage.

Yoda, who had been dubious of Karim's innocence before the bombing, asked the question the entire team was pondering. "Why did he stay?"

"He wanted to get the truck out of there. He ran to the valet office to find his keys and he hoped that he could get to the truck and get it out before the bomb hurt anyone."

"OK," Alexa added, "Let's assume that he didn't know. Doesn't that leave a lot to chance?"

"It does," Sami agreed, "But it is still a lot easier than finding four or five American Muslims to commit suicide attacks."

"He's right," Emily said. "The plan is effective because it leaves the bombing to pros, whoever detonated the bomb last night by remote. All that the Council of Muhammad members do is keep living their lives. Go to work. Go on their business trips. They are vehicles. They don't know that Karim was set up. There will be another attack. It will be the same M.O. It will happen soon."

"Won't they all get suspicious when Hasan is missing, too?" Yoda was being more than the Devil's Advocate. He was playing an important role in challenging their assumptions. Testing their analysis.

"We're the only ones who know he's here. But he had to go missing, right?" Alexa's question floated over the table before she continued. "The plane ticket was Dulles to Toronto. This morning I confirmed that the rest of the itinerary took him to Dubai."

"Are our tracks covered there?" It was Andy, speaking for the first time.

"Of course."

Alexa's was annoyed to be asked for more, but Andy inclined his gaze to show that he expected details.

"The airline rep was as concerned as me when I told her that my husband never texted that he arrived in Toronto. After I had what I needed, I told her I just had a text from him at his hotel in D.C. Hungover and embarrassed that he missed his flight. She couldn't have been more sympathetic."

Andy was pleased. "Excellent. So, let's play this out. Hasan was leaving the U.S. to encourage the next round of attacks?"

"He's a great candidate to become the new Anwar Al-Aw-liki," agreed Sami. "Al-Awliki created the archetype for modern-day YouTube jihad. His mistake was to become operational. That was how we found him and targeted the missile that killed him. But I think Hasan learned from that. Spouting bullshit about jihad against the U.S. on YouTube is much safer than carrying out jihad against the U.S. And remember, his mujahid are patsies— "

"As far as we know!" Yoda's patience was at its limit. "We know about this group. The group close to Hasan. Physically close, in Annapolis. We don't know who else is out there! We don't know what might come next. Because we're close to this group, and these attacks, we're assuming this is *the* plan. What if it's only part of the plan?"

"What's the rest?" Andy asked.

"We have him. Downstairs! We have his comms— "

Andy held a hand up to stop Sami. He wanted to tease this out. It was how analysis worked.

"Go on, Yoda. What are you thinking?"

"Think about it! Have you ever been to a hotel in Israel? India? Pakistan? A lot of them have vehicle inspections to access the garages. They inspect luggage, open the bags and hand check everything before it comes inside. There are metal detectors. American hotels don't do that."

Everyone considered the point for a moment before Andy pressed.

"Give me worst case."

"It is the easiest thing in the world to check into a hotel room with a giant roll-aboard. It's expected! No one thinks twice when you walk into the lobby like that. No one knows what's in any of those bags! Think about the Mandalay Bay shooting. What were there, two dozen long guns? I think it is probable that there are others in Hasan's group. Maybe not in the physical cell, but others here in the U.S. who are prepared to launch hotel attacks."

"And within a week, American businesses stop allowing corporate travel," Emily added.

"That's business travel," Andy nodded, "Disney would be a fucking ghost town! You assess that as highly probable— "

"This is bullshit!"

"Dost! Enough." After correcting Sami, Andy turned back to Yoda. "I asked for worst-case."

"That there are others in the cell is highly probable. That some might attack, it follows, might also be probable. I think the worst case is that they planned this well. They know they don't even need to die like the guys doing bombs in high-security areas with checkpoints. It's jihadi recycling. Instead of killing themselves in a bomb attack, or being shot by cops, they check in, set up the bombs and detonate them remotely. They do it again and again."

"If Hasan is the new Al-Awliki, he doesn't need a ton of acolytes," Alexa said.

"That's right, Lex. He coordinates with one or two at a time. Connects them to the bomb maker, and they go live. If they use aliases and are careful, it takes one or two bombings to find them. As soon as one is caught, he has another one waiting in the wings. The more successful they are, the more followers he gains, the more candidates he has and the more selective he can be."

The group let that scenario sink in. After a moment, Sami caught Andy's eyes and gestured: *Can I speak now?* Andy nodded but a raised hand commanding that he restrain himself.

"What you describe could change American life. It would grind the economy to a halt. Most frightening of all, you're right. It wouldn't be difficult to pull off. If you assume that they have access to a reliable bomb maker." Sami scanned every face to make sure they were following.

"The difference is that Al-Awliki was up to his elbows. Planning attacks, bankrolling recon throughout Europe and the U.S., training attackers. He was on the ground in Yemen. Even if you are right about there being more in the cell, Hasan's nothing but a mouthpiece. Do we agree that regardless of whether Karim and the other Council of Muhammad members know they are part of a cell, Hasan is not the operational leader?"

Emily nodded first. Then Alexa. Yoda did too, slowly.

With agreement on the team, Andy weighed in. "I'm glad we got the worst case on the table. I think it's important to start from there. But I agree. We don't have time to chase all of that now. If the person or people behind the attack are smart enough, the firewall with Hasan does not just protect the operational leader, it isolates him. As long as this isn't ego. If he doesn't want credit, he could do what Yoda described. Maybe Hasan can't tell us who his operational counterpart was. He might not recognize this Black Truck Guy. But he has information he doesn't realize he has. Something we can put into the pile with the other intel to find the source of this shit. We need to get it."

***

When Sami went back downstairs, he found that Hasan was less coy. He was more willing to listen. It was Sami's job to make him talk.

"We know you communicated with your operational counterpart through encrypted messaging. Different apps." Sami said. "How was the introduction made? How did you first make contact?"

"He is called Halif. A mutual friend arranged the first contact."

Under normal circumstances, the mention of a "mutual friend" would merit lengthy exploration, but Sami did not have time for detours. Nor did he have time to gain access to this friend even if he could determine who it was. He was focused on the discussion that had just taken place upstairs. *Find the operational lead.* He made a mental note to return to the mutual friend when possible and continued on the man Hasan referred to as Halif.

"What did Halif tell you? How did he win your confidence?"

"There were many things on which we agreed. He also watched the American Dream turn to lies. He saw that American life was incompatible with living in faith. The evils of impurity. Miscegenation and homosexuality have not just become accepted but celebrated. This is inconsistent with the principals of Islam. Women are encouraged to live in a manner inconsistent with our sacred texts."

Sami was impatient. He would pounce if Hasan got preachy again.

"His most wise counsel regarded our duty of jihad. He knew of my experiences in Egypt. He shared the feelings I experienced watching the Revolution collapse under the weight of sectarian conflicts. In a caliphate, the true home of the Ummah, those conflicts could be resolved with an eye toward the true enemies of Islam."

"Was he *Daesh*?" Sami used the Arabic acronym for the loose confederation of Salafi jihadists better known as ISIS.

Hasan smiled. Given his situation, there was not much bravado behind it, but Sami read his meaning. *Stupid American.* "He doesn't have to be *Daesh*."

"Hezbollah? Jemaah Islamiya? Come on, Hasan, they don't teach bomb-making at Al-Aqsa. He's affiliated with someone."

"He is a freedom fighter. Without allegiance to state or sect. That impressed me most. He studied the situation in the Levant. He preached that we cannot hope to win this war if Iranian proxies are funded by Iran, Saudi proxies by the sheikhs, and so on. These states have their own vested interest. Their own swollen bureaucracies and geopolitical entanglements. They are ambitious for more than a caliphate. The only answer is to win and hold territory. To put even the Sunni nation states on notice that first, we deal with America, but they are only first. Later, we will take other sovereign land. Sacred land. And it will succumb to the Caliphs."

"You had common cause. What about the bombing? Who chose the target?"

Hasan started, then hesitated. Sami lied when he continued. "Your jihad is over, Hasan. You will never leave our custody. The only question that remains is how you spend that time. You know that we have a new President with dreams of expanding Guantanamo. Bigger than ever."

"And *you* will save me from the President?"

"No. But you can save yourself."

Hasan considered the point.

"He asked me to suggest targets and find men. Did I have access to either? I told him America was full of secular Muslims, not mujahid. I was sure I could find one or two crazies to shoot up a mall, but I didn't think that was a winning strategy."

Sami nodded in agreement. For years al-Qaeda and Daesh encouraged American Muslims to access small arms in American sporting goods stores and at gun shows. These attacks were terrorizing, but not strategic.

"He agreed," Hasan said. "No gun attacks." His tone did not indicate deception. But, if he was truthful, it was a departure for the groups that had traditionally financed attacks in the U.S. or inspired domestic radicalization.

"You were discouraged from planning mass shootings?" Sami asked.

"Mass shootings are dismissed as the work of lunatics. Worse than that, they would not generate attention for our jihad. When you shoot people in the U.S., the attack gets lost in the storm of politics about guns."

Sami felt a rising wave of fear. He thought he knew where Hasan was headed, and it frightened him in its simplicity and brilliance.

"To make the conversation about Muslims, we needed real attacks," Hasan added. The pride he felt being at the center of this enterprise, even as he sat in chains, was evident. "We wanted attacks that looked like what was happening in Afghanistan and Iraq and Syria. What has happened in Lebanon for decades."

"You needed something that fit a script." Sami was nodding.

"The media already has a narrative. We needed to incorporate our jihad into that narrative. The narrative about Muslims, terrorism, American identity. We needed regular

Americans. Born here. No evidence of radicalization. No ability for the media to turn them into a curiosity. Remember that fool in Boston. Tsarnaev?"

Sami remembered him well. In the days after the marathon bombing, the FBI fed photographs of Tamerlan Tsarnaev to the media. Not the photos of Tsarnaev in a keffiyeh holding a Glock. Those only came out at his brother's trial. In the days after the bombing, America saw a parody of Borat. A preening Tsarnaev posed throughout Boston in white patent leather shoes and a scarf thrown over his neck in a way that spoke to American assumptions.

Foreign. Maybe gay?

"Our mujahid had to be faultless. Perfect. Rather than find such men and try to convince them to become warriors for Allah, it was easier to plan the attacks ourselves. Execute them ourselves." Hasan could not control the spread of a sneering smile. "I proposed finding unwitting warriors, to attack places they already had access to."

"There's a problem." Sami was trying to rally and retake control. By confirming many of Sami's own suppositions from the conversation upstairs, Hasan had shaken him. With his own hypotheses confirmed, Sami had to set his ego aside to sound out Yoda's worst case scenario. "After the first attack, your other 'Councilors of Muhammad' know. They know they're patsies. They won't be so trusting."

"This is the same concern that Halif expressed. He liked the idea, but he wondered how long we could maintain our operation. How many missions? He was wrong then. You are now. The others do not know Karim did not perpetrate the attack. They believe what the media will tell them. It may seem unlikely to them. There is no irony if it sows the same seeds of doubt in them – about their own community – that it is meant to sow in the minds of Americans. When I am gone, and my videos are released, they will assume that I was a co-conspirator. If they had been exposed to some risk, they will assume it has departed with me. They'll be unsuspecting. They won't stop working or taking business trips on airplanes or staying in hotels."

Hasan was right. It was complex and risky. The attackers could not practice any counterintelligence because they didn't even know they were part of an operation. This was an advantage that Sami would have to exploit. The attacks would also have no signatures. Even if someone were watching the cell in Annapolis, there would be no signs of mobilization. Sami and his team would always be chasing an attack that had been put in motion before their subjects knew it, and therefore before Sami and his team could possibly know. Sami tried not to betray this concern.

"We know your men. We will watch them night and day. And then we'll catch whoever is building the bombs."

"This is where Halif's experience is integral. He mistrusted my men. After the first attack, he didn't think we would have much time to mobilize the others. But he planned for that. Halif has an affinity for the strategy of Hitler." Hasan paused for a second and Sami considered the parade of horribles to which this affinity might refer. "The Nazi blitzkrieg. That's the only way to attack America. Quick, decisive strikes so fast they use the American political system's inertia against the country. American policymakers will argue. Dither. Should they infiltrate the mosque I built in Annapolis? Should they infiltrate every mosque in the U.S.? Should they infiltrate none? Preserve the American ideal of political correctness? As they dither, the media will feed the flames. In less than a week, we will have done more damage to the United States than on 9/11."

"It's ambitious. But how can you trust Halif? How do you know that he can execute the next attacks? That he will? How do you know that you weren't just another fall guy?"

"Our mutual friend." Hasan's smile changed now. It wasn't just cocky, it was sly. Knowing. "He is most exalted and beyond reproach."

Here was another mention of the "mutual friend." The one who introduced Hasan to the man he called Halif. Could he be a Muslim Brotherhood connection from Hasan's time in Cairo? It was possible. It fit some of the facts but not any intel that Sami had seen. Muslim Brotherhood was not known to have any capability for – or interest in – American homeland attacks. The door opened at the top of the stairs. There was no need for Andy to call down. If the door opened it was imperative for Sami to respond immediately. Sami rose. He would have to return to the mutual friend.

***

Andy latched and locked the door behind Sami. It could have been the lack of the sleep or the surrealism of the past 18 hours, but Sami heard Hasan's voice echoing, as if in a dream. Then he placed it. It was real. The entire team was glued to the TV. This was why Andy came for him.

"The networks have all picked it up. About ten minutes ago," Andy reported.

Hasan was standing before a plain wall. Neutral paint on drywall. Non-descript. It was the video that Yoda found on the computer and it was already transcribed and looping on every network over a text crawl of the most incendiary quotes.

Sami didn't need to see anymore. He already knew Hasan claimed credit for the attack. He declared Karim Sulemani a martyr who was fed up with America's hypocrisy, its bullying foreign policy, and "*a life lived in the shadow war of domestic discrimination against Muslims.*" And the coup de grace.

"If a normal American like Karim could attack, so might any devout Muslim. You will hear from me again," he told millions of Americans in TV Land. "Allahu Akhbar!"

Sami knew Hasan was lying but he couldn't help feeling gut-punched by the brilliant smugness of the presentation. Americans would be shaken.

"I don't get it," Alexa said. "Why put out the video? It directs law enforcement to Hasan's known contacts. The FBI will be crawling all over the Islamic Center in Annapolis and they will have every one of the Council of Muhammad members in questioning."

"Remember," Sami replied, "Only we know Hasan right now. It will take a day or two for them to build a file."

There was a file on Hasan. And there was one on the man that Hasan was calling Halif, but who he really knew as Zechariah. But not even Andy Rizzo knew that. The file had been close hold within the FBI and access was restricted completely once it crossed Gerald Seymour's desk. As a result, Sami's skepticism was understated. It would take days, or a week, to reconstitute basic information on Hasan. The Feds would be lucky to ever find Halif/Zechariah again.

"If what he told us is accurate – the blitzkrieg analogy – we don't have long before the next attack." Andy was speaking, trying to seem assertive and in control but Sami sensed a strange vibe in the room. "Guys, catch Sami up on what you discovered."

Yoda began. "All we have on the other members of the Council is open source. I will try their emails now. We have the addresses from Hasan's correspondence."

"But if Hasan is telling us the truth, these guys don't even know they are attackers," Emily said, picking up the narrative. "We don't expect the emails to tell us much."

"It's truthful," Sami said authoritatively, not wanting to re-litigate the earlier argument. "Not just based on what he told me. I was with Karim. I was looking in his eyes when he saw the bomb loaded into the truck. He had no idea— "

"Or," Yoda was annoyed. Sami felt the tension that he had trouble placing when he first came upstairs rising again. "He didn't expect to be set-up for a suicide bombing. Hasan set him up for that, but nothing else. He knew about the plot and so do all the other guys. And more guys we don't even know about, because there are five of us working the biggest threat against the homeland since 9/11. With no resources and no authority."

Andy tried to change the subject. "We have a scenario for the next attack," he told Sami. "It's plausible."

"It's a guess! Based on the half-baked intel we have and some open source." Yoda was speaking to Andy at first, continuing an earlier argument. Now, he turned to Sami. "We need to bring this back home, Sami. However this wound up with us, it is in the wrong hands. We have to tell someone at CTC what we have, and let them brief the FBI— "

"We don't have time for this!" Andy thundered. The same impartial authority that had swung to Yoda's benefit an hour earlier was swinging against him now.

"We go to jail, man," Sami said to Yoda. "If we do what you're saying." He had one hand extended toward each man, trying to calm them. "You knew that we were off the books when you joined the team. You accepted the conditions. Nothing has changed."

"People are dying!" Yoda leaped out of his seat. "Who gives a fuck if we go to jail, we can't let another bomb go off!"

"Quiet!" Sami ordered. "Maintain OPSEC." He did not want Hasan hearing their argument. He continued slowly and quietly.

"If we get taken into custody this morning, if we do what you say, and brief the FBI, there goes the only chance of stopping the next attack." He scanned everyone's eyes as he continued, trying to see if Alexa and Emily were with Yoda, or if he still had their buy-in. "We're it, guys. So, tell me why you called me up here. What did we get that will allow us to stop this?"

Yoda stormed out of the room, a streak of profane grumbles in his wake. After a moment's silence, Emily spoke.

"Tahir Hussein. He's another of Hasan's councilors. Born in California. Engineer by trade. He works for an aerospace company, out of their office in Tysons Corner. It's a large building, ten or twelve stories. There's a main entrance with the office space off to one side and a standard business travel hotel on the other. The center of the building is a courtyard. Glass, to allow light in. There's a food court and a couple of sit-down chain restaurants."

"Ok." Sami could envision it. There were dozens of similar buildings in the suburbs skirting D.C.

"All three portions of the building share an underground parking deck," Emily continued. "Because you have restaurants and a hotel it is much less secure than a parking deck at an office tower where there would be security checks."

"He's at work now, right?" Sami asked.

"We don't know," Alexa replied. "But he should be."

"Ok. And we've thought about the other guys?"

"We've tried. Nothing as obvious." Emily said. "He's the sore thumb because he has regular access to the target. He'd be known there. It fits the pattern."

"One attack and one guess. That's not a pattern." Yoda was in the doorway leading to the kitchen. His comment conveyed his resignation, but also a conciliatory tone.

"You'll stay here with Hasan?" Sami was asking Andy.

"Correct."

The Marine in Yoda could not let this pass. "Lead from behind, Oorah!"

SEVENTEEN

TYSONS CORNER, VIRGINIA

There were two points of access and egress for the underground parking. Alexa was posted at the north entrance, Emily at the south entrance. *Black pickup truck*. Beyond that, they didn't know what they were looking for. That was a huge gamble. Just because Alexa saw a vehicle matching that description deliver to Karim's truck did not mean the same vehicle would deliver to Tahir. Sami and Yoda were parked inside, within sight of Tahir's vehicle. Since arriving, they discussed the plan a couple of times and ignored all the things that might go wrong.

The plan itself was not the least of these things. Overpowering and kidnapping a grown man is no mean feat. They benefited from the element of surprise and planning, but that offered meager comfort. CIA Special Activities Officers, the people who did this professionally, practiced these scenarios. Still, in the real world, something always went wrong.

It was like the old quote from the football coach: "The other team has a game plan too."

Sami was comforted that capturing the Black Truck Guy was a secondary aim, a "nice to have," rather than a necessity. The necessity was to act quickly when the black truck arrived. Don't let him plant the bomb. Whether they grabbed the guy or not, if they could scare him off it would save this building and buy them precious time. Sami already had a plan to make the best use of that time if he could get it.

"You know, the bomb could already be in the bed of his truck." Yoda's acknowledgment broke a silence of several minutes. "He might have delivered it first thing this morning before we ever got here."

Sami considered the reasons it would have been wiser for the plotters to wait.

For the lunch crowd: maximum destruction.

To allow Hasan's video to hit the TV airwaves: for their narrative.

He decided against offering any of these responses. They were *WAGs*. Wild Ass Guesses.

He was saved from responding at all when their phones buzzed.

INCOMING FROM SOUTH.

Of course, Sami thought, *we couldn't even catch the break of him entering on Alexa's side, where she might recognize him as the same guy.* All Emily could say was a black pickup had entered.

They didn't know if Black Truck Guy would have to cruise the parking deck, as they had when they entered, or if he had a more sophisticated way of knowing where Tahir's vehicle was parked. Either was possible and they had to be ready for action.

"OK. I'm lead." Sami said.

"Copy," Yoda said, affirming that Sami had volunteered for the more difficult job. "You sure you're up to it?"

His slight smirk filled Sami with gratitude. "I think it's for the best." They were a good team. Sami owed them more resources. If things went well this morning, he would have resources within 24 hours. For now, if anyone paid a physical price for the situation they were in, Sami wanted it to be him.

A moment later, as if in a dream, Sami watched as a black pickup truck cruised past Tahir's truck, then slowed. Sami reached for the door handle. Yoda threw a hand across him, like a mother stopping short with a child in the passenger seat.

"Wait on it. Don't jump the gun. We don't get out until he does."

The vehicle pulled away. Sami nodded in apology.

The truck returned 90 seconds later. It stopped about twenty feet from Tahir's vehicle and remained still for an excruciating 30 seconds. Finally, it pulled forward, its bed lined up with Tahir's truck. The driver jumped out. He matched the description that Alexa gave last night in Annapolis.

God, was it only last night?

White male. Thirties. Dark hair in a scruffy, overgrown style.

Sami exited the vehicle and looped around the row where they were parked so he could approach Black Truck Guy from the front. The man had just opened the bed of his own truck.

Sami shouted. "Hey man, you're blocking me in!"

In devising this part of the plan, they debated whether Black Truck Guy would know Tahir's face. It was possible that Hasan had provided photos, or even that the Black Truck Guy had surveilled members of the Council of Muhammad. Sami still decided this was the best tactic. All he needed was a moment's distraction. It didn't matter if what they discussed was that Sami was not Tahir and Black Truck Guy knew it.

"Unless he shoots you on sight," Yoda had suggested. It wasn't unthinkable. Lucky for Sami, Black Truck Guy was not so decisive.

He was confused. He did have the presence of mind to slam the truck bed.

"Yeah, I only have a half hour for lunch and I'm running to Best Buy," Sami said, continuing closer.

Black Truck Guy didn't know what to do. He stared at Sami, and after slamming the bed closed, he took a few steps forward. Should he move the truck? Should he get back in his own vehicle and leave?

Yoda had exited the vehicle at the same time as Sami. He made his way to the end of the row and had been working back toward the locus of action in a low-walk that concealed him between the rows of cars. He was within earshot now. He heard the action words, "Best Buy," and sprang from his position.

In the seconds it took Black Truck Guy to consider his options, Yoda came up from behind with a spring-loaded autoinjector. Like all U.S. military personnel, Yoda was trained to use the device for self-administering atropine in a chemical weapons attack. But his skill owed more to a lifelong allergy to bee stings. He always carried his pen and had used it before.

The needle was strong enough to break through heavy cloth and he hit Black Truck Guy square on the left buttock. A stream of the same Propofol/Lorazepam cocktail that was used on Hasan now flowed into Black Truck Guy's veins. The drug required only seconds to act, but they were dangerous seconds.

As soon as Yoda struck, Sami sprang forward to take control of the man's flailing limbs. There was a second syringe if necessary, but after a few seconds that rivaled any bull ride, Sami and Yoda had their man under control.

It took another two-and-a-half minutes to carry Black Truck Guy to their vehicle, secure him inside, and exit the parking deck. They texted the confirmation code to Emily and Alexa. Both women walked toward the center entrance of the building, near the main courtyard. As they walked, Emily hailed an Uber, only four minutes away. Alexa dialed 9-1-1 and reported the bomb. The call complete, Alexa removed the back of the phone and peeled the SIM card out with her fingernail. The plastic case of the prepaid phone went into a trash can. The SIM card stayed in her pocket. She would destroy it back at the safe house. Their Uber arrived.

The entire team was gone, with their new prisoner, before the first police car responded.

EIGHTEEN

CULPEPER COUNTY

The little safe house was crowded. Never meant to serve as anything other than a temporary redoubt, with just one holding area that Hasan already occupied, the team had to make-do with their second prisoner. They stopped at a country hardware store to buy a hasp and heavy-duty padlock for the upstairs bedroom. Black Truck Guy lay across the back seat, his mouth agape and tongue lolled, like a scene from *Weekend at Bernie's*.

They didn't dare return to the safe house without a thorough surveillance detection route, but they only had one more dose of sedative and they couldn't be too circuitous. These were unnecessary risks. And unprofessional practices. They would lead to another conflict between the team and Andy. That was even before they started digging on the Black Truck Guy and discovered who they had captured.

They had taken nothing from his truck. Given the difficulty of conducting the snatch, in public, with an untrained two-man team, they agreed that trying to grab any intel from the vehicle was too risky. It was a grievous compromise. There was no telling what they left behind.

The man was sequestered in the upstairs bedroom. In addition to the hasp and lock, Yoda bought dark contact paper which they adhered to the windows. One thing that the house had in ample supply was restraints. Andy must have bought them on clearance.

And so, James Everett Clewes, a driver licensed by the Commonwealth of Pennsylvania, was trussed like a pig.

In addition to intelligence officers, cybersecurity experts, and restraints, Andy kept a doctor close at hand. She managed the drug cocktails that had been administered to the prisoners and she was called for periodic check-ups to be sure detainees were not going to die in custody. She also came in handy when the team suffered bumps, bruises or worse. The ER was out of the question.

As she examined the prisoners, Sami congratulated himself again on the selection of his team. Within hours of returning to the safe house, Emily and Alexa provided a breadth of open source intel on Mr. Clewes, nee Black Truck Guy. Even with Yoda yet to hack into his social media accounts, the public activity was providing a treasure trove of information.

They had an email address and some geo-located photos to go along with the address provided on the driver's license. These provided a sense of Mr. Clewes' origins. They also had an academic history – such as it was – and a boatload of other public information: real estate transactions, hunting and fishing licenses, gun permits, military service dates.

Were he sentient, the rapidity with which the team gathered this information would have enraged their prisoner, confirming his most deeply-held resentments against the government. The team did not have to speculate on these resentments. Mr. Clewes expounded upon them in some of the most singed corners of the tire fire that is the internet. He was a denizen of the Deep Web, perhaps less fearful of speaking without anonymity when he trolled and posted on websites that were left off search engine indexes, unknown to the general public.

By comparison to the more-widely understood physical world, the Deep Web is the internet's shady alley, a place to explore less widely-accepted proclivities. Unconventional porn, undisguised racism, unsubstantiated theories of history, sociology, and every other liberal art. Fortunately for the team, in that same physical world comparison, James Clewes did not appear to have access behind the secret doors that line the Deep Web's alleys.

Behind these reinforced metal doors with sliding speakeasy peepholes lay the Dark Web. It was still the internet, but it was protected by passwords, special software packages, or encryption.

The Dark Web was where smart terrorists communicated and Yoda was the beat cop of these precincts. It was where Halif was sending messages to Hasan. In other words, Clewes did not seem to be Halif. His internet history was clumsy. The team determined that he was, always, just the Black Truck Guy. Like Karim, and like Hasan himself, Clewes was just another pawn. But for whom?

"Given his online persona, he's either employing one of the great public cover identities since Andy Kaufman did Tony Clifton," Andy Rizzo's pop culture referenced floated past the millennials and Gen-Yers on the team. "Or, he is a person unlikely to sympathize with Muslim jihad."

"His racism is incoherent," Yoda offered. "There are bits of Zionism and then he quotes David Duke."

"That's not unheard of these days," Alexa was having tea. She swallowed and continued. "There has been a détente between Zionists and groups that are traditionally antagonistic toward Jews."

"That's right," Sami nodded. "Against Islam. The enemy of my enemy and all."

"To the extent that his philosophy is inspired by any one school of thought, it's Rebel Creek," Yoda continued. "His positions are consistent with theirs. He cites facts and opinions from their website on message boards."

"That's not our usual beat," Sami looked at Andy, then back to Yoda. "Who are they?"

"Domestic group. White nationalist— "

"Militiamen from Montana?" Alexa interrupted.

"No. From what little I have been able to find, they have mailing addresses near Pittsburgh." Yoda checked his screen to confirm the location. "Washington County, Pennsylvania. That's the good news, someone can get there quickly."

Andy raised a hand but did not stop Yoda.

"Someone has to go to Pennsylvania! I need his computer."

"And whatever else we can get from his house. We need that intel." It was Emily. She seldom spoke but she always seemed to be right.

"Out of the question." Andy had both hands up now. "First off, we don't know what we'll find there. It could be guarded. He could live with others from this group. If they are making bombs there, the place is probably guarded with arms. If TATP is on the premises, you could get killed."

TATP was the acronym for the complex chemical name of an explosive compound that avoided detection by many explosive detection scanners and had – despite its volatility and penchant for accidental detonation - become the IED accelerant of choice. The London bus bombings. The Shoe Bomber. The Manchester concert bomb. All had been TATP. And the team suspected it was used in Annapolis.

"We're just supposed to watch until the next bomb goes off?" The whole team's anger was spilling out of Yoda now. They were all tired of fighting with one hand behind their back.

Andy seemed to ignore him. "Second, we are at enormous political and criminal risk if anyone finds out what we have done."

"Save that shit! I'm tired of your spider game. You made this web: off the books, black, unacknowledged, all the bullshit, and now you keep wanting to hang that over our heads. Are we trying to stop this attack, or not?" Yoda asked.

"You all understood the agreement and you accepted it. The agreement does not exist for the jobs you like doing. Such agreements exist for when things go wrong, not when they go smoothly. I don't expect anyone to express further compunction about our approach or resources in this operation. This is the last time."

Andy stood and continued, but Sami was distracted by words crawling across the TV screen in the other room.

"In case you did not appreciate the full import of the bullshit you signed up for, allow me to explain. We are an intelligence special access program. By definition, that means that our presence is closely held. More than that, we are an unacknowledged IN-SAP, operating above the oversight of Congress. Only one person in government can authorize such a program and he decides who is read in. I don't have time to explain everything entailed by this set of facts, and I'm not taking questions, but what should be self-evident is that when you spout off about calling CTC, you're wrong. There is no call to make. No one at Langley knows that our mission exists. No one is waiting for us to come in from the cold."

"So, we wait? And play Keystone Kops again? Hope we get lucky a third time? That's three more questions on top of the one you didn't answer a minute ago. Are we trying to stop attacks? Because if we are— "

"Shut up, Yoda!" It was Sami, from the other room, where he walked to watch the TV.

"Sami, we need help! If he won't, then you need to make a fucking call and get us more bodies— "

"We won't get them," Sami said.

"Because neither of you will ask! Because of 'the agreement,'" Yoda made exaggerated quotation marks in the air with his fingers.

"No." The feeling was surreal. Sami was watching a news report he knew was fabricated. If Andy was right that few people knew about their mission, then there was a correspondingly small list of people who could have planted the false story. "We don't want help."

"Why wouldn't we— "

"You should listen to your team leader," Andy interjected.

By now only Yoda, in his state of agitation, had not picked up what was on TV.

Anonymous sources at the FBI, unable to go on the record during an investigation, have confirmed that this man, Tahir Hussien, has been arrested in connection with a thwarted bombing at an office park in Tysons Corner yesterday.

The broadcast washed over the team. They all knew the facts. Tahir was not a bomber. He never knew about the plot, and the bomb never even made it into his vehicle. There was a connection to Hasan through the mosque but there were dozens of others with the same connection. Hasan admitted that the Council of Muhammad members were hand-picked decoys, selected because they were clean.

The team knew that someone else was behind the plot. Someone who was, or at least was connected to, a white nationalist group from Pennsylvania. The real bomber, James Clewes was upstairs in their makeshift holding cell.

So why was the FBI acting like they had arrested a terrorist?

"You still want to call them?" Andy asked rhetorically. When no one answered, he continued. "Do what you've been doing. But faster."

On TV, the reporter went to a satellite feed for an interview on this breaking story. Abu Muhammad appeared on the screen. He decried law enforcement's response to "one bad Muslim." He urged the FBI to stop the widespread and intimidating investigation of the entire Ummah, which he claimed began in the past two days. In seconds, he arrayed the interests of U.S. law enforcement against the interests of U.S. Muslims.

"Faster. And smarter," Andy finished.

NINETEEN

WHITE HOUSE

The briefing was held in the Oval Office. Gerald Seymour insisted. He had been operating on the President's authority without the President's approval or knowledge. After the anonymous call came from Tysons Corner, it took the FBI the rest of the day to get Tahir Hussein on the radar. Once he was there, Seymour not only ordered the arrest, but he directed the FBI to make it splashy.

He was confident he short-circuited any connection between this Muslim terror spree and the document he reviewed in early July. The best way to be sure, was for this investigation to get big and to get there fast. To become its own thing. FBI guys got hard-ons for shit like that.

And they loved face time with POTUS. In the Oval.

The President, who knew nothing more than what the FBI would tell him today, would issue the orders Seymour had prepared. Orders that the FBI could not ignore, no matter what reservations the Director had about the inordinate amount of interest that Gerald Seymour had taken.

There was time for the Situation Room. Seymour guessed that they would reconvene there soon. After what came next.

If what came next could be avoided, if he could stop it, then he would. He would direct resources to that end. But if it couldn't be stopped, then it meant something would happen that he could not have made a first-term goal in his wildest dreams.

America would divide even further. Between Christians and Muslims.

It was a path Seymour laid out long ago, even choosing men suitable to the task. That was before he ever conceived of himself running a White House. Directing a President. Since the inauguration, things had gone so poorly that he wondered if he had chosen the right man to put in this office. But he knew he had chosen the right man for this more important mission.

TWENTY

FOGGY BOTTOM

There were bigger gay bars in D.C. And better ones. But Sami couldn't think of one more suited to his purposes than Blue-skin. Named after one of George Washington's Revolutionary War mounts and housed in a low-slung brick building on a quiet mews in Foggy Bottom, patrons had counted on its professional drag show for decades. Now a haunt for the capital's professional gays, you were as likely to see a Deputy Assistant Secretary or a Congressman as you were a well-known stage performer.

Sami made the appointment while Yoda was buying detention supplies in the hardware store, before Andy elucidated all the ways that contacting officials from any three-letter agency was a bad idea. Before Abu Muhammad appeared on his TV. Neither of these facts changed the plan.

Despite Andy's direction, Sami was meeting Brad to seek clandestine help from the FBI. Or at least someone in the FBI. He used Abu Muhammad's TV gig as an excuse to break away and break communication for a few hours. Andy had been begging Sami to talk to his grandfather since the 4th of July. Sami told him he finally was.

Sami liked Brad. They had dated once. They were gay men in intelligence with roots in the D.C. suburbs. They had that in common. Brad's great-grandfather founded the prep school he – and half of D.C. – attended. His father was a retired Rear Admiral. Sami's parents were killed in a terror attack on a Central Asian U.S. embassy and he was raised by a Muslim cleric. They didn't have everything in common.

The relationship was perfect really. It was no one's fault it didn't work, it was just that circumstances never lined up. They still met. Like this.

A few hours after setting their meeting, Sami sent Brad a text:

REBEL CREEK

When Brad replied with three question marks, Sami followed-up in-kind:

???

He knew Brad couldn't resist something so cryptic.

Sami was early. It wasn't tradecraft, just habit. Or maybe it was that tradecraft had become a habit? He threw back the first vodka martini with abandon and was nursing the second. No wonder he didn't have a boyfriend. He was meeting a guy he liked and could imagine himself with. The kind of guy he had clicked with in college. The kind of guy he liked to wake up next to.

Maybe he would wake up next to Brad tomorrow morning? He might do that. He was still considering it, and a few more martinis would make the decision for him.

Those were the things Sami was thinking.

What he knew was that he would get his PIRs. Priority Intelligence Requirements. He knew that much, and if he went into a date with that level of deceit and duplicity, then how could he make anything like a real relationship work?

A question gnawed that was less easily considered. It only surfaced when he drank, and he could keep drinking to make it crawl back under the rock in his mind.

Was he too complicated a person for anyone to love?

He was a gay man raised by a grandfather who preached the fundamental impropriety of homosexuality. He was a Muslim who fought a war against radical elements of his own faith. He was an American spy working on an operation he worried was taking him close to secrets that implicated his own government.

That shook him from introspection. Who leaked Tahir's name to the FBI? It was too big a question, so he ran through the list of PIRs again, unchanged, and now familiar.

Where did the money for the trucks come from?

Who made the bombs?

Who was the delivery man?

What was the next target?

The last question would evolve with each attack. The rest were coming into focus. James Clewes was the answer to #3. He provided – at least – a connection to #2. He had to get the bomb from someone. His online behavior suggested that the connection might be more than incidental, more than just as a courier.

Might Clewes also direct Sami to answers for #1, the Money Man? Sami didn't know a lot of white supremacist groups that had money laying around, not after they bought and assembled a TATP device the size of those detonated in Annapolis and tried in Tysons Corner. But Brad knew white supremacist groups. He was their worst nightmare.

Brad was reared in his legacy prep school when his Dad's duty station was stateside, and Anglo-American schools when the Navy took them overseas. Brad "left the dark side" for college at Oberlin, a school so liberal that the ROTC program had not been kicked off campus during the Vietnam Era because it had never even existed.

After law school at Stanford, he moved to Montgomery, Alabama and spent the next five years climbing the ladder at the Southern Poverty Law Center. He became one of the youngest senior staff members in the group's history, and the managing attorney for the former Rust Belt states.

During the economic crisis, hate groups were proliferating like foreclosures. When the Civil Rights Division of the FBI came knocking a few years ago, Brad answered. Last time Sami met him he was as committed to the work as ever, although Civil Rights was not the same priority for this White House that it had been before the 2016 election.

"They've gutted the mission! Am I going to let them gut the talent, too?" He was brave. He was committed. He was late.

Sami looked around the low-ceilinged lounge area. Banquettes were scattered around the room to favor privacy over sightlines. A handful of tables that would be well suited to a corner pizza parlor ringed the small, elevated stage. Even the most diminutive performer had to consider hairstyle choices to avoid bumping against the drop ceiling. In the reddish light,

Sami could see that the tiles pre-dated the District's smoking ban in 2006.

2006. Brad was in Montgomery, Alabama. Sami was in Samarra, Iraq.

22 February 2006. Al-Askari mosque's golden dome came down in a bombing. Sami spent the next week on foot patrols with Army infantry and MP units. House-to-house. Al-Askari was a Shia mosque, a most holy place, and he was the litmus tester. He remembered the instructions from the Lieutenant Colonel in command of the response team.

"All you do is tell me which flavor they are. The kind that blowed-up this place, or the kind that would be mad it got blowed-up."

He said that. He said "blowed-up." Sami had dialed up his best Arabic and become Samir, Your Muslim Friend in the U.S. Army. He went back and told the Colonel which doors they should knock on for information, and which they should kick down with guns drawn.

That Colonel was like the current President. He misspelled his every tweet and wouldn't know a Sunni from a Shia from a *Shiner Bock*. Which was what Brad drank, and what Sami had ordered for him ten minutes ago, and he watched the bottle sweat condensation on the bar.

Those were the people Sami fought to protect. He, a gay Muslim, was making the world safe for a country that did not understand what caused radicalization. He protected free expression for the groups Brad prosecuted when they crossed the line from expression to oppression.

Maybe he and Brad had not been doing such different work in 2006. They were each policing their own. Brad his WASPs, Sami his Muslims. The martini was on-board now. Thank God Brad walked in.

They exchanged pleasantries and Brad charmed the bartender into trading the *Shiner Bock* on the bar for a cold one from the well.

"You still have the charm," Sami observed. "Didn't even have to flash your badge."

"Oh, please. They only stock *Shiner Bock* for me." There was a mischievous glint in Brad's eye. "You are very sneaky!"

"Well, we know that." Coyly. It was amazing, Sami supposed that it was part and parcel of his professional training, but he could switch his mannerisms on a dime. Here and now, he was not the same person who met Karim in a bar less than a week ago. He was a far sight from the same person who went house to house, flavor-testing Iraqis, back in 2006.

"Rebel Creek.' And then nothing? So cryptic."

"You know how it is."

"I know, but you picked a hell of a week."

Brad was referring to the bombing in Annapolis and the near-miss in Tysons Corner. Sami didn't bite. He waved off the bartender's offer of another martini.

"Oh no, he will have another," Brad corrected. "If it's story time, you drink with me."

"I'm already two ahead." Sami jiggled his near-empty martini glass toward Brad, who frowned unsympathetically. "Fair enough." Sami gestured the glass toward the bartender, who grabbed the shaker and directed a spout of vodka in. The sight satisfied Brad. He loosened his tie and began.

"Rebel Creek are a nasty bunch. The rank-and-file are our stock-in-trade. Old. White. Male. Angry about everything that's happened since the March on Washington. Pretty typical in philosophy and membership."

"What makes them so nasty?"

"Tut-tut." Brad didn't just make the sound, he enunciated the words. "Patience! I have a narrative arc here." He swallowed a sip of cold beer. "You don't have to read *Foreign Policy* to understand the resurgence in populism, nationalism, and nativism. And it's not just here. UKIP's down but Brexit is still popular. Marine Le Pen made it to a run-off in France. The same is happening throughout Europe, even into Scandinavia. But the radical right is nothing new in this country. The Know Nothings were a national party before the Civil War – they became Republicans, by the way."

"The KKK started in the early-20th century. Everyone thinks they know the KKK, but they don't. They set the American model for organized but incoherent political racism."

"Put that on their letterhead!" Sami interjected.

"Depending on where the KKK were in the country, there were different bad guys. Catholics, Jews, African-Americans, unions. What held them together as a national movement in the 20s was Prohibition. Did you know that? Most people don't. Anyway, the thing that has always united Klansmen is the ultimate enemy. Intellectuals. Elites. They were defenders of the common American: the pure, white, Christian, self-sufficient man. Sound familiar?"

Brad was a well-trained lawyer and he made an impeccable opening statement. Other than a penchant for intricate detail, Sami could see where he was also a very effective briefer for senior FBI officials.

"There have been 31 flavors since then, but it's all the same ice cream shop. McCarthyism begat the John Birch Society in the 50s and 60s. The Skinheads of the 80s went online to create today's Stormfront. Rebel Creek is most closely aligned with the Constitutional Militia movements that spread in the 90s. Specifically the splinter movements of Aryan Nations."

Sami was familiar with modern Aryan theories, but the group was not familiar. "That's capital *A*, capital *N*?"

"That's right. Founded in Idaho. Plain, vanilla white supremacists." Brad exaggerated the pun. "About twenty years ago they were popular. On everyone's radar. The FBI called them a terrorist threat. RAND said they were the only nationwide terror threat in the U.S. Remember, this was around the time of Ruby Ridge and Waco. The Southern Poverty Law Center won a multi-million-dollar judgment against them, after some of their thugs shot and beat a woman and her teenage son outside the Idaho compound. They claimed that the woman's car backfired, they mistook it for gunfire, and they returned fire in self-defense. We kicked their asses in court. Won millions and put them out of business. It was a siren song to a young, idealistic gay man looking for a career in civil rights law. It meant that we could hold some of these groups accountable for damages, and since they were not flush with liquid assets, we could take their property."

"Their compounds," Sami nodded.

"Their safe havens." Brad held up his bottle and clinked with Sami's fresh martini glass.

"This sounds familiar," Sami added.

Brad had just paraphrased the justification for the wars in Afghanistan and Iraq. *The invasions will deprive the enemy of their safe havens*...and something about yellow cake.

"I had fun following the model a couple more times, putting other groups out of business. But what should also sound familiar are the unintended consequences. The lawsuits worked, but they don't kill the ideology. Shit, they don't even kill the bad guys."

Sami knew the unintended consequences on his side of the fence: an unstable Iraq, the rise of ISIS, an empowered Iran, Russian adventures in Syria. The devil we knew being better than the spawn of Satan that we didn't.

Brad continued. "The group fragmented. Some holdouts in Idaho. A Florida group. And a Pennsylvania group. Western Pennsylvania."

"Rebel Creek?"

"Gold star. But there's more."

"I'm all ears."

"The group was based in Washington County, Pennsylvania. South of Pittsburgh. Notable until the early 2000s only for having been the locus of the Whiskey Rebellion. It was a tax protest that turned into a brief insurgency during Washington's presidency. It was Hamilton's fault, to tell the truth. I know it's sacrilegious for me to say it because the musical is so amazing, but he was an asshole."

Brad could see Sami's patience flagging at the idea of a history lesson. "Bear with me, this is important. Revolutionary War veterans were paid in Continental paper. Hamilton tricked them into believing that it was worthless and encouraged his New York buddies, speculators, to buy up all the paper they could find for pennies on the dollar. Then he created the National Bank and insisted that those holding the paper be paid in full, with interest. To raise the money, he proposed taxing distilled spirits. Corn rots, but whiskey only gets better with age. In the absence of stable paper currency, whiskey was the lingua franca in rural areas. It held stable value. Hamilton's plan taxed farmers to pay the debts that were owed to them but had been arbitraged to Hamilton's buddies. In Washington County, Pennsylvania, they tarred-and-feathered the collectors. The whiskey rebels called themselves the Mingo Creek Rebels."

Sami nodded in recognition of the historical connection to present-day Rebel Creek.

"It got so bad that Washington saddled up his horse again and led troops. Against Americans."

"That was 200 years ago." Sami had been patient, but he could feel a break coming. He couldn't wait any longer.

"Right. Other than for being home to a handful of football players, Washington County had not been on the radar since then. It's a quiet, hilly place like a lot of others. 99% White. Kind of rednecky, but northern, right? Not Appalachia. Not the Deep South. People in my business took their eye off the ball when Aryan Nations fractured. We paid attention to the Idaho group because they had been front-and-center. We had a guy undercover in the Florida splinter group, so we watched them. But Pennsylvania was quiet. I mean, who the fuck cared about militiamen after 9/11?"

"Then came that resurgence you mentioned. Populism. Nativism. The Tea Party. The 2016 campaign."

"Would you let me finish?" Brad chugged the rest of his beer and signaled for another. "I was always told Pakistanis were insufferably formal. Tea ceremonies and the like."

"I thought the rap on gays was no foreplay!"

"I guess neither of us are a credit to our race." They both laughed. Sami raised a hand to refuse a refill of the martini he had only taken one sip from. This time Brad let him get away with it. Their business was almost done. Soon it would just be a date.

"You skipped ahead of something very important."

Brad paused. It seemed interminable. Sami caved. "What?"

"Fracking."

"Excuse me?"

"Fracking. In 2004, they drilled the first commercial well in Southwestern Pennsylvania. In 2005, Katrina and Rita wipe out the Gulf Coast gas industry. In 2006, more than 30,000 natural gas wells are drilled in the U.S. Twenty-nine in Pennsylvania. In 2010, Pennsylvania had 1,300 holes poked in it. Land that was leasing at $500 an acre in '06 was now going for $5,000 an acre. Washington County got more than $5 million from the Pennsylvania fracking impact fund in 2015. That's just the public money. It doesn't count the leasing fees paid to individual landowners. Which gets us back to where you so rudely interrupted."

"The Pennsylvania splinter group of Aryan Nations? Rebel Creek?"

Brad nodded and sipped. "Yes, led by Tom Tinker."

"That's his name?"

"It's an homage. A brief detour back to the 1790s: remember the original Mingo Creek Rebels? The intellectual rabble-rouser of the group – sort of their Thomas Payne – signed his letters as 'Tom the Tinker.'"

"We have a history buff on our hands."

"Buff?" Brad let the word hang between them before continuing. "I don't know. He's aware. But he had reasons for the name change. His name used to be Brian Lydon. He was connected to Aryan Nations leaders in Idaho but after the split, he fell off our radar. He owned 800 contiguous acres in Washington County. The leases alone were worth millions, and he struck at the right time. Took his money in 2009 and 2010, leveraged his ass off, and then turned around to buy more land rights from neighbors and family members. Pennies on the dollar. The farmers of Washington County got fleeced again. In true Hamiltonian fashion, after Lydon sold the rights off to the gas companies, he used some of the proceeds to pressure them. Remember those anti-fracking movies a few years back, about how you could light the water on fire in Pennsylvania? We traced funds used to produce one of them back to Rebel Creek."

"I'm guessing you didn't trace those funds because the FBI's getting into the business of policing Netflix?"

"That's the rub, isn't it?" Brad gestured to the bartender for another beer. Now he was the one being cryptic. Between two trained intelligence and law enforcement officers, silence could linger a while before someone broke. This time it was Sami.

"What's the rub?" They both arched their eyebrows to acknowledge the innuendo. The bar was filling up but that was not the reason Brad leaned in close before continuing, the hint of beer on his breath mixing with an afternoon sprinkle of cologne.

"I wondered when you guys would come for them," Brad whispered.

Sami was confused, but he hoped Brad read it as playing dumb. "When *we* would come? For them? Rebel Creek?"

"We gave the Aryan Nations too much credit. A nationwide terror threat? They were a bunch of whiny old white guys. 'Remember the Alamo' types. Worse than that, they had no money. The FBI had their panties in a twist about this group's capabilities and they were taken down by a tort action. They were nothing. How did we destroy ISIS? Degrade their ability to refine and sell oil. The floor dropped out on the price, too. That helped. Thanks, Saudi Arabia! But, oil money put them in the game and took them out.

"Same for Rebel Creek," Brad continued. "Fracking money bought Tinker a seat at tables that Aryan Nations could only have dreamed of. Bad tables. The kind from James Bond movies where creeps from all over the world are twisting their mustaches. We thought we had something before. The Netflix trail was a huge breakthrough because it helped us understand how they were laundering money. Their signatures."

"So, what?" Sami asked, "You think he's gone from white nationalism to funding terrorism?"

"That's not a transition. White nationalism always had elements that wanted to weaponize the culture war they were waging. And losing. They see the writing on the wall. Every Supreme Court decision since Brown v Board of Education has gone against them. But we're talking about more than funding. His vision is bigger. Think Hamas. Hezbollah."

"Sponsoring?"

"That's right. He dabbles in funding. He dabbles in arms. They have a media operation. But they have ambition like ISIS did."

"Come on! ISIS?" Sami was incredulous. He was glad he had been, because the moment called for it. Then he thought about the Annapolis bomb, and Tysons Corner, and the Council of Muhammad, and the money trail, and the sophistication of it all and he wondered how much Brad knew.

"Remember the JV comment?" Brad asked. Sami did. Everyone in D.C. did. Early in 2014, President Obama referred to ISIS as "the JV team" when the burgeoning group conquered Fallujah. Republicans still used the quote as a cudgel against the former President and his party.

"It is an apt comparison for Rebel Creek. They aspire to do things that no domestic group has ever aspired to in this country. Only Hamas, Hezbollah, ISIS. They don't just want to terrorize. They want to retake territory. Like ISIS did, starting in Fallujah. These guys live in the U.S., they have free access to small arms and the elements needed to build high explosive. They have money. They have an ideology that aligns with every other fundamentalist religious separatist group in the world. They are early-stage. Small scale. But we knew it all added up. And we saw indications they were becoming operationally effective. We never could put the pieces together. And now, you guys have."

"No, Brad— "

"I showed you mine," Brad leaned in even closer. "Now it's your turn."

Sami allowed the entirety of what Brad said to wash over him. Now was not the time for deep reflection. He needed to stay "on" until he left Brad. It was more concern for Brad than deference to Andy, but the more he heard, the more certain he became that he could not give Brad any indication of what his team had already discovered. Sami needed to shift gears quickly. James Clewes was locked up back at the safe house.

This wasn't a date anymore. Brad read the hesitation as re-luctance. Sami hoped he misinterpreted the reason for it.

"My bet?" Brad said, sitting back onto his stool. "It's not funding. I don't think you can connect Rebel Creek to this homegrown cell in Annapolis. They're all U.S.-born. They ap-pear to be middle-class guys. They didn't need anyone to fund an apartment or whatever. So, they self-radicalize. Online. And thanks to this imam, Khalifa. Who is missing, by the way. He had a ticket, but we know that he never boarded a flight to Toronto, and we have not seen him transit any other interna-tional border. He's the connection to Daesh. But he's not operational. He couldn't blow up his microwave with a Costco roll of tin foil. And, this ain't France. Not with this President. They know that if any of these Annapolis guys visited Syria, or anywhere they can train with active Islamist groups, they'll never get back into the U.S. So they need someone to train these guys. Bombmaking material. Detonators. Tradecraft."

Brad was closer than Sami expected. Closer than Sami wanted him to be. Sami wanted to ask the next question: Did the FBI have anything on Tahir Hussein other than being a known associate of Hasan Khalifa? But he couldn't ask that question. It would tip his hand too much. Instead, he showed some leg.

"If you think this American white supremacist group is con-nected to Islamists there has to be more. We know Hasan Khalifa, and he's not the cutout. There's someone else."

Halif. But Sami didn't say the name. He knew it was a meaningless alias anyway.

"Tom Tinker isn't a simpleton like the old Aryan Nations leadership. We've known he was making bombs for 40 years. An FBI file on him back in the late 80s had that and it brought him down. Before that file made its way around town, Brian Lydon was connected in government. Remember the Moral Majority? It was Pat Robertson and Jerry Falwell and all these televangelists in the 80s? Well, they split after '88, but Bush 41 had his own group of religious advisers. Less well-known, less publicized. And non-sectarian. It wasn't just Christians. Don't forget, Bush was connected to the Saudis— "

"Oh, come on!" Sami cut him off.

"What, too Michael Moore for you?"

"Worse!" Sami said. "You sound like some walk-in to a CIA station, spouting crap from the *National Enquirer*."

"Look, the connections are there. Those are indisputable. I'm not saying Bush. I'm not. Or even his White House. It doesn't have to be anyone we've heard of or anyone in a visible position of power. There are people around the Presidents and Princes." Brad shook his empty bottle at the bartender and another bottle materialized too fast to be anything other than the bottle opened when Sami ordered earlier. Brad was too dialed-in to notice.

"You have to win the Electoral College, right? The people who get you 270 electoral votes get White House jobs. Carville, Begala, Stephanopolous. Rove and Hughes. Axelrod, Plouffe, Favreau. But before 270, you need precincts. You have to win primaries in every little shitheel county in Iowa and New Hampshire. Between Iowa and election night, you have to win in South Carolina and on Super Tuesday. And in Pennsylvania. There are a lot of people involved in that. We might not know their names. They're not on Sunday shows. But, a lot of favors go out. A lot of access is granted. Running a familial monarchy, a kingdom, is the same."

"From the Al-Sauds, you draw a line to the Wahhabis," Sami said.

"And from the Bushes, you draw a line to the fundamentalist Christians," Brad continued.

"Then you're drawing a line that connects them?"

"Actually no," Brad smirked, "Gerald Seymour drew the line."

The name was familiar to anyone in the Beltway, but Sami had to run through a mental checklist. Seymour wasn't a household name. Not Carville or Rove or Axelrod. He had been profiled once or twice, but reluctantly. He was well-known among insiders for things that were said about him and could not be proven. That he spread racist rumors about one candidate in South Carolina. That he leaked when another candidate's wife had been in drug and alcohol rehab. He was rumored to cut deals with reprehensible people who led fringe groups. All of this was coming to Sami, but Brad blanched at the glacial pace of Sami's recall.

"Senior Advisor to the President. He organized back in the 80s and 90s, but he was more niche. Religious groups were his specialty. And not Methodist churches. There was an article about him on Breitbart a few years back. They got him to talk about how he corralled these fundamentalist groups. He said, 'It wasn't hard once I showed them all they had more common ground than just the Temple Mount.'"

"Meaning?"

"Meaning that Muslims and Christians have plenty to fight over in Jerusalem. Throw in the Jews and Palestine, on it goes. But in America, the fundamentalists all thought gays were evil. They all thought the American melting pot was a cesspool of miscegenation. They agreed on the proper role of women. Salafists and evangelical Christians agree on a lot."

A chill shot down Sami's spine. Brad was paraphrasing Hasan's conversation with Halif. Sami knew he had gone as close to the line as he could. He was grateful that Brad's intel had been so enthralling, or he might have had another martini. He stood.

"Wow!" He accompanied the exclamation with an eyebrow raise that said, *You have overwhelmed me.* "I need to pee. I'll be right back." He walked toward the back of the club, where the bathrooms were. And the back door.

Just before he entered the hall leading to the bathrooms, Brad called his name and Sami turned.

Brad raised the *Shiner Bock* in salute. "It was good to see you."

TWENTY-ONE

CULPEPER COUNTY

Back at the safe house, the team was working their areas of expertise and their personal networks to fill in the blanks on James Clewes. They continued to exploit Hasan's PC and phone, examine his internet history and access whatever accounts they could. As it had been since they grabbed Hasan almost two days ago, the TV was tuned to 24-hour cable news.

They monitored the news in shifts because it was their best open intel source, but they had stopped calling out to the other members of the team whenever something new "broke" because the breaking news never stopped: the attack in Annapolis, Hasan's video, the thwarted attack in Tysons Corner, the arrest of Tahir Hussein. The breaks were almost all the result of several daily FBI press conferences.

Between breaks, there were the talking heads, of two types. A steady rotation of former officials speaking as experts on everything from terrorism and explosives to geography and theology, and the advocates with an ax to grind. Republicans playing to the cheap seats back in Red America. Democrats vying to show Blue America the limitless bounds of their political correctness. And Muslims. Muslim political groups. Muslim theology scholars. A few clerics.

It was too much to process and Andy only wanted "substantive" updates in real-time. The rest could wait for team meetings, held twice a day. So, Yoda was barely listening to the TV when familiar words washed over him like the shower he needed.

He glanced up to see another imam on camera. A familiar one. Famous, even. If Yoda were asked to name an American imam, first he would say al-Awlaki. If he were restricted to the living, he would say this guy, Abu Muhammad. It was his third or fourth interview in the last day. Yoda had no idea that the imam was Sami's grandfather. Though it had been a point of contention between Andy and Sami, it had not been discussed in front of the team.

The beginning of the interview was predictable enough. Abu Muhammad dispatched questions and insinuations about his connection to Hasan Khalifa. But then Yoda noticed something. Something familiar.

"We wish to be supportive of the law enforcement community. We have long partnered with them. Local agencies and the FBI. But this is different. Over the past two days, intelligence agencies have been pouring into our mosques. Accosting our members. And this stokes latent resentment in the American Ummah."

The speech, and the term "American Ummah," had a vague familiarity. Yoda was squinting at a hunting scene hung on the opposite wall, trying to place the memory, when Sami walked in.

"Where's Andy's car?"

Yoda punched the MUTE button.

"Gone. With Andy."

"He left?" Sami continued through the living room, looking for Emily and Alexa. With their present guests, calling the women's names out loud was an OPSEC risk.

Yoda waited for Sami to return before answering. "Took off not too long after you did."

"OK." Sami met Yoda's gaze. He saw the fatigue. They needed formal rest breaks, working in shifts, no more hurdling from crisis to crisis. He waited for Alexa and Emily to enter the room before he began.

"Starting now we work in a rotation of 18 on and 6 off. Everybody's strung out. We need to get control of that. And make sure you're eating." Sami checked everyone's face. They were all still in. He hadn't lost them yet. He knew that debriefing the meeting with Brad would only help to lift their spirits. Or, at least, focus their energy.

Concealing the source to protect Brad, and – by extension – the fact of his insubordination of Andy, Sami told the team everything Brad said. They were good listeners, there were no interruptions. Sami saw Alexa scratch a few notes as he spoke. She met his nod with an affirming gesture, the notes would be destroyed as soon as their conversation was over. Other than that, there were no distractions. Sami just told the story. It took about ten minutes.

"He mentioned Gerald Seymour?" Alexa asked.

"He did. To illustrate the point that these groups have common ground," Sami said.

"But we know that the 'line drawn through' Rebel Creek and Hasan's Council of Muhammad is Halif," Yoda added.

"No," Emily corrected. Sami considered the same question on the drive back from D.C. He understood what Emily meant but also understood Yoda's confusion. The data was running together for all of them now.

"Emily's right. Halif is someone from Rebel Creek, presumably. Maybe even Tinker himself. Remember the intermediary?"

"The 'mutual friend," Emily added, quoting Hasan.

"OK, fine," Yoda said, "But the 'mutual friend' doesn't matter. Right?"

"I'm not so sure— "

Yoda continued over Emily's soft-voiced objection. "Tinker or Lydon or whatever we're calling him. He's the driving force. We stop Lydon."

Alexa nodded and picked up the point. "Right. We need to focus on him. We already know what no one else does. The Muslims are patsies. This is all Rebel Creek. Hasan was just herding scapegoats. Whatever connections there might be to radical Islamic groups, they are irrelevant. At least now. Tinker and Clewes, they were the ones blowing up buildings. And still trying to."

"I think that's right. We need to exploit Clewes more than just open source. Get whatever else we can on him."

"But we can't go to the house," Yoda complained.

Sami spoke up over him. "I'll talk to Andy as soon as he's back. We have to find whatever we can that might indicate the next attack. Where. When."

***

It was just before 11 PM when the team adjourned, and Yoda took the first sleeping shift. Armed with her computer, a 24-ounce Diet Mountain Dew, and the information on the shell company that produced the Netflix documentary, Alexa went to the back porch to unpack Rebel Creek's finances. Emily took a laptop to the chair designated for guard duty, watching Hasan and Clewes on a split-screen monitor.

Two hours later, she found Sami by the blue glow of the muted TV.

"You need a bathroom break?" he asked her.

"No." She said no more but lingered over him.

"What's up?" Sami hoped Emily wasn't leaving the team. He couldn't deal with a personnel shuffle and she was the best person he knew for the role she played on the team.

"I looked back at the group you mentioned from the early 90s. Gerald Seymour's campaign project. The fundamentalists."

"Yeah?" Sami sat forward.

"Look, Sami, it's not my business..." Her confidence wavered, but she found it again. "I don't care that you didn't tell us. OK?"

"Tell you?" The problem with living a life of so many secrets was that Sami didn't know what Emily was referring to. No doubt there was something.

"About Abu Muhammad." She paused, painfully. "He's your grandfather."

"Emily— "

She spoke over him. "I won't tell the others. If you don't want me to, I guess there's no reason I need to."

"OK." Sami was relieved, but hesitant. Emily was not finished.

"I won't tell them about your relationship. There is something you need to know. And them, too. He's connected to Tinker. Through the group in the 90s. By Gerald Seymour."

"What?" Sami was shocked.

He was young then. Too young to remember much about his grandfather's organizations and activities. Emily turned the laptop screen toward him. There was a grainy scanned image from a newspaper archive, alongside an Op-Ed decrying the rise of religious influence in Republican politics.

Sami wanted to read the story. He wanted to see more. But he knew that Emily was good. She was thorough. For her to have come forward in this way, he knew the connection was rock solid. The photo of his grandfather, standing in a group of men, was unmistakable.

Emily was right. On one side of Abu Muhammad stood Gerald Seymour. On the other side was Tom Tinker.

"He's connected to Lydon, which we couldn't have known until now. Then there is the peripheral connection to Hasan. Why aren't we talking to him, Sami? What's going on?" She pleaded.

"Andy has been telling me to reach out since day one—" He stopped himself to explain that he hadn't spoken to his grandfather in years, but Emily interrupted.

"Andy knows?" She asked.

"I'm not sure how much. But he was pushing me before we made any connection to Hasan, much less Clewes or Lydon."

"Now you found out about Lydon, from someone. Andy ran off at the same time. And all of it is connected back to Gerald Seymour. Sitting in the White House." Her face was a mask of fear.

"Whatever Andy's doing, it has nothing to do with my information. That came from..." Sami didn't want to compromise Brad. It was not his right to. "It came from a friendly service."

"If we rule out Seymour himself, and I'm not sure why we would, but if we do," Emily said, "then it seems obvious who the most likely candidate for the 'mutual friend' is."

Sami wondered how the conclusion had escaped his own notice. He realized it was because he didn't want it to be true. Not because of anything as understandable as paternal affection. None remained. There had never been any. His grandfather had always been cold and distant, and not without reason. Not based on what Emily discovered, and not if her supposition was correct.

Sami didn't want to consider this possibility sooner because he was afraid. It was no longer fear of censure or reproach, but fear of confronting what he discovered was true about himself. Not that he was gay and a Muslim and an American. That was a reality that others could not accept, not him. But he was his grandfather's blood and there were facts about his family that he was not prepared to confront.

Sami forgot that Emily was before him. After a long silence, he gathered his thoughts.

"You're right," he started.

Emily could see the pain and fear in his eyes. "It's OK," she said.

Sami saw fear reflected back. They were in danger and Sami had put them there.

"I'm sorry."

"I know. It doesn't matter now though, does it?" she asked. "Whatever connection Abu Muhammad represented, it is behind us now. We need to focus on Clewes and Rebel Creek. Tinker."

Spies are trained to be dispassionate. Calculating. But no amount of training can make them inhuman. Sami grabbed the emotional lifeline that Emily threw with every ounce of his strength.

"You're right. It doesn't matter anymore."

TWENTY-TWO

LOUDON COUNTY, 2001

It was a Friday in May. The cherry blossoms had bloomed, and Washington was in the glory of its springtime. Few of its transplants – neither the Southerners who resented its snow storms, nor the Northerners who complained of its sweltering summers – could find complaint with the climate.

Sami was supposed to be at school. If he had been there, he would have spent the afternoon playing basketball at the College Rec with Karim. A gaggle of undergrads, law and med students, and young faculty members ran pickup games every week. They cleared the court when the serious ballers, former high school varsity players, borderline walk-ons, and local non-GW talent showed up. Sami and Karim would have showered back at the dorm and then hit the cafeteria before hitting a party or a movie.

Sami told Karim he had an interview for a summer job. An odd excuse for a Friday night, but Karim didn't ask. Sami's own whereabouts might have been a matter of uncertainty, but he knew just where his grandfather would be. His grandfather would have led Jumu'ah just after noon and the evening after Friday prayers was a time Abu Muhammad reserved for solitary reflection.

Sami took the train to Fairfax and then a taxi to the top of the cul de sac where his grandfather lived. His own home. Or, at least, where Sami lived ever since his parents died. He approached the house on foot. He walked around the back and keyed into the door off the small deck. Sami winced as staccato cracks issued from the old stairs on his climb to the second floor. He was sure his grandfather would have heard them.

The landing at the top was in a wide-open area with a small bedroom to the left, a bathroom straight ahead, and a hallway running off to the right. A right U-turn took him down the narrow corridor that ran parallel to the stairs, back toward the rear of the house where his grandfather had converted a bedroom, study, and bathroom into a multi-room office suite.

Stealing his nerve, Sami breathed deeply outside the door to the office. On the train ride over he drank two airplane bottles of vodka, knowing he would need the boost of liquid courage for this moment. Even that nearly failed. But he thought of his parents' faces and their voices, how he had been deprived of a chance to say goodbye to them, to ever hug them again or tell them he loved them. He pushed through into the outer office.

The walls were lined with books. One wingback chair sat in the corner, next to a floor lamp. On the floor, by the east-facing window, lay a prayer rug. The door to the inner office was closed. As a child, Sami never would have pressed on. This is where he would have stopped and called "Grandfather!"

Sami had never seen the next room, but he knew when he opened the door his grandfather would be in there, sitting behind a desk. When he saw Sami standing in the threshold, the imam's eyes widened in surprise, and then lit with rage.

"Samir! Your impudence— "

"Quiet, grandfather!" Sami interrupted.

Nothing like these words had ever passed Sami's lips. There was shocked silence as the same realization settled on them both. Sami was no longer a little boy. Abu Muhammad was well on his way to becoming an old man. His grandfather had never been violent with him, but there was no longer the physical intimidation that freighted interactions between small children and larger authority figures. Especially those authority figures who wanted to intimidate.

"Samir," the old man said again as he rose, and very much wanted to intimidate, "You will leave this office now! This house! Leave now!"

But Sami didn't leave. He didn't take a step back. More than physical intimidation was lacking. Obedience required respect. There was none left.

Sami said a name. And then others. They were names that his grandfather thought he had forgotten; or perhaps never realized that Sami knew. With his grandfather staring, flabbergasted, Sami revealed why he mentioned those people and what he had discovered about them. And what they did to his parents.

Sami listened as his grandfather did the one thing Sami never thought he would do. Beg forgiveness. That was when the old man told the lies that Sami had not unpacked for two decades, until now.

"You are correct. I knew these people and I arranged the meeting."

"But you never told the FBI?"

"How could I?" His grandfather asked. "You must understand. You must forgive me. Samir, this wasn't the same country it is today. If I were connected with those people, people who had just attacked the American embassy, it would have been the end of everything. I knew these people, but I knew nothing of their attacks. In America, as it was then, guilt by association—"

"It might have prevented another attack!"

"I would have been arrested. And imprisoned. Our community. My reputation. I had already lost my son, should I lose all of that, too? Worse yet, Samir, you were so young, and you lost your parents. Could I let you lose your grandfather as well?"

"Shut up! You lied." Sami had never spoken to his grandfather that way. For twenty years, he wondered why Abu Muhammad allowed it. Now Sami realized it was to cover up something even worse.

TWENTY-THREE

CULPEPER COUNTY

Andy messaged ahead of his arrival.

BLACK SUV IS ME.

A moment later, an American-made SUV pulled up in front of the safe house. It was so de rigueur in its appointments as to lack only a CIA vanity license plate. The tinting made it difficult to identify any faces, but Sami could see that Andy was not driving. There was at least one other person on board besides Andy and the driver.

The others stayed in the SUV as Andy swept past Sami into the house. He jerked his shoulders and head to indicate Sami should follow. Alexa was roused from her sleep. It was about halfway through the 6-hour break she began just after 5 AM. The team assembled in the living room of the house, in the same positions they had occupied hours before for Sami's debrief.

"We've done well. I know that we all wish we could have prevented the first attack, but we must prevent the next one. You've all worked with us before, you are familiar with how this works. Sometimes, we resolve these issues on our own. But, when we have done all we can..." Andy caught himself and thought about how much he wanted to say, "When I have briefed that our team has done all we can, the decision can be made to bring the operation back home. It doesn't happen often, but it happens. Not unlike Trident."

Trident was the code name for the operation that concluded with Sami watching a drone strike on his laptop from a Georgetown coffee shop. Sami and Andy - working with a different group of contractors like Yoda, Emily, and Alexa – provided targeting for the Yemeni redoubt that housed Chitre Al-Fazl. A German national, Al-Fazl was responsible for coordinating a series of low-tech but high-profile mass killings in Europe.

Trident was different. It always had been. On that operation, The CIA presented BND, its German liaison, with exquisite intelligence on Al-Fazl. In its ongoing post-World War II effort to absolve itself of the unforgivable sin of National Socialism, the Germans had one of the worst cases of moralism ever seen in the global intelligence fraternity, and they would not act against one of their own citizens on the U.S. intel.

The information was passed to the BfV, which would be Germany's corollary to the FBI, except that its agents did not carry weapons or even have the authority to make arrests. CIA pitched a plan, but German politics foreclosed a local operation when the target traveled back home. High-ranking individuals within the German government worked through backchannels to indicate that no great diplomatic sturm und drang would result if Al-Fazl were eliminated by others, when he was elsewhere.

The Americans were happy to oblige and even had a model for the operation. In 2015, a drone strike killed Junaid Hussain, a British national and ISIS black-hat hacker who was located thanks to exploitation of a secure messaging app. The plan was a go.

Even with German go-ahead, the CIA wanted the legwork off the books to protect the liaison relationship. Allies appreciated plausible deniability when it came to their prior knowledge and tacit approval of plans for U.S. intelligence to kill their citizens. Cue Andy Rizzo. INSAPs, or Intelligence Special Access Programs, afforded the cover of darkness.

Sami knew Andy's comparison of that mission to this one was false. The goal of Trident had always been to Kill or Capture Al-Fazl. That was how Andy briefed it from day one and Sami had yet to see a mission with a plausible capture scenario. Andy was making it sound like the CIA had only taken Trident back because Andy's gang didn't do drone strikes. Andy was dissembling.

"Why now?" Sami asked. "This should stay black."

Sami left unsaid what he and Andy both knew: INSAPs could only be authorized by the Director of National Intelligence, so only the DNI could formalize Operation Home Game under the CIA's authority. Only the DNI, or his boss, the President. To make that call, the DNI would have to read POTUS into the operation. Not unlike their European counterparts, Presidents didn't like that sort of knowledge. They preferred to let dirty deeds stay in the dark.

"Special Access Programs still are accountable to overseers. Those are the people who provide the structure that shades the dark side, and they remain in charge." Andy said, a little too pedantically. "We maintain control, but they give us resources to stop this guy."

"It's too soon, Andy," Sami responded.

Much of his meaning remained unsaid. INSAPs were often pulled back into the fold just before they were concluded. This not only allowed them to be put into the record, but for that record to be sanitized. The outcomes were reported nice and neat, without the complicated case history that would be present if the entirety of the operation was recorded in cables, status reports, interrogation records, and other contemporaneous accounts.

Andy ignored the comment.

"We are running Rebel Creek," he said, confirming that U.S. leaders did not share all compunctions with our allies – such as targeting domestic suspects when they were terrorists. "The FBI will stay on the Muslim issue."

"There is no Muslim issue!" This time it was Alexa, speaking before Sami could. Emily cut her eyes toward Sami, but no one noticed.

"Something's not right here, guys," Yoda said, so disenchanted by Andy's leadership that he spoke to the whole group in a breach of decorum that approached insubordination. "We know Tahir Hussein isn't a terrorist. That's what the FBI is saying on TV every chance it gets! Neither was Karim Sulemani. Someone else is pulling the strings here!"

"Twenty-four hours ago, you were the guy up my ass to take this to Langley!" Andy shouted.

"That was before we opened the connection between Tinker, Rebel Creek, and Gerald Seymour! Seymour, as in the fucking White House! Which is something we have not even discussed!"

For Andy, who had not been present for the debrief of Brad's information, the mention of Seymour's name was a shock. He didn't hide it well. He lost the last of his composure.

"Excuse me!" Too loud. "We serve at the pleasure of the DNI. We always have, and everyone here knew that. Do not think because what you do is not briefed to the Intelligence Committees, you are above the law of the land."

Sami caught himself before he listed off the violations of the law that had been committed just during Home Game, much less Trident, and a dozen other Ops. Andy was making a mistake by getting emotional. Sami would not do the same.

"No one is taking you off of it," Andy continued, staring at Sami, whose first thought was: *Because you may need someone to hang it on.* He pushed the impulse aside. He owed Andy more than that.

"You haven't done what you needed to do from the beginning," Andy continued. "You didn't with Karim. And you still haven't with Abu Muhammad." There he was again.

Why was Andy so obsessed with my grandfather? Unless he knows about Seymour? Or, worse, knows what I know about Baku in 1996?

When Sami cleared his head, he saw Emily watching him, trying to gauge his reaction. Her eyes willed him to speak, but he didn't.

"We'll have security on the safe house. These detainees may be moved, but that is no longer your concern. You'll head back to D.C. later today. I'll need you to brief personnel that are reading in for the move on Rebel Creek. Pack your things."

***

Time was warped. Like a bicycle tire bent by a curbstone, the last few days had lost their circadian shape. As they stood on the front porch of the house, Sami checked his watch to confirm that the twilight discernable over Virginia's hills heralded a new dawn and not the ending of an interminable day that began in Annapolis.

The country was still in shock, but the proximity Sami had to the events of the last few days afforded him perspective. Practical concerns were returning. The rental car that Alexa drove to the scene in Annapolis was parked behind the cabin and needed to be returned to BWI. Then they needed to rendezvous at the keyman office in Alexandria to wait for their briefing. Andy would summon them when he was ready.

Yoda sat on the steps. Alexa nodded back to sleep in a rocking chair. On another chair, Emily was thumbing her phone. Sami was watching the sky to the east, hoping to catch the first ray of sun coming over the mountains. It was the least active they had been and yet when they looked back on Operation Home Game, this was the moment of their biggest break. When Sami's phone buzzed. It was a 703-area code. Northern Virginia.

"Hello?"

"Good morning, sunshine." It was Brad, but he wasn't calling from the cell phone where he and Sami exchanged texts yesterday. He was at home, Sami thought, remembering it was early. He caught himself. Brad lived in the District. 202.

"To what do I owe the pleasure?" Sami asked. Maybe it was time for that date. Maybe he would finish this whole mess in time for tonight.

"If you cannot speak freely for two minutes, tell me 'It's been a while,'" Brad instructed. It was a modified duress code, a signal to confirm that Sami was safe and could discuss sensitive matters.

"No. It's good to talk again so soon," Sami responded. He didn't say Brad's name, but he wouldn't hold anything else back. He trusted the members of his team.

"Something's not right, Sami. About that matter we discussed yesterday. Now it's a hot potato. And the FBI dropped it."

"As ever, I'm just a soldier," Sami said. He walked off the porch and away from the house, out of earshot of the new team of guards. "But," he continued, "things sure look different from the front."

Sami explained the three-letter agencies seemed very interested and his team had just been pulled off Home Game. "Not pulled off. They were clear about that. But we have been staff-augmented into irrelevance."

"Someone to hang it on," Brad responded. He was quick and perceptive.

Sami wanted to hear more. "Give me the context," he said.

"I mentioned that we have been working Aryan Nations for years, and that we lost track of Tinker and lost the plot on Rebel Creek. Well, we had picked it up again. The information I shared with you last night came from an ongoing investigation. It's been multi-faceted, but about a year ago we caught a break with a CW." Brad was telling Sami that the FBI had someone inside Rebel Creek, a Cooperating Witness. "That's how we got wise to the weapons angle. Not to stockpiling. We knew that. That's typical militia and no violation of the blessed second amendment. We didn't know that Tinker was seeking training, cooperating with some nasty dudes to get some of his people trained."

"How nasty?" Sami asked.

"Globally nasty."

"Trained? To attack in the U.S.? At scale?" Even for the 1990s militias, a movement that spawned the Oklahoma City bombing, this would be a bombshell.

"Trained in bombmaking. But not for their own attacks. At least, that's not what we were told. In exchange for the training, he offered support. Logistics. These groups, who had the knowledge he wanted, needed something from him in return. Access to the U.S. Houses. Cash. He becomes the armorer of choice for domestic attacks in the U.S. It makes sense. For Tinker, it was a beautiful marriage of his ideologies: capitalism and racial nationalism."

"Elaborate on the nationalism for me." Sami was following, but still a little muddled. He needed sleep. "How does arming radical Muslims support his objectives?"

"That's the same question that came up in the Bureau. It's what I asked the guy who showed me the intel from the CW. 'What's the end game?' And we short-changed Tinker. We figured he hates Muslims, but he agrees with the idea that they should have their caliphate. White Christians should have theirs, too. In America. But we missed the forest for the trees. He's a devious motherfucker, Tinker. That wouldn't be enough for him, just the idea. He's not a dreamy-eyed revolutionary. He's a revanchist racist."

Brad stopped himself, but Sami could feel the idea that had formed in his friend's mind. Sami knew Brad was right. He had pieced together the facts that Sami and the team had watched unfold and that Hasan confirmed. He might not have known that Karim and Tahir were set-ups, but he had deduced that Tinker was supporting the attacks because they would destabilize America's delicate racial politics.

"The guy who showed you the intel, who—" Sami began.

"Don't even take us there!" Brad interrupted. His source was off limits. "But I saw the interrogation notes. It was a redacted copy with the CW's identity minimized, but I saw it. That's what I'm calling about. It's gone."

"Gone, how? What do you mean gone?"

"I mean the report I was not supposed to know existed, much less have seen, is no longer present in the files of the FBI. I should be walled off from it, but I should be able to see it exists. Someone panicked. They panicked, and they dumped the file, and by doing that they left a trail."

"You are saying someone within the FBI is— "

"Is trying to cover up the only solid indications we had of the cooperation between Rebel Creek, a domestic white nationalist group, and this domestic Muslim cell that attacked in Maryland and Virginia this week."

Sami hesitated and then said, "There is no domestic Muslim cell." He felt he owed that much to Brad. "That's what I plan to tell the FBI when I brief them today."

There was a brief silence as Brad processed Sami's information. Sami loved him for not asking the questions that were swirling in his head about how Sami discovered it.

"So, your Op is Rebel Creek then?" Brad asked.

"Yes. Although as of this morning, the Rebel Creek Op has gone back to Langley."

"S.A.D.?" Special Activities Division of the CIA, the paramilitary arm directed by Langley.

"I assume so," Sami said. His confidence level was 90 percent.

"They do it with black helicopters and the Rebel Creek raid never makes the news," Brad said. "But the Muslim round-ups going on now? That's front page."

"They might get the explosives, Brad. They probably will. We needed their resources for that, to stop another attack. But someone's heart is not in the right place."

"Governments don't have hearts, Sami. Only heads. Remember that."

Brad was right. The CIA, the FBI, the White House; they were organs of government. The new White House spoke about combating terrorism and had a strong-armed foreign policy, but they were untested against a U.S. attack.

"Wherever their head is at," Brad continued, "I'll tell you this: FBI agents are crawling all over National Harbor today."

National Harbor? Sami was puzzled.

How could he have forgotten? Today was the opening of the annual convention of the Association of Muslims in America. The event was a three-day gathering of Muslims in the U.S., but it always attracted global attendees and attention. If the FBI decided to make hay at that event...Sami did not have to finish the thought. The whole operation was coming full circle to where Andy first read Sami in.

"National Harbor is going down in history with Selma and Montgomery," Brad said. "The White America that voted for this President, that wanted to ban Muslims, will get their moment. The FBI using the proverbial fire hoses, this time on uppity Muslims. The government will be wrong this time too, like they were then."

Brad was right, but Sami didn't have time to dwell on the historical ramifications. Or the question of why the FBI was ignoring information, much less disappearing it. There would be another attack. One that Rebel Creek would pin on American Muslims. And Sami knew where it would happen.

TWENTY-FOUR

NATIONAL HARBOR | CULPEPER COUNTY

One notable thing about the convention of the Association of Muslims in America was how much it was like every other D.C. convention. Poster boards throughout the hotel lobby directed attendees to one of the many ballrooms with appropriately historic names. A long registration table was hung with crisp white linen and displayed a long grid of nametags waiting to be claimed.

Some attendees had driven their expensive, but not ostentatious, cars from Beltway suburbs. Others arrived by Uber, after landing at Ronald Reagan National airport. As the conference opened, they were being borne down from guest rooms by elevator. Nearly all were dressed in conservative suits from up-market men's clothing stores.

In a brown suit and open-collared ecru shirt, Abu Muhammad needed no nametag. His current role with the board of AMA was ex-officio, but he remained the de facto host of the annual convention. He offered introductory remarks welcoming attendees to Washington and then delivered his longer remarks as a closing address on the last day of the meeting. This year, the agenda was different. Events required it.

He acknowledged a few friends and acquaintances as they arrived but retreated to a small conference room opposite the main ballroom, which had been modified to function as the green room for panelists and speakers. A table by the door was stocked with bottled water. A prayer mat was spread out in the center of the small room, and two others were rolled up by the wall. There were two pairs of chairs, each sandwiching a small end table. Abu Muhammad selected a chair. He had issued instructions at the door that he was not to be disturbed.

He wrote the speech longhand, but he no longer possessed the original. He had given it to Hasan Khalifa. He reviewed a copy and wrote a word or idea in the margin to serve as cues when he spoke. As he reviewed, he remembered much of what was written verbatim. But, now that he would be the speaker, the speech needed editing. He changed specific words to reflect his own preferences. He adjusted the pace and cadence to match his own speaking style.

An unfamiliar feeling settled in his stomach. He was nervous. The stakes of the speech would not be obvious to others until later, but he knew these words would be shown endlessly on news programs. History was not linear, not the history of the movement he represented, but someday his speech would be written about in history books. Today marked a turning point.

It was time to speak. Abu Muhammad crossed the hall to the small waiting area behind the curtains. He could not resist the childish urge to pull the curtain aside and look at the ballroom. Hundreds were crowded around circular banquet tables, chatting. The room was full. He nodded to a young woman from the Association offices who was the convention's logistician. In turn, she nodded to a round-bellied employee of the conference hotel, who handed her a microphone and flipped a series of switches on the audio board.

"Sabaah al-khayr. As-salamu alaykum. Please have your seats. The program will begin shortly."

In less than a minute, the murmuring on the other side of the curtain was replaced by the shuffle of chairs. And then, silence. The crowd was ready. The young woman parted the curtain and Abu Muhammad walked on stage.

***

Yoda was flipping through TV stations, past all the news channels with their "Attack on America" graphics, but no network was going live at the AMA meeting in National Harbor. He found C-SPAN, but a hearing of the Tax Policy Subcommittee of the House Committee on Ways and Means, in recess, took precedence. The team stared at the TV as he changed stations.

On C-SPAN 2, they saw a podium set against a black curtain and the logo of the AMA. A man was standing at the podium, completing introductory remarks. Abu Muhammad. His voice was clear and resonant, possessed of a slight accent that reflected education in English, rather than American, schools. He offered a cursory note of sympathy for those killed in the Annapolis hotel attack.

"Coincident with our sympathy, the community assembled here must also feel apprehension. Even as we gather, in peace, we are surrounded by the FBI."

A few heads in the crowd turned, scanning the room as if to ask: *FBI? Where?*

"In the country we have adopted as our own, but which seems unwilling to claim us, we see violence everywhere. In city streets, between warring gangs, hundreds are murdered every year. And yet, the FBI does not infiltrate the African Methodist churches. In those same cities, violence is directed at Americans by the police departments sworn to protect them. And yet, the FBI does not suspect the chaplains of those police departments are fomenting these killings. In so-called 'red states,' for years the bastions of the Ku Klux Klan's ideology of supremacy, each day brings another in a string of mass shootings. Massacres committed with readily-available guns. And yet, the FBI is not targeting the conferences and conventions of the Baptist or Pentecostal or Presbyterian or Episcopal churches."

Perfectly divisive. Abu Muhammad was carving up American culture by identity groups. Picking at old, unhealed wounds.

"To our brothers and sisters in other countries, what is America any longer? Is it the country I came to? The beacon of light? The city on a hill? No. America is the destroyer of worlds. With precision-guided GPS missiles. Unmanned aircraft. Special Forces entering sovereign lands to kill sovereign citizens and skulk away under cover of darkness. Never too concerned with who has been killed, or how many, America has become Death."

Sami registered the allusion to the *Bhagavad Gita*. Quoted by Robert Oppenheimer in the moments after the first atomic blast – "Now I am become Death, destroyer of worlds" – the *Gita* was a Hindu holy book and core text of Indian philosophy. *Indian*. It was no secret that Pakistanis and Indians did not play well together. The implications may not have registered for the rest of Sami's team, but he understood what his grandfather was doing. No doubt the AMA audience did, too.

Before Sami horrified his grandfather by admitting his homosexuality, an endless string of family embarrassments resulting from Sami's behavior confirmed that he was a disappointment. One such embarrassment came during high school, when Sami – a below average player, but avid fan of basketball – played in a Washington-area Indo-Pak 3-on-3 tournament. When Sami made the mistake of wearing the tournament t-shirt at home, his grandfather treated him to a screed, explaining that India had chosen Western secularism over Islamic orthodoxy after the fall of the British Raj.

In 1947, the Maharajah of Kashmir targeted Muslims for ethnic cleansing and the world watched in silence as India suppressed Pakistan's attempts at aid. In 1971, the Indian army undermined Pakistani efforts to quell an uprising of Bengalis in East Pakistan, which resulted in the dissection and creation of Bangladesh.

Abu Muhammad hated India. He viewed the state as traitorous and the people as apostates. Yet, he had quoted one of India's most well-known philosophical texts. The message might have been subtle for an impassive listener, but as Abu Muhammad used every wedge possible to divide Americans, he was making concessions to India's 180 million Muslims. The Ummah was more important than any nation or historic conflict.

Cycling through the implications of his grandfather's words, Sami was distracted. He continued to hear the words his grandfather spoke, but he wasn't listening.

"Holy shit, Sami," Yoda said, shaking Sami from his reverie. Sami assumed that Yoda had also caught the India implication.

"It seems, therefore, to be incontrovertibly true that America is a violent country," Abu Muhammad continued. "And yet, each time one incident of violence is perpetrated by someone with a name, or a skin tone, that appears 'Muslim," Abu Muhammad used air quotes, a cheap pantomime that Sami had never seen his grandfather employ before. "Our entire faith is attacked. It leads us, many of us, to conclude that there can be no such thing as an American Ummah. That the community of believers in one of the world's great faiths can no longer find a home— "

"In the lands of the world's once great superpower." It was Yoda.

He spoke the sentence just before Abu Muhammad did. Everyone in the room turned their eyes away from the imam on TV to the Marine cyberwarrior. Yoda opened his laptop and typed his password.

"Holy Fuck!" He clicked once, and then again, and opened his documents tray. "Holy Fucking Fuck! Guys! Andy! Fuck!" Yoda was clicking frantically. He found the folder he wanted and opened a video file. It was one he had watched three times. He had listened to it on headphones another half dozen. He knew bits by memory.

It was Hasan's second recorded video. Abu Muhammad was giving the sermon meant to be released after the Tysons Corner bombing on national TV.

***

Using the DVR, the team compared Abu Muhammad's speech to the video on Yoda's computer. They watched the two speeches back-to-back a handful of times. They showed Andy the videos juxtaposed. There was no doubt. The video that Hasan pre-recorded to be released after the second attack, when he was supposed to be out of the country, was nearly identical to the speech Abu Muhammad just delivered.

"The portions of the speech that refer to the bombing in Tysons Corner were changed," Yoda explained. "Somehow, it almost makes the thing worse. Instead of justifying the bombing, it turns into a screed about overreach. The FBI sweeping in on every Muslim in the country in reaction to Annapolis. But other than parts that had to be changed, it's identical."

Sami agreed. He could see Andy trying to catch his eye.

"The really clever part is the end." Yoda clicked PLAY and Abu Muhammad's frozen face was animated.

"I call on the FBI, and I know that my friends in the U.S. Congress who have long supported me, and my congregation, who have received our support in return, will join me in calling for the release of relevant evidence and information, as soon as possible, to prove that the arrest of Tahir Hussein is based on something more than innuendo and what – sadly, in today's America – is the misfortune of being a Muslim."

Yoda stopped the playback.

"He's hanging his ass way out there," Andy said. "Maybe it's just bluster, but we know – and we might be the only people who know - he's right."

"The FBI knows," Yoda offered. "He's fucking smart. He's making them put their cards on the table and they don't have shit."

"The Annapolis group was a plausible cover story," Sami said. "To hang domestic terror attacks on U.S.-born Muslims. 'Normal' ones. To plant the seed that any Muslim might be dangerous."

Confused faces looked back at Sami. Abu Muhammad didn't seem to be supporting a thesis that Muslims were dangerous. Sami pressed on.

"But the seed needs to be nurtured. The FBI needs to be goaded for the plan to work."

"It doesn't take much for the FBI to suspect a bunch of Muslims," Alexa responded, sharp but still bleary-eyed from her nap.

"Agreed. That's the easy part, right? But Muslims need to be brought along, too. That's the hard part. The Muslims. Hasan Khalifa did his job with creating the window dressing, but he was always leaving the country. Someone has to stoke them. Fire them up. Direct their resentments. Someone has to lead a public campaign of revolt."

"Someone who has the cache to lead the Muslims and the profile to attract the FBI," Emily said. "Someone who was the nexus between Rebel Creek and Hasan Khalifa."

Sami didn't know if she told the others about his grandfather, but she went no further now. The implication was clear between them.

"The mutual friend," Sami responded.

He stalked out of the room and toward the basement door, the one that opened down into Hasan's cell. Alexa followed.

"What is it Sami?" she asked.

Sami unlocked the door and headed to the makeshift cell downstairs.

TWENTY-FIVE

WASHINGTON COUNTY, PENNSYLVANIA

The large concrete and rebar house was hidden in the hollow of two hills. The setting was not unlike the safe house in Virginia, but where the Culpeper County farmhouse was inconspicuous, this house was much larger, newer, and more imposing. There were three stories, all in poured concrete, each with small windows placed high in the walls. The place resembled nothing so much as the Abbottabad, Pakistan compound made famous as Usama bin Laden's safe house; a resemblance that was inspirational rather than coincidental.

In a centrally-located room on the second floor, which smelled of bleach, a small command center was set up. This too was not unlike the one now in use at the Virginia safe house. There were screens tuned to TV news. Others showed live feeds from security cameras around the house. A half dozen AK-47s hung from a tactical gun rack. In the center of the room, a kitchen island held stacks of TATP explosive packets. Wrapped in plastic and sealed with duct tape, they only needed to be transported to a plastic footlocker for delivery.

Tom Tinker waited for the go-sign. He was also watching CPSAN2, though he had required no channel surfing. He was prepared for the broadcast. If the speech was not shown on TV, he had one of his men in the room right now. The stakes were too high to permit a technical difficulty to interfere.

They were waiting to hear the words that Tinker told Hasan Khalifa to record. When Khalifa went silent, Tinker contacted their mutual friend. His old friend. He was told to proceed with preparations and tune into this broadcast. If he heard the line about "the American Ummah," the plan would move forward.

As soon as he heard the words, he grabbed the remote and clicked off the TV. Old friends though they might have been, Tinker didn't care to hear any more of Tahir's shit about

Muslims. Or America. The basis of their alliance was the agreement that neither of them should ever have to listen to someone talk about a false God. Not in a caliphate. Not in a Christian America.

Tom Tinker would set his country free again. But first, he needed to blow more of it up.

TWENTY-SIX

CULPEPER COUNTY

Hasan was reclined on the cot, one knee bent and his head resting on a rolled blanket that was the sole luxury he earned for his cooperation with Sami's earlier interrogation. With clear disdain, he began to speak, but Sami didn't acknowledge the words. Even in his haste, Sami was careful not to tip his hand. He didn't want Hasan to know that they had stopped the second attack.

"The second video? The American Ummah. Who helped you write the speech?"

Hasan frowned, disappointed to admit he might need help writing his sermons. He remembered his place and thought better of challenging the question's premise.

"That video is very important," he said. "The most important of all. On this, like all areas of this plan, I was aided by our mutual friend."

Sami swallowed hard. The video was a "go" sign for another attack. There was little doubt in his mind where it would take place.

"The mutual friend who connected you with Halif." Halif, not Tinker. Sami didn't want Hasan aware of any of their progress.

"Yes, but you are not listening. You have been ignoring my construction. It has been vague, I admit, but then we are..." Hasan gestured toward the camera mounted high in the room's corner "not alone. I was trying to be discrete, in your own best interest."

Sami could feel his proximity to the answer he sought but he also felt himself losing grip. He was not in the mood for Hasan's tortuous and contrived manner of speaking. Manufactured, to sound like some fictional version of a wise, old man of Allah.

"Why don't you make it clear?"

Without hesitation, Hasan responded.

"*Our* mutual friend." He enjoyed the emphasis on the first word. "Yours and mine. Abu Muhammad."

It was what Sami suspected. It had been possible someone sent Hasan's video, or a transcript, to Sami's grandfather, but now it was confirmed. Sami's lungs filled with a deep breath.

"When you were told to record this video, you went to Abu—
"

"Your grandfather," Hasan interjected and looked at the camera.

The team knew the truth now. Unless Emily had already shared what she deduced, but she would not have. Yoda and Emily, already uncertain about this operation, would also be confused about their leader.

"You went to my grandfather and told him you were working on this video— "

Hasan interrupted again. Sami was losing control of the interrogation. "He often helped me with khutbah." Sermons.

The team, watching on camera upstairs, filed that additional tidbit of information away. "Often helped." The connection between Hasan and Abu Muhammad was not as tenuous as Abu Muhammad implied in his TV interview.

"But this time, you revealed the entire speech to him?"

Hasan delighted in the question. Laying on his side, propped on his elbow in Sami's direction, he reclined, placing the rolled blanket back under his neck.

"What are you asking?"

The words had been swimming in Sami's thoughts for years. Since college, when he discovered the truth about his grandfather's connection to the men who blew up the embassy and killed his parents. He asked himself the question, but he had never spoken out loud. He was afraid of the answer.

Sami's parents were gone, and the truth would not bring them back. It would be hard to ask the question, harder still to wait for the answer, to watch his grandfather formulate a response, to see the deception in his face. He was afraid to hear what he had never proven but always suspected, the words that made his grandfather worse than an estranged stepparent. Sami looked at Hasan and saw the thing that he feared in a new face.

Only this wasn't about Sami's parents. The truth mattered.

Still, he could not ask the question that mattered, and he tried another oblique approach.

"Did Abu Muhammad see the entire speech?" Sami asked.

"He wrote the speech."

"Then he knew about the bombings?"

"Knew about the bombings? No, my friend, you misunderstand."

Sami felt a rush of relief, but there was more. Hasan relished the moment, sensing it would be his last contact with anyone for a while, and his last chance to spring a surprise.

"Abu Muhammad planned our jihad."

TWENTY-SEVEN

LOUDON COUNTY | WASHINGTON COUNTY

The cul-de-sac was picturesque. A grassy center island was lined with white oak trees. The front yards boasted mature persimmons, hollies, and redcedars. Scaley-barked shortleaf pines poked their sparse crowns up along the back of the homes. Visitors often remarked on the vague familiarity of the place. In the 1990s it had been a popular backdrop for filmmakers. When a Senator's or Supreme Court Justice's home was needed, they came to Sami's Northern Virginia neighborhood. Sami would watch out the window and think: *You should film what's going on in here.*

Sami was standing on the small back deck, peering through the glass terrace door into the kitchen. His grandfather was somewhere inside – in his upstairs office, Sami guessed – but the grandson was not inclined to knock. Walking into that office and confronting his grandfather again, in the same place where they had the conversation that drove Sami away for good, would be hard enough. He preferred to retain the element of surprise and the illusion of control.

The spy removed a simple pry tool from his back pocket and forced open the door. Stepping a few feet inside to quell the sound of cicadas from the surrounding trees, he heard nothing, no acknowledgment of his presence. He closed the door and replaced the pry tool in his back pocket. His arm brushed against the 9mm Sig Sauer secured inside his waistband. The magazine held fourteen hollow point cartridges. Sami never carried a loaded gun, but before holstering the weapon, he had racked a round into the chamber.

He was coming home.

***

It was nearly August. Even in Pennsylvania, it was too hot to be sitting outside on a 36-can cooler, trying to dent that capacity as much as possible and taking shots at the dove not yet in season. But there was Larry Day, in the mosquito-filled depression that he called The Bottom, a remnant of one of his Grandad's old coal seams.

The coal mine was long gone. And this wasn't his property anymore. When the Lydon kid bought it a few years ago, Larry's debt on the place was paid off. No more collection calls, foreclosure letters, visits from the Sheriff's Department. Lydon gave him $10,000 cash, off the books and he let Larry stay in the house rent-free.

"Just keep an eye out for me, Mr. Day," the kid said. "I like privacy as much as you."

Lydon also told him he might see people on the property now and then, and he shouldn't be alarmed.

"Men from the gas company, working on the wells," Lydon told him. "Maybe even a buddy or two of mine. Training."

Larry Day knew all about the Tom Tinker moniker, and all about Lydon's politics. Larry Day was an American first. He didn't think much of someone who talked about destroying the government and all that. But he was also a Washington County man, which meant that it was none of his business.

That was what he liked about the place he lived. Larry Day could shoot dove whenever he wanted, and the Lydon kid could dream about religious wars. Larry knew there were always goofy ass kids over on Lydon's side of The Bottom, shooting at old refrigerators. Sometimes he heard the concussive boom of an explosion ripping through the junk cars Lydon stockpiled.

He didn't think much of it when a half dozen guys came strolling up the dry bed of The Bottom, armed to the teeth. In spring, or after a big rain, the bed would hold water for a few days, breeding the mosquitoes and attracting the doves. It was dry enough now that these guys barely had any mud on their boots.

Larry Day wasn't worldly. Since he got back from Vietnam, he had only left Pennsylvania once, for a three-day weekend in Vegas that he funded with the cash Lydon gave him. But he was observant, especially about things country people know. These guys' boots weren't just dry, they were new. Expensive. They were leaner than the doughboys that ran around shooting Lydon's guns and blowing up his junkers.

Lydon's pals favored cheap AR-15s modified for fully automatic. The guys passing through The Bottom had a variety of firepower best suited to an infantry platoon. Tricked out ARs, a large caliber automatic that was something like an M249 SAW, only it wasn't American. Larry had seen them on the computer, and he guessed maybe it was an H&K. Each of the boys had a 1911 strapped to their thigh and a subcompact Glock secured in a chest holster. Then there were the grenade launchers, flash-bang canisters, and Kevlar.

They were trying not to look like soldiers, but they were. If it wasn't obvious enough, as soon as they saw Larry and realized he had seen them, one of them called it in. On a throat mic.

"Sorry, buddy. Hope we don't scare 'em off," one of them said. "Fella who owns the place said we could pass through."

Larry waved nonchalantly. Thinking that he hadn't seemed natural enough, he added, "Haven't got a damn one all day anyway."

The half dozen members of CIA Special Operations Group had already moved past, and not registering a threat from Larry Day, had already forgotten about him. Larry wasn't a threat. Not to them. Not to his country. He didn't go in much for that overthrowing the government junk. But Washington County people stuck together, and he had promised the Lydon kid he would keep a lookout.

Larry Day plucked the phone from his breast pocket and typed out a text message.

***

Tonight, Sami would correct every mistake he made the last time he confronted his grandfather. He began by widening his stride to the outer edges where the stairs wouldn't creak and climbed to the second floor. He found the door to the outer office open.

This was unusual to Sami, but he did not know whether his grandfather kept the outer door closed – as he always had during Sami's childhood - now that no one else lived here. Sami did not expect to find his grandfather on the other side of that door anyway, in the small sitting room where he took meetings. Whether visitors or family, all were relegated to this room.

Only Abu Muhammad passed into the next room, the imam's sanctum sanctorum. The room was only accessible through the outer sitting room. There were no outside doors. It was small and spartan, with a simple desk and chair, a floor lamp, and a window facing East, at the base of which lay a prayer rug.

That was where Sami surprised Abu Muhammad twenty years ago with what he had learned about the embassy bombing that killed his parents. As he had done that day, Sami would catch his grandfather off guard and uncomfortable, seize control, and not relinquish it. It worked then. His grandfather admitted to arranging the meeting that led to one of the worst terror attacks on U.S. interests prior to 9/11.

And killed Sami's parents.

Sami heaved a deep breath and shouldered through the door into the outer sitting room. There, waiting as though he expected company, sat his grandfather.

"Come in, Samir," he said behind a sickly smile. "I thought we could chat here this time. It is much more comfortable."

***

Larry Day's text message was brief and cryptic. When he heard the sounds of a firefight over the hill, he wondered if he had done enough, but he didn't wonder long. He had done his duty to his neighbor. To Washington County. Let the chips fall where they may. The chips had not fallen well for Larry in Vegas. He turned Lydon's ten grand buyout into $850 before boarding the plane home.

That was Larry Day. A simple guy. The kind of guy who thought he might go on a lucky streak and beat the house. The kind of guy who would not have guessed that his message was not the first warning Tom Tinker received.

Another text arrived only moments before Larry's, from another man who had known Tinker when he was just Lydon. Gerald Seymour. When Tinker received Larry's text, he was already in an old pickup, with cargo, headed out the back side of his property on another dry creek bed.

Gerald Seymour was a less simple man than Larry. He was gifted at understanding and managing the complex. But now, Tom Tinker had dragged him into something so complex that he might not get them both out the other end. If they got out the other end, the country would never be the same. It would be better because it would be more like it used to be.

Simple men like Larry Day didn't care. They would carry on with the simple illusion of their false patriotism.

If Seymour failed, he would become subject to a media firestorm, then he would become a prisoner, and finally, he would become a cautionary tale. But it was so predictable.

Like any chronic disease, the whole sequence of events that would unfold were symptoms of the larger sickness. A malignancy, which needed to be excised. Tom Tinker would do his part today. Just as he hit the gravel of Rural Road 371, he heard the first distant shots.

Rebel Creek would fall in dusky twilight and tomorrow a new day would dawn in America.

***

"Sit," Abu Muhammad urged. His manner was discomfiting for its mock-welcoming effect.

Sami planned the infiltration, parked blocks away and approached on foot, broke in through a darkened backdoor, and crept upstairs. Yet it was his grandfather who sprang a surprise.

"You were always a sneak," The grandfather said in response to his grandson's expression. "Perhaps not always but beginning in your teenage years and ever since. It demonstrates that sexual prurience is not a sickness itself, but symptomatic of a larger behavioral disorder. Somehow you thought you fooled everyone. You still believe that. Man is what he hides, Samir."

Sami could not place the quote, but it was not from the Qur'an. Rather than ponder the source, he thought of an appropriate retort. But Sami didn't utter it. Not right away. Instead, he entered and sat in a chair across from his grandfather in the small library. Even when he sat, he paused in silence. The pace of the conversation was good. His grandfather was an impatient man. Sami felt the Sig pushing hard against the small of his back, but silence would be his weapon.

His grandfather was wearing the same clothes he wore on CSPAN, the brown slacks wrinkled. The jacket hung on a corner rack. Abu Muhammad's skin was the color of blanched coffee, his aged complexion more ashen than in Sami's youth. His hands also showed concessions to time and arthritis, gnarled and clawlike in his lap. He had a prominent forehead, giving his eyes a deep set that could appear meditative or sinister. The shirt sleeves were short and with the collar hanging open, Abu Muhammad looked every bit the cleric from Sindh.

To calm his nerves, Sami ran through a mental Abu Muhammad dossier. He was trying to sequester his resentment and his anger, make this like any other job. Andy had been right all along, doing his job meant Sami had to talk to his grandfather.

Annoyed, Abu Muhammad broke the silence.

"Surely you have not come here, after many years, to say nothing."

"It's nothing to do with my words that brought me back," Sami replied awkwardly. "It was your words."

That was all. He said no more. Sami's existence was an affront. His mere presence was an instigation. The grandfather could not brook even these minor irritations from his grandson.

"Speak, boy! Say what you have come to say or slink off as you did before – I thought permanently." Despite the exhortation for Sami to speak, Abu Muhammad showed no sign of stopping himself. "You are a traitor to your family, your people, your God— "

"You made a mistake."

Sami's interruption infuriated his grandfather. Again, the old man waited for more. Sami kept him waiting. After ten seconds of huffing, puffing and rearranging himself in the chair, the old man's patience was at its limit.

"Say what you have come to say! Or do what you have come to do!"

Why aren't you telling me to leave? Sami considered the question as he watched his grandfather boil over. Having driven his grandfather to distraction, and to the brink of fury, Sami began.

"You made a mistake— "

"You've said that— "

"You'll listen now." Sami held up a censorious finger. The little boy inside flinched, but the Spy's poker face held. "Perhaps the mistake was not making adequate changes to the speech after Hasan Khalifa was captured? If not for that oversight, we might not have made the connection. But no, before that you erred in writing the speech. Someone who knows your style could still detect your fingerprints. The biggest mistake was conceiving this plan at all. Once you did that, the path was inexorable. That was your original sin, and now you're beyond your depth. You are not a tactician and you cannot overcome that shortfall. You were always going to make mistakes. Mistakes that would lead me to you."

"Please, tell me about this plan."

"You thought if you found a bombmaker, it would be enough. If they can make and conceal a bomb, how hard can it be to deliver? To detonate? Your plan relied on entrusting that to your partner. Someone who had limited experience, and even then, his experience was dated. It came from a time when we needed phone taps and other physical surveillance to monitor communications. It came from a time when we could not track the sale and movement of bomb-making materials."

Abu Muhammad smiled sickly, but his eyes betrayed him. Sami continued.

"You knew your partner was inexperienced. Not as experienced as those with whom you worked in the past. In the Middle East. The mujahideen of your own faith, too many of whom in your own network have made themselves experts at waging war against the innocent and defenseless. But you couldn't risk involving them. It would take too long and be too costly. There were too many obstacles. It was far better to have American Muslims hang for this anyway. Good, middle class, Americans who were Muslim. If some mujahid - some kid who had been to Syria or who was in chat rooms going on about the jihad - could be connected, then it would be the same old story. The media would cut-and-paste the same narrative with a new name. No, you needed wholesome names and faces. You needed America to fear every Muslim. And in that yearning, you found a partner. A friend from your past. His organization had some operational shortcomings, but he made up for it in this shared goal. And you trusted him."

Sami's suppositions elicited a chortle. Not a sinister laugh, like in the movies, just a single, sibilant exhalation and a curl at the corners of Abu Muhammad's lips.

"That's what you have? The speech?"

"I have the speech. Your words matching Hasan Khalifa's version." Sami paused before he continued. The next piece of information was a giveaway, but he gave it for a reason. "And I have Hasan Khalifa."

The information did not surprise his grandfather. The lack of a reflexive reaction was a tell.

"I have Tinker's delivery man. I have a special operations team in the hollows of Western Pennsylvania. They will get the people and the materials that are there. Capture or kill. If that does not neutralize the threat, if we still sense that people are at risk..." Sami paused, to see if his grandfather's face would tell him whether the bombs were already on site at National Harbor. "Then I come for you."

"Do you?" Abu Muhammad said in Sindhi. He preferred the intimacy of Sindhi. With friends, they spoke the more common Karachi-area language of Urdu. The fluidity with which they switched languages had been a hallmark of Sami's childhood. Sami would not let Abu Muhammad continue to infantilize him.

"If it is necessary to come tonight, or tomorrow, to neutralize any ongoing threat, I come with the gun. After we have compiled all the evidence implicating you, the FBI will come anyway. With handcuffs. Either way, someone comes for you."

His grandfather laughed again. This time, he was genuinely amused.

"You will do this, Samir?"

"I am not alone."

"Ah, but as I understand it, you are very much alone. You don't control this mission. You do not even represent your country on this investigation. Not any longer. Isn't that right?"

Sami's mind cut to Andy. The weeks of insistence that Sami talk to his grandfather. The reluctance to follow Sami's leads. Outside of Sami's small team, who else knew that Sami was no longer lead on the bombings?

"You have no one behind you. You have no authority. You criticize my tactics, Samir, but you haven't done your own homework. The FBI doesn't answer to you. I know this. Your threats are grandiose dreams. There is only you. You have no plan and you have no power. You don't even have the handcuffs about which you speak."

The certainty and smugness stung Sami, as much for its cumulative effect after a lifetime as for the recognition that Abu Muhammad might be right. He might get away with it. Politics might protect him. The law might not assess his culpability beyond a reasonable doubt. Would a jury convict and sentence an old man to the punishment he deserved for killing Karim and targeting innocent people?

All of that was fiction. Politics, law, sentencing. It was for lawyers and lawmen inside the Beltway, not for Sami. He had learned one thing going door to door in Samarra with Army Rangers. The law, the rules of engagement, none of it meant shit when a gun was drawn. When that happened, the person on the other end did what they were told. That was real.

Before he knew it, Sami had the Sig leveled at his grandfather's head. For the first time that night – or ever - he saw surprise in his grandfather's face.

"I have everything I need to do justice."

Abu Muhammad tried to rally. He smiled but Sami could see beads of sweat spreading a stain across his shirt.

"You will shoot me? You, Samir? You have betrayed your family. Your people. Allah. In these acts, you demonstrate that you are a low form of life. But not a killer. You are also something else, something worse. A faggot."

The sting of the word pulsed through Sami's body and his finger jerked the trigger. He felt sick. In his own home, the place where he had grown up, the person who had given him food and shelter called him that name. Without a punch thrown or a shot fired, Sami lost ground. It was as if the air had been taken from his lungs.

The reality of his Samarra epiphany came into focus again, and he realized that it took more than a gun. Someone had to pull the trigger. Someone had to be defenseless, merciless, hopeless. That was what it took to pull the trigger. Without guile, without planning, he spoke.

"You're a politician. Worse, you are a demagogue. You do it from this room and so the consequences are invisible to you. You have a theory about everything. Your religion and your biases have concocted those theories, but they mean nothing. To kill takes anger. It is the activation of hatred. You're right, I am gay. All over the world, there are people who hate me for that. Worse yet, I am a gay Muslim. Hated among some of my own people. Hated in my own home. In my own agency, in my own army, in my own country, there are others like you. They hate me for everything I am. You want to activate that now, in me."

Sami lowered the gun, silently dropping the hammer.

"America is not perfect, but it stands for the proposition that people can try. You teach some of your own people to hate and Tinker teaches some of his. You feed into ignorance that makes Americans afraid of Muslims and Muslims afraid of Americans. I won't let you succeed. That is not my oath of allegiance to this country, which welcomed you and which you now hate. It is not a measure of my commitment to the military and intelligence agencies you see as crusaders. The kafiri. What you think makes me weak is what makes me strong. I cannot let you succeed because I am a gay, American Muslim. Thanks to you and your kind, I know what a future without hope looks like. I will prevent that future. I will preserve my hope. Or, I will kill."

In his grandfather's face, Sami read something he could not place. For the briefest moment, he interpreted an expression of bemused pride. He was focusing on his grandfather's face so intently that he barely noticed when Gerald Seymour entered the room.

***

"I'm sorry to alarm you," Seymour said. "I don't suppose you will surrender it, but it would give me great comfort if you would holster your weapon." He was smiling. Playing the politician.

Sami had never seen another person in his grandfather's inner office, the room from which Seymour emerged. With no other way into or out of that room, Seymour must have heard the entire conversation. The White House advisor seemed to read the young intel officer's mind.

"There were several instances when I might have preferred to reveal myself, but the timing never seemed opportune. I trust you understand the dilemma." He spoke softly, more like "a grandfather" than *my* grandfather, Sami thought. "I have been privy to this conversation, and given my position, I think you'll understand that I have an obligation to expound upon it."

Seymour finished on an up note, though it was not a question. Whatever else is happening here, Seymour seemed to imply, you are a U.S. intelligence asset and I am a senior ranking official of this government. *You are subject to my command and control.*

"What you have been discussing is serious, and in some ways personal. Abu Muhammad has long been a friend, I care about him, and so this concerns me. Alas, graver concerns impinge upon my sentimentality. This is not a family matter. It is an issue for all Americans. About security. Not just this week, but in the long-term. And for all Muslims, too. The accusations you have made against your grandfather are grave. Sometimes our friends make mistakes, and when the mistakes are..." Seymour sought the precise phrase, "of a certain kind, it is incumbent upon people who have accepted certain duties to set aside personal relationships and do their duty."

Sami didn't remember replacing it, but he felt the weapon holstered at the small of his back. He was sitting in the room with a person he knew to be a terrorist co-conspirator, and another whom he suspected of complicity, but he hadn't searched anyone, or asked them whether they were armed. And now, he had holstered his own weapon. It was the instinct that had driven him all of these years. He could not kill these men now. He didn't even know if he was able. But he knew that if he did, he might never have the truth about his parents.

"You have done your duty, as you see it. The threat to our country is being taken care of right now, in Pennsylvania, by Americans whose duty it is to bear arms in our defense. You have done your duty. They are doing theirs. But yours and theirs are not the same as mine. 'Uneasy lies the head that wears a crown.' You know it?" Seymour asked.

Sami nodded. *Henry IV, Part 2.* He was impressed that Seymour had quoted Shakespeare correctly, rather than the common misquote "heavy is the head," but Sami didn't speak. Seymour waved away the question as a distraction.

"My duty is to all Americans, for the preservation of their long-term security. This duty requires the synthesis of complex factors. Our allegiances, the partners we select, do not share our narrow self-interest. At times our interests are at odds, friends and allies do things we cannot endorse. And so do we, in their eyes. To preserve our allegiance, we sometimes look the other way. Anyone on the internet can spout off about this. It's rather easy to see, isn't it? Why do we support one regime which violates human rights while we vilify another? Allegiance. Security. Self-interest. What people fail to see is that it is often in our own self-interest to…" Again, Seymour grasped for the right word, "permit activities that are unsavory."

"You knew about the attack? The White House knew?"

"Son," it was the first note of condescension from Seymour, "did Winston Churchill evacuate London when he knew bombs were coming? No. He used the deciphered Nazi codes to misdirect the German bombing campaign. He allowed British citizens to die because he knew it was in the long-term interest of his country, all its people. That is war. We are at war, too. Do you see?"

"You don't need to tell me about our war. I was there."

"So you were. True enough. You are upset and you are failing to understand nuance. That being the case, it behooves me to stop here." Seymour drew a deep breath. "Not stop but shift tactics. Your work is done. You should not be here, and you should not be armed. There are professionals who will handle the issue from here."

"I shouldn't be here?" *This is my home.* Sami didn't say the words, but he felt the full load of their resentment. "What should I be doing then?"

"You should forget everything you discovered, too much of it you were never meant to know. I have been briefed throughout and as I understand your role in this affair you are an intelligence analyst. You are afforded access to secrets of our government. Whether you agree with the policy choices that are made in consideration of that information, you are trusted to keep those confidences. I trust you will do that now."

"This is different— "

"So said Edward Snowden. And so said…" Seymour paused, his expression changed to that of a person who had just tasted something unpalatable, "Oh God, what do I even say about that reprehensible Manning? He? She?"

Seymour's ploy was crude but effective. He compared any action that Sami might take to counter Rebel Creek's attack to the cases of Edward Snowden and Chelsea Manning. Whistleblowers? Traitors? Whatever the merits and demerits of their actions, in intelligence circles the two were considered to have breached an understanding. Analysts are not policymakers.

Few people, and no one at Sami's level, had all the information they would need to put policy into context. They knew what they needed to know to do their jobs, nothing more. It was why Andy had been so strident they maintain their focus, and it was an argument so familiar and so sympathetic to most in the intelligence community that Seymour was very astute to deploy it.

"You have become emotional because your work is enmeshed with personal matters. Only that can explain why you are confronting your grandfather, and now a senior White House official, with a gun. Without anyone's permission. You and I know, son, that the men with guns, the men who know how to use them, are somewhere else right now. You have your ass way out over the side of the boat. You know that too. I am here to tell you that the shit is flying." Seymour paused and stared hard. "I run this government. All its power resides in me. You have seen that power brought to bear on others. You know its might. You don't want it to come down on your head."

There was a moment of silence. The hum of cicadas from the backyard rose. It all seemed so mundane. Life went on.

When Seymour continued, he was professorial instead of prosecutorial.

"As is always the case, I am sure you will agree, operations have gaps of information. There are things you know and things you don't know. Fragmented information is impossible to draw conclusions from. At least, accurate conclusions. As on each of your previous missions, there are people in our government who are afforded all the information. People who have all-access clearances. People who sit daily in the Situation Room of the White House and deal with one crisis after another. Unemotionally. Like Churchill. That is our job. Your job is to keep our secrets. Go back into the dark. That is where you thrive. You have lectured your grandfather here tonight to know his depth. Take your own advice. And now, take mine. Keep your secrets." Seymour breathed in, seemed to rise to his toes and raise his shoulders, seemed to look down his nose before adding, "Keep all of your secrets, lest they come back to haunt you."

That was it. Seymour and Abu Muhammad stayed. Sami left through the same back door he had entered. He began a surveillance detection route to his parked car before he realized the tradecraft was needless. His cover was already blown and his adversary was among the most powerful men in the world. He was in shock.

TWENTY-EIGHT

NATIONAL HARBOR

The first call came at 3:30 AM. Later investigation revealed it came from a prepaid mobile phone, a burner, bought months ago at a convenience store in Anacostia. The hotel clerk was watching Netflix on his own phone, which was propped up behind the front desk. He described the voice on the phone as "matter-of-fact," and "yeah, kind of foreign."

"You have a hotel guest, Abdullah Ibn Abdullah. He picked up a rental car at Dulles airport yesterday, loaded a two-hundred-pound bomb in the trunk, and it is now parked in your garage. Before the morning news, it will explode."

The ensuing series of calls to increasingly responsible hotel personnel were each more frantic and fragmented than the last, like a child's game of telephone. When events were pieced together, it took longer than the hotel preferred to admit, until 4:25 AM, for someone to call 911.

"There's a bomb!"

"You saw a bomb?" The operator asked in a strained voice. Given the events of the past week, the level of seriousness given to bomb threats had risen right along with the number of fraudulent and erroneous calls. A perfect storm.

"No, I didn't see it. But they told us it's there."

"Who told you?"

"He didn't leave his name!" The hotel caller became unhinged, but the call was credible enough to merit a response. Within minutes, every black-and-white and fire truck within 10 miles was in route to National Harbor. The FBI's bomb squad was close behind. Anyone with a police scanner heard the news. Some TV trucks beat the bomb squad.

At 5 AM the scene commander ordered an evacuation. By then, the helicopters were circling overhead. By 5:15 authorities had ordered them back. But they got the shots, which ran on the local broadcasts that were already live and went national when the morning shows started at 6 AM. Another hotel. Another bomb. There happened to be a convention of American Muslims meeting at the hotel.

Sami may have been pulled off the operation by Andy Rizzo and warned off by Gerald Seymour, but his credentials were still enough to get him through the roadblocks that were set up at the entrance to National Harbor. There was nothing more he could have done after Seymour ambushed him last night, but he knew the White House aide would be nowhere near National Harbor if there was a bomb.

Seymour's complicity confirmed there was no play working this through proper channels. Sami was alone again, just as he had always felt in the Army barracks and on his prayer mat at the mosque. An outsider. This was Sami's best chance, and maybe his last, to confront his grandfather and stop the attack. His identity and his mission had finally come together.

The scene was surreal. Everyone had been on high alert for days, and now it was happening again. This time, authorities hoped they caught it. The energy was the closest that Sami had ever felt in the U.S. to a war zone. That sense was heightened by the hard, angular impression the Sig made in Sami's lower back. Yesterday was the first time in months he carried the pistol. This morning, he tucked the gun into the holster at the small of his back by instinct.

He approached the command center at 6:41 AM and was not the least bit surprised when he saw Andy step down from the command RV a moment later. He flagged his boss down, afraid he would receive a sneer in response.

But this was when Andy's pressure valves released. The tension of an operation was in the uncertainty. Wondering when to pull the trigger. Wondering how long to keep the secret. Once things were back in normal channels, it was someone else's problem.

"Nothing," Andy said when he approached.

"Nothing to it?" For a moment, the tightness in Sami's chest eased.

"No, there's a big ass bomb. But nothing for us."

That's not true, Sami thought and almost said aloud. But Sami knew things that Andy didn't. It felt wrong and it was. The only way for Andy to know what Sami had discovered was for Sami to tell him. He trusted Sami to do that. That was how information flowed, up the chain. This was different because Sami knew what waited at the top of the chain.

"It's a clusterfuck," Andy continued, unable to contain his amusement even as a bomb threatened to explode at any moment. "They evacuated the building, but they don't want guests to leave. Or get away, I should say."

"Suspects, you mean?"

"It's in a car, rented to an imam from Detroit. Abdullah. Anyway, it took a few minutes to find him, but they got him under hot lights now."

"Does someone have the guest list? By room?"

"Hey," Andy's expression changed towards sternness. "Not our monkeys, ain't our circus."

"It's fucking bullshit, Andy. Some imam from Detroit? I'm not saying it isn't him, but we have the MO. The other attacks were plants— "

"By Rebel Creek, who we shut down last night."

"Last night! Whatever's in that trunk was already in there. And I wouldn't say we shut them down. We got a handful of guys, right?"

"They aren't Hezbollah. We got the guys. And a shitload of explosives!" Andy was annoyed. They had slid back into the recriminations of the past 48 hours. Then his brow furrowed, too. "We didn't get Tinker."

This was news. Through backchannels, Sami heard the raid was a success.

"We didn't get him?"

"No. He wasn't there."

"Where is he?"

"No one knows. We were looking, and then..." Andy gestured to the building.

"Get the guest list, Andy. We need to check the names against our Rebel Creek list."

"Oh, come on!" It wasn't objection, but regret. Andy knew Sami was right.

"They need to match the list against the evacuees. They need to be sure everyone is out of the building— "

"That's impossible!"

"We have to."

"We can't. Anyway, the list only has registered names. Right? Not their wives, children, boyfriends, girlfriends, hookers, whatever."

Andy was right, but Sami had already moved to the next question.

"They have to go room-to-room."

"What?"

"Before they let anyone back in— "

"Sami, right now they are just trying to get the bomb defused in the garage. Don't get ahead of yourself."

Andy was walking towards the command center, so Sami shouted.

"They cannot let people in until we have gone room-to-room. It's the easiest thing in the world to check into a hotel room, or five hotel rooms, with big rolling suitcases filled with explosives. Spread them around and coordinate the detonation. It will make Annapolis look like nothing."

Sami's voice was loud. People on both sides of the rope line were watching now. Andy stalked back.

"Are you out of your fucking mind? Even this White House isn't that crazy! Go room-to-room? Inspecting the suitcases and hotel rooms of Muslims at the national Muslim convention? Even if we could get approval to do it, it would take forever, and then it would be an absolute media circus."

Andy pulled the rope up, nodding to a police officer that Sami was allowed through.

"I'll get the guest list." He gestured for Sami to follow. "Stay with me. Keep quiet. Don't make me regret this."

***

The next two hours proceeded with perfect normalcy for people whose lives were anything but normal. There was brief but spirited debate over whether to detonate the bomb in place, which posed the least risk to the bomb squad. Over increasing protestations from the resort's owner – who only seemed to increase the FBI's tolerance for a detonation with each self-interested plea – the commander decided that the damage to property and potential risk to life was too great.

The bomb would be loaded into a concussion containment unit and trucked to a safe area for detonation. This was fraught with peril but unlike the bombs over the past week, scans inside the package showed the device was not rigged for remote detonation.

The process took time, and though Sami had no role in the discussion or execution, he almost screamed: *The signature is remote detonation! Why isn't this one the same? Because it's a diversion!*

Once he had the guest list, Sami headed to the grassy area 300 yards from the hotel where the FBI was holding guests. A grid of sawhorses and police barricades encircled people in pajamas. As the sun climbed in the July sky, some guests were shedding the blankets they wrapped themselves in for the predawn evacuation.

With all the action and munitions just 300 yards away, the big swinging dicks from every local, state and federal agency left junior agents and traffic cops guarding the quasi-prisoners. Sami flashed a credential with attitude and a minute later he was overseeing an effort to quantify – by registered room guests – who was and was not accounted for among the guests.

By the time Andy Rizzo located him, the task was nearly complete.

"This isn't what I told you to do."

"I know, but I did it because I know what you're going to tell me next."

"Which is?"

"Now that the bomb is gone, they're letting people in."

Andy jerked his head and walked away, indicating Sami should follow so they could continue at a distance from the guests.

"These people aren't guilty of anything." Andy offered. "We can't keep them out here forever— "

"Not forever, but they could clear the building."

"We're not going room-to-room!"

"What about dogs? At least send them in, see if they signal."

Andy rolled his eyes. "Finally, our plan is to your satisfaction. That is happening right now."

"And then?"

"And then we let them back in."

"You're kidding?"

"I'm not. And neither is the White House. They got involved an hour ago. This is the third real bomb and three-hundredth threat this week. The country is shitting a brick, Dost. Big businesses might stop corporate travel. The White House wants this normalized.

*The White House wants...*Sami wondered how far Gerald Seymour was from that directive. Instead, he asked, "How much time do I have?"

"An hour, maybe two."

"I need to grab this list." Sami took the list from a cop guarding the prisoners. "Get me to a phone."

Andy breathed a sigh of pre-regret. "Let's go."

***

Sami texted Yoda, Emily, and Alexa. Ten minutes later all three were in the makeshift Alexandria ops center. He called back on a secure phone Andy provided, with the list in front of him.

"I have some names. I need you to run them on every database."

"For?" Yoda asked with a conference room's echo.

"Anything weird."

"Can you be more specific?" It was Alexa.

"I am most interested in names that get zero hits."

"Aliases?" Yoda echoed back.

"That's what I'm thinking. But not well worked. Cheap aliases. Unprofessional. Disposable."

Sami read names and the team frantically typed and clicked through windows.

At the end of the exercise, Sami had four names highlighted on the sheet. A combination of two criteria merited highlighting. First, the identity had no hits on any database. Second, they were not present in the guest corral.

"Meaning that either they did not evacuate, or when they did, they didn't stay," Andy said when Sami explained the criteria.

"Or, they weren't here to evacuate," Sami added. "They checked in with an alias, dropped a bag in the room, and left. Look at the room numbers, all on different floors. Two are near the center of the building, one on a high floor and one on a low floor. Each of the others are on opposite wings, mid-height of the building. This hotel allows pre-registered guests to check in with an app and choose their own room. I'll bet you my car that if we check with the hotel, these guests used online check-in and chose these rooms themselves."

Andy breathed deep, a sign of impending action. "I don't want your fucking car."

"Double or nothing with my condo that all the rooms were registered and paid with the same credit card. It's like you said, this isn't Hezbollah. What Rebel Creek had was access to the munitions and some training in building them. Otherwise, they've been sloppy from the beginning. That's the only way we caught on."

"I can make the case," Andy said. "What am I asking for? Make it quick!"

"Evacuate the hotel."

"For good?"

"Until we can go in with trained people. Like this was in theater. Military munitions experts. Room-to-room."

Andy turned in a slow circle and rubbed the meat of his palms deep into tired eyes. He gave a mirthless chuckle when he noticed the bench where he met Sami less than two weeks ago, only 200 yards away. Neither man was happy, but they smiled at each other.

"You're right, you know. I think you're right," Andy said. "Committing career suicide is going to be easier since I am doing the right thing." He walked toward the command center. Sami followed.

"Coach."

"Dost?"

"One more thing."

The chuckle was a snort this time. "Yeah, what?"

"Get me someone from the hotel."

"What do you need? Breakfast?"

"Maybe later. I have one more question about the list." Sami showed Andy the paper, placing his thumbnail below a room number and scanning across to the name, listed as *Hotel Comp – Conference Organizer*. "I need to confirm who is in this room."

Sami said "confirm" because he already knew. Andy's eyes radiated no censure for how long it took, only gratitude that Sami had gotten there.

***

Standing outside the RV-cum-command center, Sami watched through a window as Andy Rizzo explained, then cajoled, and now shouted. He wasn't getting buy-in. The men and women in the command center were post-9/11 homeland security pros. They knew the directive: minimize risk. But when the White House sent specific instructions that the risk was understood and would be taken, the job description changed. There were few government officials who would have risked pushing back.

Sami was glad he worked for one, but rather than ponder his luck, Sami found the hotel manager that Andy cornered moments ago and approached without introduction.

"That room is reserved for the conference organizer," she said, before adding a ceremonious but uncertain "Sir!"

"I know that, that's what it says on this paper, but who is staying there?"

She frowned. "Well, it's weird." And then to herself, "I guess this whole thing is weird though, so who knows— "

"Ma'am! Who is in there?"

"It's just...see, this is not the group comp room."

"The list says it is."

"I'm sorry, I'm nervous. I mean it isn't usually."

"You're doing fine. Just explain what you mean."

She took a deep breath, shook her hands before her, and then continued. "The room we comp for groups of this size is on the top floor. It's a large suite. It's perfect for that purpose because it has a sitting room and a dining room. Conference organizers often use it for receptions or to host smaller meetings."

As she explained, Sami looked down at the list and checked the room number again. Center of the hotel. Mid-level floor.

"He didn't want that room. He said he would seldom use it anyway. Only for 'emergencies' was what he said, so..."

"And 'he' is? Abu Muhammad?"

"That's weird, too. Usually, we deal with an executive assistant or something, but— "

"Yeah, weird." Sami cut in. It was the final piece of the puzzle. His grandfather was in there. He hadn't just come up with this entire sick campaign, he was the final bomber.

Sami made one more request, which the hotel manager obliged uncomfortably but without hesitation, and then he left her standing there muttering to herself. He walked back over to the command center. Through the window, he saw things had calmed, but the tension was still visible. Andy Rizzo's jaw was set in a bulldog expression. The group was listening to a speakerphone. Without the benefit of hearing the voice, Sami knew it was Gerald Seymour.

Unless the dogs hit on something, the scene commander would have no choice but to let people in. Because TATP was so volatile, there were no dogs that had sufficient training to detect the explosive. The scene commanders didn't realize they were running down a clock they controlled. Sami had already memorized the important room numbers and he tucked the list into the back pocket of his jeans, next to the pistol he had never fired in anger.

Sami was going in. He did not share the rest of his plan with Andy, or anyone else on scene. But someone knew. Across the river in Alexandria, listening through the app she had uploaded onto Sami's phone, Emily heard him running.

***

Though the hotel was presently the world's most famous crime scene and surrounded by cops and Feds, the building was not entirely locked down. Inside the perimeter that authorities had established – which Sami breached with Andy's authority – credentialed personnel enjoyed freedom of movement. This augmented everyone's ability to move about and do their job without the constant need for security checks and clearances.

Still, Sami did not plan to waltz right through the front door of the hotel. He made his way down a sidewalk that circled the building away from the command center's line of sight and the throng of high-ranking lookie-loos. There would be a perimeter guard, and so as he walked, he pantomimed looking up at the building as though examining something. It wasn't much of a cover but if someone asked, he would report that command ordered a "visual inspection." Leave it at that. Sounded official and reasonable. Elaborate only as needed. The Spy had learned that the ambitions of a lie should be narrowly-tailored to just do the job, and no more.

He did not need the cover story. Standing at the corner of the building to cover two sides, an FBI agent cradled an M4 rifle. Sami couldn't see his eyes behind the shades, but when he gestured to say "just looking," the FBI man returned a thumbs-up. Sami saw what he was looking for: a side door, accessible only by hotel card key. The kind of card key he had taken off the hotel manager's lanyard and stuck into his back pocket. He held the card to the magnetic reader, saw red change to green, and was inside.

There was a stairwell adjacent to the outside door. He started up and the realization dawned that he was following the route guests had taken out of the building in the early morning hours. The exit door and stairwell were for evacuation of the property. In an emergency. He was following the other route. Going up, into danger. As he climbed past the third floor, he thought of the firefighters on 9/11, doing the same. Climbing up into danger. They were heroes, which was their job. He wasn't sure what his job was anymore.

He intended to save this building and these people, but not with the consent or support of the people who employed him. He wasn't sure who those people were anymore. He had not been for a while.

Nations and armies and laws were powerful. But they were abstract. They were symbols. A person needed to accept them to appreciate their significance. Everyone in a society had to accept them for their power to be meaningful. The consent of the governed. That was what this plot tried to undermine.

He was employed to preserve those ideals, but that was not his mission today. He had been involved in counterterrorism for a decade, fought heinous terrorists, uncovered ingenious attacks; and yet he had never taken it upon himself until today. He climbed the final flight of stairs and came to terms with the facts he uncovered back in college and the suspicions that had swirled since he confronted his grandfather. Never had he placed himself face-to-face with evil, a gun in his hand.

There was only one difference on this mission. It was personal. But why? Was he motivated because his grandfather was threatening violence against the country? Or was it that his grandfather had been complicit in his parents' death? Whoever he worked for, the first conclusion equated to him doing his job. Serving his country. Protecting the ideals.

The other conclusion amounted to revenge. The thought had been swirling through his thoughts and dreams for weeks, and he could reach no conclusion. Only one person could confirm the truth. He confronted a tailor-made villain. He undertook a struggle inseparable from whether he bore some responsibility for the evil himself. In countering the threat with lethal force, would he end it or just subsume it? If he pulled the trigger, was he a good Spy? A good son? Either way, was he just a murderer?

Ya Allah! I am Prince Hamlet and Grandfather is King Claudius!

Only his grandfather knew. It sickened him that the man still had power over him. Not patriarchal power over a child, but power over his soul. Control of his destiny.

He reached the floor where he knew he would find his grandfather and scanned an emergency escape diagram hanging on the wall. It showed the floor plan and he determined which way to exit from the stairwell and how many steps it would be to the door of the room.

The hotel manager's key card should open the door. Sami hoped that he would not walk into a hail of gunfire. His grandfather was not the type to be standing behind the door with an automatic and he was confident that there was nothing behind that door that could hurt him. But as he pressed the key card to the door, he had never been so scared.

***

Tom Tinker met Abu Muhammad in 1989, in the private dining room of a Washington restaurant. A future President was there. And a half dozen present, past and future Cabinet officials. And Gerald Seymour. Seymour brought them together then and they hoped he would save them now.

Tom Tinker met Abu Muhammad for the last time in a gas station parking lot near the Navy Yard at 3 AM. It was only hours before Sami would arrive at the hotel in National Harbor and only hours after he left Abu Muhammad and Gerald Seymour in Virginia.

The bombs were delivered to the hotel the afternoon before, long before the raid. Seymour delayed the raid on Tinker's compound by hours when Tinker said he needed time. When there were no more clarifications or briefings for the White House to request, Seymour texted Tinker that SOG was coming.

Tinker carried the detonators. He and the imam drove together from the Navy Yard. After he called in the bomb threat, Abu Muhammad threw the burner phone into the Potomac as they crossed the Woodrow Wilson Bridge. The old friends entered the hotel together in the quiet predawn.

The sun was up, and they were drinking coffee now. They watched TV news. They peered out the window. Tinker brought earplugs for the time when the hotel alarms were screaming. Someone stopped the sirens an hour ago.

Soon after they arrived, they discussed the plan if there was an infiltration. When they heard Sami's key card in the door, and the electronic lock cycling open, Tinker grabbed his gun and entered the bathroom to the left of the room's entrance. As Sami walked in, the gun was trained on his head. Tinker flipped off the safety switch. Red. Dead.

***

"These dramatic entrances are a growing annoyance, Samir."

"A distraction, you mean." But Sami spurred himself. He didn't need snappy repartee. Andy was right. Today, Sami needed to be the man of action.

Abu Muhammad, the great intellectual of American Islam, his grandfather, sat on a couch and gestured to the coffee table before him.

"In either case, it is a trend that will be short-lived."

Sami's training fired his instincts and for a moment the emotion was subdued. Four cell phones sat in a neat row on the table. Four detonators. This affirmed his assumption about the phantom guests from the ledger, the number of bombs, and their placement. He needed to get that information to Andy.

Did his grandfather intend to detonate the bombs? It would only take one phone for a trained operative to detonate all four bombs, so the presence of four phones suggested that the plan had always been for Abu Muhammad to detonate the bombs. A specific number would be pre-programmed into each. Click

SEND twice to redial it and the corresponding bomb detonated. That could be done by anyone, with little training.

"You've crossed a line," Sami said. "Again."

"A line?" Abu Muhammad looked over his shoulder. Ever the literalist, he pretended to scan behind the couch for evidence. "Was it a red line? Or a 'line in the sand?" Sami had never seen his grandfather use air quotes until the speech on CSPAN yesterday but now he did them again. Uncharacteristic behavior. Manic. The suspect was emotional. Maybe unhinged.

"A few favorite metaphors of American presidents. An imaginary line for brown people to cross before the artillery rains down."

"You are the one with a direct line to the White House." *Grandfather.* The last word almost escaped his lips. He hadn't spoken the word as a form of address in years. Sami cursed himself. Forget the emotions. Forget the personal connections. That was history and now it was a distraction. And yet, he couldn't forget.

He was an intelligence analyst. A cog in the American spying apparatus. He wasn't James Bond. No one's trained killer. No assassin. Then, even assassins weren't assassins. All of them were just human beings, like him. Like his grandfather. Flawed. Emotional. He could no more set aside the emotions coursing through him now then he could have set aside the emotions that coursed through his teenage body. When he realized that he didn't like girls. Very much the opposite, he liked boys. He was gay. Apostate. Outcast. Embarrassment.

He swung his hand to the weapon holstered at the small of his back.

"Gerald Seymour knows nothing about this." Abu Muhammad lectured with a pointed finger.

The comment seemed out of place, the rebuttal to an argument Sami had not made. And didn't intend to make. Seymour knew something. It wasn't Sami's job to piece together intel anymore. Nor to analyze it. Nor to advise action. He needed to take action.

"There's a sickness in this place," Abu Muhammad began. "Within a week, that is all anyone will be interested in. 'What did the White House know and when did they know it?" Again, the air quotes. "This city, this country, would rather focus on its own fetishes. The arguments reverberating in its own echo chamber are more important than the reality outside the window. The rest of the world. The *real* world. There is no real world. There is America, and everything else is for tourism or target practice."

Sami's fingers tightened around the pistol grip, but the gun remained in the holster. He had not come here to listen to a sermon. Not from this man. He had heard too many. He focused on the substance of the discussion. His grandfather changed the subject off Gerald Seymour. Sami recorded the questions for later. *What did the White House know? When did they know it?*

"It was you." There was a trace of childlike disappointment in Sami's voice.

"'It' was never me. I have watched for years, yes. I have been supportive, in whatever way I could be. But what choice did I have?" He rose and whirled away from Sami toward the window. "Open your eyes, Samir. You are a guard, standing at the warm, radiating door to the incinerator."

Though his grandfather was never a virulent anti-Semite, the reference was a clear reference to the Holocaust. It caught Sami by surprise. It was not a Qur'an analogy. It was modern. Western. American. It marked a similarity that Sami and Abu Muhammad shared. One of the few. They slid between worlds.

That skill accounted for his grandfather's ascension as America's leading authority on Islam, his political dexterity, and his connection to people as disparate as Hasan Khalifa and Gerald Seymour. It was also the skill that defined Sami's career, and his success as an agent of America in its battles with extreme Islam.

"You have chosen the side of the aggressor. Of the brute. America is a global criminal enterprise. I came here in pursuit of the elusive American Dream, only to find that America is a tragedy clothed in myth. It began in genocide and when the

Indians were finished, it imported black Africans to slaughter, and when it finished with them, it turned to the rest of the world."

"I've heard the speech," Sami interrupted. As it had the night before, the impudence rankled his grandfather. "I have it on tape, actually. From my first interrogation of Hasan Khalifa. He gave it better. I see why you attached yourself to him. He is a gifted communicator. He'll make a great witness."

"He'll never see the light of day— "

"Stop! Don't presume to exert control over things beyond your grasp. If you make it out of this hotel alive, you won't be dictating the events of your prosecution."

"Remember, Samir. I am the one with the direct line to the White House." This was followed by a knowing half-nod. With his head declined, Abu Muhammad narrowed his gaze over his spectacles. "He will go to Guantanamo Bay. Which is where I would go 'if I make it out of this hotel alive.'" Another set of air quotes.

Sami was certain that this was mania. It was only then, and only because of how intimately he knew his target that Sami was sure what happened next.

Abu Muhammad would detonate the bombs.

Unless Sami stopped him.

It had been the plan all along. Khalifa and the Council of Muhammad and whatever else were negotiable. If they succeeded, great. If not, all that was essential were Abu Muhammad's appearances on TV news. The raising of his profile. The footage the world over of a man who had appeared on Sunday talk shows and been the friend of White House insiders. Those pictures running over a news crawl that said he had blown up a hotel in Washington.

A trained assassin - one that worked in a different dark corner of U.S. intelligence from Sami, the corner the U.S. government denied in the polite company of diplomatic board rooms – would have extracted the Sig now. Target confirmed. Pump three bullets into the target, center mass, and then evacuate the building. Call in confirmation when out of local law enforcement's reach.

But Sami was not a trained assassin. His determination to kill would be tested, but that was not what faltered now. Instead, he succumbed to the only unforgivable sin of an assassin. His curiosity. And worse, his emotion. But not for his grandfather.

Now that Sami knew the truth about the events of the past week, the case was closed. But another cold case remained very much open. His memory jogged, and for a moment Sami was a ten-year-old boy again, sitting at the kitchen table of his grandfather's home.

"Sami, there has been a horrible tragedy..."

"How long?" Sami asked now.

After a moment of confusion, his grandfather responded. "Don't be ignorant, child. Use complete sentences."

The question Sami wanted answered overtook every other thought and impulse, and yet he still could not speak it.

Now he was in college, sitting in the library, piecing together facts from government and news reports. The names and faces in them were swimming in his memory and they were familiar. They were faces he had seen when traveling with his grandfather.

"How long?" he muttered again. "When did you start?"

His grandfather laughed. "The great American spy!" He retook his seat on the couch, before the neat line of cell phone detonators. "People are being allowed back into the building. The time is near. And they send you?"

Unable to conceal his alarm, Sami ran to the window. His grandfather was not bluffing. A line of guests were outside of the hotel's main entrance, snaking back a hundred yards. They were conducting some kind of security screening to permit re-entry. Andy had prevailed upon the incident commander to do that much.

It would be meaningless. The threat was already inside. Like so much post-9/11 American security, the screening would be counterintuitive. It would only admit innocents to become victims.

"This will be the first to explode." Abu Muhammad said from the couch, indicating the phone furthest to his right.

Right to left. Most Americans would have arranged the phones the other way, as they arranged written words or numerals. His grandfather went right-to-left. Like the Qur'an. Like their native language.

"It's an inconvenience because it is the weapon set on the high floor. I will have to wait for these people to reoccupy the building. To filter back upstairs." His finger straightened and he moved it to the left. "Then this one. And this one. We flush them downstairs and then these explode. They are near the middle floors, on the ends of the building, near the evacuation stairs. By now, the carnage already great, whoever has made it to the lower levels, near the exits, and all the emergency personnel. The police. Everyone will feel this one." He pointed at the last phone, all the way to his left. "It is the largest. A single bomb that will have a place in American history. 'Fat Boy.' 'Little Man.' A bomb that will have a name."

Sami knew that Abu Muhammad's comparison was inept. The bomb dropped on Hiroshima, Japan on August 6, 1945 – whatever else it had been – was an expression of power. It may have been pragmatic. It may have saved the lives of some U.S. service members by preventing the need for an invasion of Japan, but it traded those lives for Japanese civilians. It was, undoubtedly, bullying. A new global superpower flexed its muscles.

His grandfather's bomb would express something different, something expressed by the rash of global terror attacks that any person could list: London, Madrid, Barcelona, Nice, Paris, 9/11. And now, this hotel.

The scripture, the icons, the prayers, the bombings. The path to eternal peace, somewhere else. They thought it was their hope. It was all so hopeless. Sami never understood suicide attacks. He respected the IEDs in Iraq. They were strategic and effective. Asymmetric warfare. He had to counter it, but he respected it.

The suicide attacks? The bomb vest? The truck attacks? Desperate. Weak. When you have resigned yourself to minimally effective, low casualty attacks against soft targets and the only way you can attack them is by suicide, you are staring failure in the face.

His grandfather had been in that stare down since Sami's parents died. Blowing oneself up to kill innocent people was evil, but there was something worse about how Abu Muhammad had planned this. He wasn't walking into a market and blowing himself up. He had planned a detailed attack, for maximum casualties. He wouldn't just kill shoppers and shopkeepers and families, he would strike at the core of American values.

He would undermine American values and exploit American domestic discord. It was an attack only an American could conceive and execute. A traitor. Like the attack on the embassy. The one that killed Sami's parents.

All of this flashed through Sami's mind in a second. History, politics, religion, and emotion, flying on the wings of neurons.

Just as quickly, he was back in his grandfather's study. Not last night, but years before. On the night when he confronted his grandfather.

"You introduced them to the bombers, didn't you? You arranged the meeting?" He asked then.

His grandfather confessed. The truth was more than Sami could handle and he did not press. But that was years ago.

With unconscious quickness, Sami swung his hand around to the small of his back and unholstered the Sig. His grandfather had lied. It had not been misplaced trust. Not a horrible mistake. Abu Muhammad was the one. He planned the attack that killed Sami's parents.

Sami wouldn't listen to any more pontification. He fired.

***

Sami expected more. He thought blood would cover the pale-yellow shirt, but there was only a small tear. Blood spread in an irregular brownish splotch, but slowly.

"Samir!" Even now, his grandfather was preparing a lecture.

"You lied! There was no confusion. No accident. You planned the attack that killed them!" The spy had not become an assassin. He had not fired three quick rounds center mass. It was one bullet fired by a vengeful son. A scorned grandson. "You used your own son to gain access."

Gasping for air, his grandfather replied. "These people, they are serious. For them, for me, the jihad is not a political set piece as it is in this country. Something for the Sunday talk shows. It is jihad. War. Life or death. American bombs are raining down on their homes, on their children. They wanted to know if I was serious. How serious? Would I sacrifice what they had sacrificed? Would I sacrifice everything earthly for Allah? Your parents betrayed their God. Look at you! You can have no better example. You were young and don't remember your father's work, but he was a conciliator. He was committed to betraying Allah for some elusive peace. I saved him. And I tried to save you, Samir. But this place. This sick, hedonistic, materialistic, immoral place already had you in its maw." His grandfather coughed and lie on the side where he was shot, blood staining the couch.

Now Sami knew. His grandfather had not just been connected to the people who had killed his parents. He hadn't just been duped by a friend who used access to the embassy to detonate the bomb that killed Sami's parents. No, Abu Muhammad made the introduction and planned the meeting for the bomber to kill Sami's parents. He was the mastermind behind the terror attack that would kill his own son. Knowing that his grandfather had done that, Sami was left with no doubt that Abu Muhammad would kill himself and everyone else in this hotel.

And the grandson panicked. He stepped over to the couch where his grandfather lay moaning, and without paying attention to which detonator went where, he stuffed the four phones into his pockets. He ran to the window to see if anyone outside heard the shot. The line to reenter had shrunk. Guests were back inside now, but there was no indication of alarm. It was orderly.

No one heard the shot that was still ringing in Sami's ears. If not for the ringing, he might have heard the bathroom door slide open. Instead, he felt a bullet bury itself in his shoulder and knock him against the window like the kick of a mule.

***

Sami thought about God at the oddest moments.

Abraham Lincoln said: "I have been driven to my knees many times by the conviction that I had nowhere else to go." Religion as desperation. Deathbed conversion. Epiphany in crisis. Born again behind bars. Rock bottom.

And it held. It comforted. Day after day, every whispered wish, each tearful request for reprieve.

Not for Sami. The moments when he thought of God were the moments when he was so overwhelmed by a sense of cosmic gratitude, and so unable to figure out who to thank for it, that he thought of God. Then he checked himself.

I'm lucky: a gay Muslim, in America, in the 21st century. If God had anything to do with it, then what did God have against the Congolese who were hacked to pieces during the Belgian conquest less than 100 years ago? Or, the Jews who died by the millions in Europe 75 years ago?

What did God have against the people about to walk in the front door of the hotel?

God had nothing to do with it. Sami owed his debt to the place he called home. To the people, White, Anglo, Christians who might have hated him, but who made the trip across an ocean, worked their hands to the bone and died at forty-five so that their kids – and their kids' kids – would not know another pestilence, famine, or genocide. He couldn't thank that person, so he thought about his good fortune and his gratitude, and he became overwhelmed at the randomness of it and he thought about God.

These were founding myths, yes, but neither was Abu Muhammad right. Nor Tom Tinker, nor Gerald Seymour, nor the man who sat in the White House having wet dreams about a wall. Whatever they intended, those Seventeenth Century

WASPs invented a place that others would come to, others they never hoped to live alongside. And they were still coming.

Not only his grandfather, and his parents, but others. They were coming because they wanted what he had. They wanted what overwhelmed him with gratitude. The ones coming now would be outcasts just like the Irish and the Italians and the Jews, and the Chinese, and the Latinos. They would be hated, and they would live miserable, poor, unhealthy lives picking other people's strawberries or mowing their lawns. But their kids would be Americans. And God had nothing do with it. They made that luck.

That was what he honored: he represented a place where anyone could do that. Make a life. Change the future. That was why he did what he did, which his grandfather never understood. That was why he didn't regret it – any of it. The bombs over Baghdad. The millions displaced. The creation of ISIS. The drone strikes that sometimes kill children. He didn't regret it because America intended none of those consequences. Collateral damage was a painful euphemism, but it wasn't a lie. America tried.

Sami resented anyone who chose the alternative.

Drop to your knees in the conviction you have no place else to go and flip the switch. Religion as pathology. It was a crutch. Don't worry that your life is hard, that you don't have the discipline or intelligence, or creativity to change your reality. Or the patience to let it happen. America could be bad, but he had never seen it be evil. Until today.

He had done his best for America. He was down now, bleeding onto a hotel carpet while Gerald Seymour sat in the White House conspiring with terrorists. Sami didn't know how he felt. Or what was real. His mind was bending. The pain in his shoulder was like nothing he had felt before. Starved for oxygen during training at The Farm, the searing pain in his lungs then was sharper, but not as heavy. The pain of alienation from his grandfather, and his friends, and his mosque community was deeper, but not as urgent. The pain of losing his parents...His parents.

Abu Muhammad killed Muhammad Lakhani. My grandfather killed my parents. Now he shot me. Shot his own grandson. Sami knew what he hadn't been sure of as he climbed the hotel stairs: he was not here for America. Who gave a fuck about the USA? He was here for vengeance.

He rolled onto his good shoulder and slid his hips back toward the wall. He propped himself onto his elbow and the pain burned like a thousand matches lit against his skin. He winced and paused. The pain did not abate in the slightest and he sucked in a deep breath and pushed himself straight up against the wall. He saw his legs in front of him, but he couldn't feel them. They were props in this drama. For a moment he thought he was paralyzed before he realized that his legs were numb because so much feeling was concentrated near the gunshot wound.

His parents.

Sami should never have left his grandfather alive. The Assassin would have fired those three shots center mass. The vengeful son?

Muslim. American. Gay. Soldier. Spy. Terrorist. Grandson. Orphan. He had lectured his grandfather about the American melting pot. Maybe Abu Muhammad and Seymour were right. Maybe multiculturalism was a failed experiment. Sami sure was tired of juggling his various identities. The vengeful son should have emptied the magazine.

Sami was determined to do that now. He hooked his good arm onto the window sill and heaved himself upright with a pained growl. It was only then, facing back into the room with a view over the back of the couch where his grandfather lay, that Sami saw they were not alone in the hotel suite.

TWENTY-NINE

NATIONAL HARBOR

Sami stared into the eyes of the man who shot him. Somewhere between middle-aged and elderly, their color was washed out in grey, but they remained the blue eyes of a white man. The skin was wrinkled and pale. There was no beard. It was not the face of any terrorist that America knew. If Gerald Seymour won, they would never know the face of Tom Tinker.

Tinker wore a lightweight button-down fishing shirt and khaki cargo pants over hiking boots. For all the world, he could be a guy on the way back from a summer fishing trip. Which is what he hoped the TSA agents would think - without a second thought - when he boarded the plane. He was holding a ticket in one of his myriad pockets, but first, he needed to finish this.

The only accessory that marred the angler look was the pistol he held in a perfect triangle firing position. Sami tried to focus on his training rather than the pain. The gun was a subcompact. But large caliber. Maybe a .40? Glock 27.

"Stand up and put your hands on your head," Tinker commanded.

Sami complied, but slowly. "I can stand, but the hands-on-head thing will be a little tough since you shot a hole through the right side of my torso."

"Turn around and face the window. I am coming over to..." Tinker hesitated. "No. Walk in front of the couch and place the detonators back on the table."

Sami played things out. The options were to be shot again, and die; or, be blown up along with this building, and die. The relative hopelessness of his situation imbued his impertinence.

"Let's not make this Hollywood. Just shoot me again and you can take them out of my pockets yourself."

Tinker steadied his triangle position and raised the barrel. "I could."

"But you won't." Sami walked toward Tinker, cradling his right arm across his body, in an invisible sling. The left was still aloft as Tinker instructed and Sami nodded toward it, a gesture meant to emphasize his compliance. "You won't shoot me again, because he might die."

They both looked down at Abu Muhammad on the couch. The blood had spread, and the front of his shirt was now a damp, rusty brown. He was silent, seemingly unconscious.

"And if he dies," Sami continued, "Then you need me. Because you need a live Muslim when the bombs go off. All the better to cover your tracks if it is me they find alive and Abu Muhammad is found with a bullet hole through him."

"Just put the detonators on the table." Tinker's expression said Sami was wrong. He could shoot him. Sami fished the four phones from his pockets, one after another. When he was done, Tinker marched him to the far corner of the room at gunpoint.

"Stay here, facing the corner. If you turn, you're dead. I am getting out of here alive and that means you might too, if you do what you're told."

Before returning to the table, Tinker scooped up Sami's pistol which had fallen when Sami was shot. Sami listened as his hope dwindled away. He didn't dare turn to look. The anger was gone. He was afraid.

Tinker walked to the couch and tried to revive Abu Muhammad.

"Tahir!" he shouted in the old man's face. "Can you hear me?"

Abu Muhammad moaned.

"Tahir, you have to sit up." Sami heard Tinker snapping his fingers in front of the old man's face. Slapping him. "Tahir! Come on. We're almost there, old friend, but I need your help!"

What help could he need? Sami was perplexed. Was Tinker that much of a coward? He would not shoot Sami. OK, pulling the trigger to end a life was not easy. Was he not prepared to blow the bombs he had built and then delivered to this building?

"Tahir, people are back in the building now. Just as we planned! You need to tell me which detonator is for which bomb. Dammit, Tahir! Come on!"

Tinker did not know the sequence of the detonators. Sami's grandfather had been specific: first, they would blow a bomb at the top, then on the middle floors - two bombs, one to a side - and then the big one at ground level. Abu Muhammad had them in order when Sami arrived. But now, in and out of Sami's pockets, replaced on the table in a jumble, Tinker could not distinguish between the identical phones.

In the corner, Sami closed his eyes and listened.

"Come on, Tahir! Tahir!"

"I caaan't..." The words came out of Sami's grandfather in one combined exhalation. He did not have strength for words. If he didn't get help soon, he would die. Sami would not be far behind. He was bleeding less than his grandfather, but steadily. He was lightheaded. Dizzy. He opened his eyes again, trying to orient himself to the walls and floor.

"You son of a bitch! We've come too far!" Tinker shouted. He gave up on reviving the wounded imam.

And then the world was upside down.

***

Sami was face first on the carpet. Uncomfortably so. Unnaturally. He had been thrown there by the blast. The room was a kaleidoscope of swirling dust and broken glass was all around him. The window was blown out. The wall on the opposite side of the room was gone.

Frustrated with his accomplice's inaction, and in his haste to execute the final stage of his plan before the clock ran out, Tinker had chosen a detonator at random and blown the first bomb. It was one of the two on a middle level, placed far enough away to avoid killing the bomber in this room. But the Rebel Creek men had cut it very close.

Tinker's impulsiveness had been a mistake. Any doubt in the minds of the state, local and federal law enforcement waiting below was erased. The political brake that Gerald Seymour had put on aggressive action would be released. Wanting to move before he ran out of time, Tinker had started the countdown.

Sami tried to raise himself from the push-up position, but his shoulder wailed in agony. He had to get up though. He had already concluded that if the opposite wall was blown, then the blast must have come from that direction. Tinker – standing toward the center of the room – would have gotten the worst of it.

Sami stumbled to where the couch and table were moments ago. The couch, with the added weight of a man, had not moved far. Abu Muhammad was still drawing shallow breaths. The table had been upended, and Tinker, looking as groggy as Sami felt, was on his hands and knees trying to locate the detonators. The blast had thrown them from the table.

Sami needed to get them first. No matter how disoriented he was, Tinker realized his own mistake just as Sami did. The cavalry was coming. If Tinker didn't know which of the remaining detonators was which, then he would blow all three.

Tinker was patting the floor by the couch. Sami guessed they were thrown further, and he looked to the spot on the floor where the table was standing before the blast. He knew which direction the explosion came from, and he tracked his eyes across the floor to the spot where he guessed the detonators might have been thrown. There was nothing but dust settling.

It settled over the carpet like a heavy dusting of snow. Across the room, it settled on the shiny granite countertop of the small kitchenette. It settled on the couch, and onto the motionless form of his grandfather. His grandfather's chest was not moving. Sami saw no sign of breath. No sign of life.

The tableau knocked the wind from his lungs. The feeling was worse than the gunshot or the blast that knocked him unconscious. Tinker, his face inches from the floor, continued to pat and feel like he was working his way through a minefield. But Sami backpedaled into the corner. From there, he could see it all.

He smelled the explosion and heard the wail of sirens. He was in shock, but there was something more. This is what it was like. He was living the moments his parents never had, experiencing the seconds after they were torn to pieces by another bomb in another building on another continent, detonated for the same reasons.

The bombs had exploded for decades. In Beirut and London, left by Palestinians and Irish Nationalists. In Madrid, left by separatists Basques and revanchist Muslims. In Baghdad and Kabul, dropped by U.S. planes. If there were answers, if there was truth, it evaded him. There was only suffering and dying. In Baku and Washington, D.C. He'd seen enough. Clarity settled over him, like the dust.

The choices were so clear, they seemed divinely communicated. If he went on, he would have to conjure with all this again. Bad people, or at least people who get bad ideas; bombs and their wreckage; the post-traumatic stress of his parents' death and now his own shooting and bombing; and his grandfather. His abandonment. His betrayal.

Or, he could stop here. He could sit down in this corner, cover his eyes and ears, roll into the fetal position, and wait. Wait for Tinker to stop patting the floor and find the detonators. Wait for the next explosion. Wait for the gunshot between the eyes. Wait for all the pain to go away, and he wouldn't have to be anymore. Orphan. Gay. Muslim. Spy. Soldier. Terrorist. Grandson. Victim.

Sami's grandfather fought the battle for identity by rejecting any alternate interpretations of himself and embracing the radical. Sami considered seizing the opportunity to resolve the inner struggle that had defined his life by another expedient: surrender.

The wafting chunks of drywall were gone. Only small particles floated on air that was returning to something like transparency. For the first time in minutes, Sami breathed without a grimy film coating the inside of his mouth. There was light again. Not the grimy yellow haze of the last few moments, but bright, clear sunshine.

The new day that his parents never saw. They did not know before and after. There was life and then there was the bomb. Sami was left with the rest. The anger, the guilt, the depression, the trauma. The after. Life. He always felt that his story was different. That had never been a good thing.

Until he looked down, with tears streaming down his face, and saw three detonators at his feet.

Right there, in the spot where Tinker sequestered him, Sami saw the three devices. They were blown in this direction by the force of the blast and stopped from traveling further by the corner where Sami was confined. He scooped the dusty phones up and put them into his pockets.

He won. He survived the bomb. He had beaten his grandfather, beaten Tinker and Seymour, beaten back hate and beaten his own past. He had the detonators.

"I have no time to waste. This time, I will shoot."

Sami realized that Tinker had not been searching for the detonators. While Sami struggled with undercurrents of feeling, Tinker understood the dynamics of control. The detonators were secondary. He had been looking for the guns. The small, black Glock would have been near impossible to find. But Sami's own Sig was in Tinker's hand.

Tinker leveled the gun and Sami closed his eyes. This time, Sami heard the shots clearly. Three rounds. Center mass.

THIRTY

NATIONAL HARBOR

Sami's eyes were sealed shut like a corpse, but the gunshots rang in Sami's ears. Tinker staggered forward, as though pushed from behind. He fell to one knee, then the rest of his body crashed to the ground.

"Let's go! C'mon!" Sami felt hands grab him, but the voice barely registered.

"Where are the detonators? C'mon, do you have them?" The hands pulled at him again, trying to move him from the corner where he was rooted. "Let's go Sami, we need to get out of here." At the mention of his name, Sami opened his eyes to see Yoda.

The Marine still held a gun in his hand. On the floor, Tinker lay with one knee shoved up under his torso, his body contorted, and his mouth lolled open like a fish on ice. Three rounds to his vital organs had the effect Sami had expected when he shot his grandfather. Deep burgundy arterial blood was spilling from the exit wounds and onto the carpet.

"Sami, do you have them?" Yoda could see his friend's shock, and he spoke slowly while looking into Sami's eyes.

Like a child waking from a nightmare, stunned into silence by the fear that any movement or sound might rouse the beasts from his imagination, Sami did not speak. But he nodded.

"You have them," Yoda confirmed. He was holding Sami under the elbow now, guiding him toward the door. "All of them, right?"

Sami cleared a heavy slab of dust-choked saliva from his throat. "Yes," he croaked. "All three."

"We need to go. Are you OK to move?"

Sami nodded.

"They got you good, buddy." Yoda noticed the gunshot wound to Sami's shoulder and switched to his other arm, where he continued to lead his friend toward the door. "We'll get you some attention, but it's through and through. You should be OK. You're lucky."

Sami didn't respond.

"That's not the only way you're lucky. If Emily hadn't put her app on your phone, we might not have found you."

Sami was distracted and he tugged free of Yoda's control. The Glock was still missing, but Sami's Sig had fallen at the floor near Tinker's feet. Sami picked it up. He fumbled at the small of his back but failed to reholster it. He tried and failed again.

"I can take it." Sami ignored Yoda's outstretched hand.

His focus had shifted to the couch, where his grandfather was drawing shallow breaths. He might have been roused by the trio of gunshots, perhaps imagining they were the sound of his own demise, just as Sami had. Or this might be his death rattle. Whatever the reason, he was awake now, his eyes pained but lucid. The old man's position, askew on the couch like a ship run aground, confined his field of vision. Sami walked closer until it was clear Abu Muhammad saw his grandson.

Sami held the gun by his right thigh and looked into the eyes of the man who left Lahore for the U.S. and built a community of worshippers, and a family. An American family. An American religious community. The American Ummah.

Sami discovered the truth about his parents only moments ago, but that painful realization had been suppressed as he fought for life. Now it surged back. More than that, what rose was the resentment of a man made to feel unworthy. Unnatural. Dirty. Subhuman. The locus of that resentment was Abu Muhammad.

Sami had known better than to listen to the hatred in his own home, he had known enough to leave, but his flight had always been a survival tactic. Deep down, he could not help but yearn for this man's approbation. A Soldier. A Spy. A Muslim. A Man. Whatever he had become, whatever he mastered,

Sami could not help but feel that something in him was broken because he could not be a Grandson.

Now that he knew the truth about his parents, and about his grandfather, he could deal with the reality. Not of who he was, but what had been done to him. The wounds of his childhood could be excised. It was Abu Muhammad who was evil, because of what he had done. Not Sami, because of who he was.

Sami raised the gun. Would it be merciful to kill the old man, to end his suffering? Sami dismissed those ideas as dramatic. It would be murder. Vengeance. For his parents and for himself. It was what brought him up to this hotel suite and it was what Abu Muhammad deserved.

His grandfather looked up in desperation. His blood stained the couch. He drew another ragged breath, expecting it to be his last.

Sami lowered the gun.

He followed Yoda down the stairs. There was mayhem outside the hotel. The perfect conditions to slip away unnoticed. Like an assassin.

SANTA MONICA, CALIFORNIA | AUGUST

California was far away. It had sun and beaches and other stuff Sami supposed might keep his mind occupied. He put the condo in Georgetown on Airbnb, and even with the asking price of accommodations in D.C., he rented a more expensive apartment at the beach on the way toward Malibu.

His days began with the physical therapy Andy's doctor prescribed after she treated his gunshot wound. Yoda was right. The bullet went through and through, mainly traumatizing the muscles connecting Sami's shoulder and neck. He stretched every morning and then replaced his arm in a sling.

He went to Santa Monica Pier, strolled through Pacific Park, leaned on the trusses under the roller coaster and felt it rattle his chest as it passed overhead again and again. Sun, sand, sea air and the only thing he noticed was how soft a target the park was. No security of any kind. Families clustered in lines all day, waiting for their turn on the rides, and then teenagers came at night.

Groups. Clustered. Drop a gym bag by the Frog Hopper and another by the Ferris Wheel.

Sami left a bag by the entrance to the Wave Runner. No one said a word. He sat on a nearby bench for ten minutes and watched. Not a second glance. A pressure cooker bomb would work well because you wanted flying shrapnel, low to the ground. More casualties and they were simple and cheap.

At the Griffith Observatory, even as he listened to Leonard Nimoy describe the multimillion-dollar renovations, all he could think of were the vulnerabilities. No bag checks. No metal detectors. Single point of vehicular access and egress. The balconies overlooking the city were always crowded with people. This would be perfect for a small arms attack. Two or three guys with ARs. Two on the observation decks start the shooting, and one on the wide expanse of green grass out front, to pick off runners fleeing for the shelter of their cars.

The Dodgers had a long homestand and Sami attended every night. He took great comfort from the setting. Loud and crowded, but orderly. Security in green jackets. Metal detectors standing at each gate like sentinels. But he found weaknesses. He formulated a plan. The team left for an East Coast swing and he was glad.

He drove to Vegas on a three-day/two-night promotion at a hotel on The Strip. He didn't even last eight hours. The place was begging to be attacked again.

He was amazed at how America had returned to business as usual, as though the hotel bombings had never happened. As though the places that Americans ate and played and stayed had done anything to make themselves safer. He was not in Beirut. Not in Jerusalem. Not even in London or Paris. When America saw danger ahead it didn't stop, it accelerated. If the hit and run left carnage on the road behind or did damage to the big black SUV, that's what insurance was for.

This realization increased Sami's alienation from his work and his country. That was a long time coming, and not unexpected, but another feeling overpowered that reaction and caught Sami off-guard. He was an orphan. His grandfather, his last connection to his parents, was dead. Sami was alone. He cried for hours, though he was not always sure for whom or for what.

The aftermath of the attacks was predictable in Washington. Abu Muhammad's role in the plot was revealed. And so was Tom Tinker's. The networks and cable news shows let that marinate until Nielsen said America was losing interest, and then they detailed the connection to Gerald Seymour. With a gentle push from material that Sami left behind with specific instructions on when and to whom it should be released, the story broke.

What did they know? When did they know it?

What did the White House know and when did they know it?

WHAT DID THE WHITE HOUSE KNOW AND WHEN DID THEY KNOW IT?

A hurricane near Orange Beach, Alabama provided a brief distraction. But it wasn't enough. The press corps hated the President, they hated Gerald Seymour more, and they smelled enough blood in the water for a feeding frenzy that would consume both. Less than 72 hours later, the most unorthodox of American Presidents, the man who prided himself on rejecting conventional wisdom, did the most conventionally wise thing of his presidency and threw Gerald Seymour overboard.

About three weeks after he arrived, Sami returned to the Santa Monica apartment with a fresh six-pack of Pacifico and two limes to cut. He threw open the sliding door to the beach and turned on TV news. Seymour's termination had only been the beginning. He had enemies. He was hated, within his party and without. Even among those employed by the administration he brought to power, there were those with scores to settle.

Revenge was exacted. It came from the FBI, where the report Brad could not find had reappeared. It came from the intelligence community, which resented being manipulated in support of a terror plot against Americans. It came from House and Senate committees, and it came from a Washington Establishment gleefully reasserting itself.

When Sami saw the news crawl, he was holding a paring knife. A squirt of lime juice had just sprayed his hand and the scent of citrus was in his nostrils. Gerald Seymour was indicted. Gerald Seymour was arrested. Gerald Seymour was likely to be the first American tried for treason in a very long time. Gerald Seymour might cut a deal, but then again, Gerald Seymour's old boss sure liked talking tough. He liked looking tough even better, and a conviction for treason came with the death penalty.

Talking heads entered the drama. Would he, or wouldn't he? Plea or no? One former White House aide was inappropriate enough to suggest that Seymour might be found hanging in his cell long before any of those options could be played out.

Sami cut two sections from the lime and inserted them into two longneck bottles. It was a two-beer night. He took a long pull from one and then threaded the bottles through his fingers and walked toward the deck. He paused in front of the TV and watched.

He felt vindicated. Karim was dead. Sami had not saved him, but the scales on which a spy balanced justice were different from a lawyer's or judge's, and they inclined toward vengeance.

But Sami didn't feel any safer. The world was still a dangerous place. While he finished the beer, he packed his bag. Twenty minutes later, he left the keys to the apartment on the kitchen counter and he went back to work.

ACKNOWLEDGMENTS

I must begin by offering thanks to Lawrence Knorr, Chris Fenwick and the team at Sunbury Press for the time and effort they put into improving this book. I am so grateful that Sami's first story found the right home.

Long before any publishers or agents saw the manuscript, a select group of beta readers contributed their time and provided cherished feedback. Thanks to Roy Brooks, Michael Young, Laurie Walker and Jane Nolette for brining your own sparks of innovation to the table -- many of those sparks became the best parts of this book.

Realizing the dream of publishing this story would not have been possible without the support of everyone who pre-ordered a book. Special thanks to Colleen and Kevin Honan, David and Betsey Stewart, Burke and Adrienne Ewers, Chris Elias, Gary McAuliffe, Kelley and Chris Ruthstrom, Roy and Sue Brooks, Wendy and Chris Jennings, Ian Thomson, Jane Chmielinski, Andrew Kelleher and Brooke Bassinger, Asa O'Sheal, Betsy and Scott Miller, Brandon Knight, Bruce and Andrea Jeffrey, Carl Garofalo, Chad Solomonson, Gerry Walsh, Jan and Beth Bialach, Janine Coppola, Julie Yingling and Rick Davids, Kay Murray, Laurie Walker, Marnie and Tom Donoghue, Matt and Misty Davis, Maureen and Jack Kiely, Mike and Kate Orroth, Mike and Amy Young, Mike O'Sheal, Pamela Zamora, The Shrigley Family, Stephanie Baker-Watson, Ted and Jill O'Shea, Terry Yingling and Jim Candelet, and Vanessa Lane and Jack Easley.

No one pre-ordered this book (or sold pre-orders) with more enthusiasm than my parents, Joe and Debbie Walsh. When waiters and waitresses ask my parents if they are celebrating a special occasion, Dad always says he won the lottery...the day he met Mom. In truth, that was the day I hit life's lottery by being born to parents who are truly kind and loving people.

I am sad that my brother Ted did not live to see either of our names across the cover of a book. It is a testament to his caring soul that I know he would be as tickled for me as he would have been for himself. I miss you, Ted.

For me, writing is about a passion for telling stories, a need to be expressive and creative, and the desire to use the written word as an art form that can weave a tapestry of entertainment and education. And, writing is about sacrifice: a lot of late nights, early mornings, and Saturday afternoons spent at a desk instead of in the pool or the park or on Netflix.

My sacrifices pale in comparison to those of my family. My parents gave me life, my earliest readers gave me a chance, but my family made this happen. God only knows what I'd be without you.

Sam – Thank you for being the most supportive partner.

Natalia, Ben, Charlie and Abby – Thank you for letting your Dad chase a dream. May all of yours come true.

ABOUT THE AUTHOR

J.A. WALSH worked in intelligence and counterterrorism after the 9/11 attacks, before embarking on a career advising the U.S. military on energy security strategies. He has degrees in Russian, English literature, and Environmental Law. He lives in North Carolina with his family.

Made in the USA
Middletown, DE
30 May 2019